KELI GWYN

Family of Her Dreams

HARLEQUIN® LOVE INSPIRED® HISTORICAL

Recycling programs
for this product may
not exist in your area.

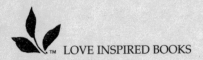 LOVE INSPIRED BOOKS

ISBN-13: 978-0-373-28317-0

Family of Her Dreams

www.Harlequin.com

Printed in U.S.A.

A man's heart deviseth his way:
but the Lord directeth his steps.
— *Proverbs* 16:9

For my mother, Patricia Lannon,
who instilled a love of reading in me at an early age,
introduced me to Harlequin romances when I was a teen
and rejoiced with me when my dream of writing for
their Love Inspired Historical line came true.

Chapter One

July 1866
Shingle Springs, California

"Look out, ma'am!"

Tess Grimsby jumped back to avoid a fellow about fifteen pulling a baggage cart with far too much speed for the bustling rail station. She collided with a mother herding her four youngsters, causing the weary-looking woman to drop her wicker basket. Several children's books slid across the wooden platform.

"My apologies. I didn't mean to bump into you." Tess stooped to pick up the books that had landed at her feet.

The woman made sure her children were all right, dropped to her knees and reached for a copy of *Little Bo-Peep*. "It wasn't your fault." She scowled at the baggage handler. "He needs to watch where he's going."

The young man parked his cart beside the baggage car and sprinted over to them. "Sorry 'bout that. It's my first day on the job, and my boss said to hurry. I've got to make a good impression." He grinned, reminding Tess of one of the many boys she'd befriended when she lived at the orphanage.

She smiled. "No harm was done."

A man with a voice as rich as Belgian chocolate addressed the teen. "Be more careful next time. Getting the baggage moved quickly is important, but Mr. Flynn wouldn't want you to endanger our passengers, nor would I."

"Right, sir." The lad left.

"Come, children. We need to get home." The mother took the books Tess had gathered, muttered something about troublesome teens and hustled her children across the crowded platform.

Tess slid her satchel back on her shoulder, straightened and found herself face-to-face with a broad-shouldered, golden-haired gentleman. He was younger than any of the men she'd worked for—and far more handsome with his strong chin and arresting sky-blue eyes, currently clouded with sadness. If he was Mr. Abbott—the widower she'd come to see—she could understand.

He held out her journal and said nothing for several seconds as he gazed at her, his expression unreadable. No doubt the tall man wasn't used to looking a woman in the eye.

"Sir?"

The frown he'd worn faded, giving way to a hint of a smile that caused her breath to hitch. "I believe this is yours. It fell out of your bag during the commotion."

"Thank you." She took the diary from him, its pages so full of her hopes and dreams—as well as the mementos she'd tucked between the pages—that she had to grip it tightly to keep items from falling out. She would add her train ticket to the collection of memorabilia, a symbol of the new chapter in her life she was eager to embrace. "You must be Mr. Abbott, the stationmaster."

His forehead furrowed. "I am, but I don't believe we've met."

She shoved the bulging book into her satchel. "Not in person, although we've corresponded. I'm Tess Grimsby, Polly's friend. I've come about the housekeeper position."

"Ah, yes. She told me you'd arrive today." He clutched a notebook with sun-bronzed hands that obviously did more than complete paperwork, and scanned the platform, where several passengers lingered. "I need to see to a few things. Could you come to my office in ten minutes?"

"That would be fine." She could use the time to compose herself.

"Actually, let's make that twenty. I need to see if anyone requires my assistance, and then we can take care of the interview."

He certainly didn't sound eager to meet with her. Not that she could blame him. Hiring someone to care for his motherless children could be difficult. "Very well. I'll see to my trunks and meet you there." She should have time to rent a room at the hotel.

Tess set off for the baggage area, weaving her way through those waiting to board the train for its return trip down the hill. As the end station of the Placerville and Sacramento Valley Railroad, the depot was one of the busiest in the state. While it handled a great deal of freight, a number of travelers passed through Shingle Springs, too. However, few remained there, which she hoped to do.

People watched as she swept past them. Some even craned their heads to follow her progress. As much as she'd like to fade into the bustling throng, she couldn't. Everywhere she went she encountered the thinly veiled surprise and outright stares of strangers. You would think they'd never seen a tall woman before.

Peter Flynn, Polly's russet-haired husband who worked

at the station, saw her and hustled over, a smile on his tanned face. They made quick work of their introductions.

"Polly said you were tall, but…" He tilted his head to look at her. "You could dust the ceiling at our place with the feathers on that hat of yours. Just how tall are you?"

Most people didn't come right out and mention her height, although she would prefer that to whispers behind fans. Polly had warned Tess that Peter spoke his mind. Since she tended to do the same, she didn't take offense. "Six foot."

He whistled a note of surprise, drawing the attention of several freight men, who viewed her with curiosity and made some less than flattering remarks. Indignation straightened her spine. She wasn't *that* much taller than other women. Why must everyone make such a fuss about a few inches?

She lifted her chin and gave the workers the impassive look she'd practiced in the mirror until she'd perfected it. Once she had, she'd pasted it on whenever the sharp-tongued orphanage director maligned her, unwilling to let him see her pain. Nearly nine years had passed, but the recollection of Mr. Grimsby's cutting remarks left a bitter taste in her mouth. Thank the Lord she'd been able to leave the orphanage the day she turned sixteen, having secured a position caring for the children of a family heading West.

"At least you and Spencer will see eye to eye." Peter chuckled at his play on words but quickly sobered. "And speaking of him, I'd better get back to work. I'll have one of the boys deliver your trunks to the hotel." He doffed his hat and returned to his duties.

Standing on the platform in front of the depot, Tess surveyed the small town. Shingle Springs sat at the foot of the majestic Sierra Nevada mountain range, which rose up to meet the cloudless sky. The steady stream of wagons headed east had dug deep ruts in the wide main street. Most of the businesses and houses lining it were made of wood, but an impressive stone building on the south side stood out.

She crossed the street and made her way to the Planter's House hotel, a two-story white clapboard building with a balcony that shaded the porch below. With the temperature approaching triple digits, she would welcome getting out of the early afternoon sun.

A glance at the watch pinned to her bodice caused her to move quickly. She'd have just enough time to change and dab on some rosewater to mask the lingering smell of the ashes and soot that had rained on her. Not that a railroad man like Mr. Abbott would notice the smoky scent.

From what Polly had written, he'd become so preoccupied since his wife's passing he could barely get himself to the depot on time. Once there, all he had time for was work—to the exclusion of everything and everyone else. Tess understood. Grief could immobilize a person. How many times had she seen newly orphaned children go through their days as though encased in a fog?

If all went well, she'd soon be caring for Mr. Abbott's two little ones and helping them deal with the loss of their mother. She looked forward to easing their father's burden and helping him cope with his grief, too.

"If you'll step inside, Mr. Drake would be happy to send a telegram for you." Spencer Abbott directed the elderly couple to his ticket agent's cage and resumed his perusal of the platform.

Other than the new baggage handler's mishap, things had gone smoothly that morning. Spencer had been able to eat the meager pickings in his dinner pail in peace while rereading the letters Tess Grimsby had sent.

Although she had glowing recommendations from two of the families she'd served, her most recent employer had dismissed her. From what Spencer could tell, the banker had no complaints about her work but had taken issue with her personality. Such things happened. Spencer knew that from experience. But a trait one employer disliked another might value. He believed in giving a person the opportunity to prove what he—or *she*—could do. Most people showed their true colors fairly quickly.

What troubled him more than Miss Grimsby's employment history was his reaction to her. When she'd stood and he'd looked into her eyes, speech had eluded him. Rarely had he encountered a woman that tall. She must be at least six foot, although with her hat the size of Texas, she appeared even taller.

While her height had come as a surprise, what had captivated him was the compassion in her warm brown eyes. Clearly she was a caring person. Rather than rail about the young man who'd almost barreled into her, she'd defended him and shown him kindness, which spoke well of her character. A woman like her should be able to take Luke's antics in stride.

What had kept Spencer riveted to her had nothing to do with her personality, though. He hated to admit it, but the reason he'd gawked at her like some smitten schoolboy had everything to do with her lovely features, from her delicately arched brows and high cheekbones to her rosy lips lifted in that mesmerizing smile. She was the first woman to capture his attention since he'd lost—

Focus, Abbott. He had no business thinking about another woman. Trudy had only been gone three short months. He was a widower in mourning who'd loved his wife, not a man in search of someone to take her place. Not that anyone could. She'd held a special place in his heart and always would. It must have been loneliness that led his eyes to stray, that's all.

Well, he was master of his emotions. When Tess Grimsby returned, she'd see a man in control of himself. If he chose to hire her as his housekeeper, he would keep things strictly professional.

Tess emerged from the hotel wearing her favorite dress, a cobalt-blue calico that matched the three peacock feathers atop her hat. She tugged on her gloves, crossed the busy street and strolled alongside the tracks until she came to the railway station.

The depot was a hive of activity as men prepared for a freight train's arrival. Drivers seated on sturdy wagons waited for their cargo in front of three warehouses east of the station. Horses whickered and shook their heads to rid themselves of the ever-present flies.

Although the platform was large, the wooden building at the heart of the action was small. Somewhere inside sat the man who would determine her future. Mr. Abbott must hire her. If he didn't, she'd be forced to return to Sacramento City and pray she found another position before the last of the money in her reticule was gone.

She shook the small handbag dangling from her wrist, the jingle of the few coins inside lacking the reassurance she sought. While Polly had said she and Peter would welcome Tess, she couldn't impose on them, not when they were expecting a second child soon.

Given her recent dismissal, Tess hadn't been able to secure another governess position in the city, despite spending two weeks searching for one. Polly's letter with news of Mr. Abbott's need had been most fortuitous. If he hired her as his housekeeper and her work pleased him, she'd be able to restore her reputation and replenish her depleted savings.

A bell tinkled as she entered the depot. The man in the ticket cage peered at her through the wrought iron grate and smiled. "Good morning, ma'am. May I help you?"

"I'm Tess Grimsby here to see Mr. Abbott. He's expecting me."

The ticket agent nodded. "Welcome, Miss Grimsby. I'm Mr. Drake. I'll let you in."

She waited at the door he'd indicated. It opened, and he pointed out another on her right. She paused and said a silent prayer.

"Don't be scared. He doesn't bite…often."

She wasn't afraid of Mr. Abbott, but she was concerned about her reaction to the appealing gentleman. Despite his rumpled frock coat and limp collar, it could be all too easy to cast admiring glances his way, and that would never do. She must act like the professional she was and keep her goal of being hired first and foremost. "Me? Scared? He's the one who ought to be. Men have been known to run from me."

Mr. Drake chuckled, the curled ends of his heavily waxed handlebar moustache dancing. "You've got spunk. That's good. You'll need it if you're to work for him. He's a fine boss, but he can be a mite intimidating on his best days. Lately…well, let's just say losing his wife three months back changed him." He inclined his head toward the door to Mr. Abbott's office. "Give it a rap, and he'll invite you in."

Tess peered through the small window inset in the door. Mr. Abbott sat at a desk in a painfully clean office with a ledger spread before him and his head in hands. Like Mr. Drake, who had a shock of wiry gray hair, Mr. Abbott had a full head of hair, as well, although his was the color of ripe rye at sunset. Unlike his ticket clerk, who had a ready smile, Mr. Abbott sported a frown, as he had earlier. Not a promising sign.

She knocked.

"Enter."

She stilled her trembling hand and opened the door. He jumped to his feet.

"Miss Grimsby. Please, have a seat." He held out a hand toward the bentwood chair facing his desk.

"Thank you, sir." She sat, folded her hands in her lap and drew a calming breath. "I trust you received all the documents I sent."

"I did." He remained standing, resting his hands on the windowsill with his back to her. Several seconds passed before he spoke. "You're not what I expected."

Her nervousness fled. She didn't appreciate being challenged at the outset, but she wouldn't let him fluster her. "Neither are you, but I can do the job, I assure you." She'd worked for some prominent families in Sacramento City, the last one having a name anybody in the state would recognize. The wife of the widely respected banker had written her a letter of recommendation, albeit reluctantly. Not that Tess could blame her. The woman's husband had found Tess's direct manner problematic.

Mr. Abbott sat on the corner of his desk with his long legs draped over the side, forcing her to look up. She caught a flicker of feeling in his eyes. Curiosity perhaps? Or was it concern?

"Why would you come to a small town when you're used to living among the elite? I lead a simple life, and I don't want my children exposed to any newfangled notions."

His manner and tone rankled. If she were to work for

him, she'd have to show him she wouldn't tolerate his high-handedness. "I'm a simple person myself, eager to leave the bustle of the city behind. I was most recently employed by a family of means, true, but I hail from humble circumstances."

Please, don't let him ask me to explain. She had no intention of educating him about her past. Humble circumstances didn't begin to describe her miserable childhood.

"Your circumstances don't concern me. But your methods do. I contacted your most recent employer. He said you have a tendency to speak your mind. Is that true?"

That was a more tactful description of her supposed failings than the domineering man had used when he dismissed her. "I have opinions, but doesn't everyone?"

His blond brows rose, and he pressed a fist to his mouth. She thought she saw his lips twitch, and it gave her hope, but when he pulled his hand away, the frown was there as before. "Can you cook?

Mr. Abbott's abrupt change of subject took her aback. "I assume you mean can I cook well, and the answer is yes. I can keep house, do laundry, sew, garden and care for animals, too. But the most important thing is that I'll do all I can to help your children through this difficult time." The Lord had used her to minister to countless youngsters who'd lost their parents, and she could put that experience to good use—provided Mr. Abbott hired her.

He folded his arms and took his time studying her, as though she were a horse or a milk cow. Well, two could play that game. She tilted her chin and let her gaze rove over his fine features, drinking her fill.

At length he nodded. "I'll give you one week."

A week? Her previous employers had offered a one-month trial period. Torn between a desire to laugh or shout, Tess gave an unladylike snort, which she covered with a cough.

In her experience overbearing men like Spencer Abbott responded to a show of force. She couldn't resist the urge to slip in a hint of sarcasm, too. "How generous—but entirely unnecessary. I'll prove my worth to you in a day."

Chapter Two

Spencer wasn't one to refuse a challenge. If Miss Grimsby was bold enough to claim that she could impress him in a day rather than asking for a month as he'd expected, she deserved the opportunity to try. The sooner he found out if her assertion was valid, the sooner he'd know if his search for a housekeeper was over.

As much as he detested the thought of a woman he didn't know helping raise his children, Peter's wife had vouched for Miss Grimsby. Polly had never steered him wrong.

While Spencer was certain Miss Grimsby could fix better meals than those he'd eaten lately, how would she deal with Luke? The poor tyke had taken to misbehaving. Having a different woman watching him every few days didn't help matters.

Miss Grimsby seemed to have the strength of character necessary to tame his spirited offspring. Not that Lila would pose a problem. She'd not even begun to walk. Ever since Trudy's dea— Ever since the service his little girl had been content to play quietly with her blocks.

"You may start now. I'll run you out to the house and

return at suppertime. Mrs. Carter, an elderly widow from church, is with the children now. She'll show you around."

She gave a decisive nod. "That would suit me just fine."

Spencer stopped his wagon beside Miss Grimsby a few minutes later and hopped down to help her onto the seat. She climbed aboard before he reached her. Her independent streak didn't surprise him, but her agility did. He wouldn't have expected a woman that tall wearing boots with three-inch heels to move as quickly or gracefully. But there she sat looking as composed as any woman of leisure, the smooth plane of her neck exposed as she peered over her shoulder at the shops across the street from the depot.

"I noticed a general store earlier. Would you mind if I run inside for a moment before we get underway?"

Spencer groaned inwardly. "No, but make it quick. I've got work to do."

"I'll be back in a trice."

He slipped his gold watch out of his waistcoat pocket. He'd give her five minutes. If she wasn't back by then, he'd hitch his team to the post and tend to some paperwork. Waiting on a woman wasn't something he had time for. He closed his eyes to block the bright summer sun and made a mental list of all he had to accomplish that afternoon.

The wagon rocked as Miss Grimsby climbed aboard. "I'm sorry I took so long, but someone was ahead of me."

Three minutes wasn't long. Three minutes was astonishing. Unsure what to say, he grunted an acknowledgment. He pocketed his watch, took the reins and started the one-mile trek to his spread.

With each clop of the horses' hooves, the stabbing pain he experienced every time he saw the place intensified. Memories abounded, as sour as they were sweet. He and Trudy had worked hard to make the house a home.

Although she was gone, he could see her everywhere. Why, he fancied he could even smell the rosewater she'd favored.

"What was she like?"

"Huh?"

"Your wife. You looked sad. Were you thinking about her?"

An inquisitive housekeeper was not what he needed. "That's not something I care to talk about, especially with a stranger."

"I'm sorry. I thought—"

"You thought wrong. I need a job done. Nothing more." That had come out harsher than he'd intended. She was only trying to help. Even so, he didn't trust himself to talk about Trudy without choking up. Silence was safer.

"I'll pray for you. I know what it's like to lose a loved one and feel that vacant ache."

He bit back a retort. How could she possibly understand what he was going through? She'd never been married and left with two children to raise alone. "Pray if you like but no more questions please."

She bowed her head.

For some reason her gesture comforted him. He'd reached the point where he no longer knew what to pray and trusted the Spirit to intercede for him "with groanings which could not be uttered," as it said in Romans. If Miss Grimsby's prayers could help, he wouldn't turn them down.

When she opened her eyes, they held unasked questions, but the compassion he'd seen before was there, too. She smiled, and the future didn't seem quite as bleak as it had. Perhaps she was as capable as she'd said and would solve his immediate problems. He'd know soon enough.

* * *

Tess remained silent the rest of the way to Mr. Abbott's place. He'd made it clear her attempts to offer sympathy were unwelcome. She could understand. Each child who'd come to the orphanage handled grief differently. Some wept. Some talked about their losses, while others kept their own counsel. Some blamed themselves and suffered guilt, while others lashed out in anger. And there were those like her soon-to-be employer who did their best to go on with their lives despite the near-crippling pain.

As she'd prayed, a sense of peace had descended on her—along with a sense of purpose. She wasn't here to get what she wanted. She was here to give of herself to this hurting family. All those years comforting others had prepared her for this. She would offer the care and comfort Mr. Abbott's motherless children needed, and she would lift some of the burden their grieving father carried.

Above all she would guard her heart. Even though she was drawn to him, she mustn't let herself care too much. This was a job like any other, and she would do well to remember that.

They approached a two-story ranch house painted bright red with white trim. All the windows were open, curtains peeking from beneath the raised frames. A wraparound porch beckoned her to slip into one of the ladder-backed rocking chairs gracing it and spend time sipping lemonade with a friend. She'd often dreamed of having such a house, although the one in her dreams was blue—a lovely slate blue with burgundy trim.

Mr. Abbott parked the wagon, and she was on the ground in a heartbeat. He held out a hand toward the stairs. "After you."

She passed through the open front door and nearly gagged. What was that horrid stench? It smelled worse than the rotten eggs some of the more daring boys at the orphanage had hurled at Mr. Grimsby's carriage once— before he'd meted out the swift punishment he was known for.

"Luke!" Mr. Abbott bellowed and charged inside.

That didn't bode well. Tess followed on his heels. They reached the kitchen where a full-figured woman with white hair attempted to wipe a squirming baby girl's jam-spattered face. Mr. Abbott's four-year-old son ran circles around the dining table in the adjoining room, whooping like an Indian on the warpath.

Everywhere Tess looked, chaos reigned. Soiled shirts had been draped over chair backs, newspapers and toys were strewn about and a path had been worn through the dust coating the floorboards. Although she'd only been there two minutes, she itched to get to work restoring order and a sense of harmony.

Mr. Abbott addressed the older woman, raising his voice to be heard over the din. "What happened?"

"That boy of yours snuck up behind me when I was checkin' the fire and chucked some salve in the stove."

"What next?" He raked a hand through his thick blond hair, causing a swatch of his long locks to stand on end. Tess suppressed the urge to smooth it for him.

The older woman lugged the baby upstairs, and Mr. Abbott strode to the cookstove. Tess tore her gaze from him, entered the dining room and stepped in his son's path. She caught the little fellow's raised arm as he passed. "Whoa there, young man."

He came to an abrupt stop and stared at her with eyes as big and round as washtubs. "Who are you?"

"I'm Tess, and you must be Luke."

"What're you doing here?"

"Your papa is going to see if I'm the right person to look after you and your sister."

He shook his head wildly. "No! I don't want you here. Go away." He flew out of the house.

She took off after him, hitching up her skirts with one hand, holding on to her hat with the other and running as fast as her high boot heels would allow. He dashed into the barn. She found him crouched in the corner of an empty stall, tears flowing over his flushed cheeks, and her heart went out to him. She approached slowly on tiptoes, but she bumped into a shovel leaning against the wall and sent it crashing to the floor.

Luke prepared to bolt, but she caught him by the shoulders and held him tightly as he twisted and turned. She squatted so she wouldn't tower over him. "I'm not going to hurt you, but I won't let go until you settle down. You can't run off like that. A ranch is a big place. You could get hurt."

"No, I couldn't!"

The little fellow showed no signs of giving up his struggle. He flailed his arms as he attempted to break free. "You're coming with me, Master Luke." She planted him on her hip and headed to the house. His fists flew, coming uncomfortably close to her face. Her ears rang from his shrieked protests.

She reached the kitchen, where Mr. Abbott knelt in front of the stove filling two metal pails with glowing embers. He'd shed his coat and rolled up his shirtsleeves, revealing muscular arms. She had little time to take in the unexpected—albeit pleasing—sight because he turned toward her, exasperation etched in every line of his attractive face.

"Quiet down, Luke," he said in a firm voice. "Do something, Miss Grimsby. *Please.*"

The mischievous boy ceased shouting long enough to send her a triumphant smirk.

She'd had enough of his antics. No four-year-old, however unruly, would keep her from securing the position. She'd dealt with his kind before and knew just what to do. "I guess you don't want to see what kind of candy I brought. I won't give it to a boy who's pitching a fit. I'll set you down—if you agree to stay put. Will you do that?"

He crossed his arms over his chest in such an adult manner Tess hid a smile. She rummaged in her reticule with her free hand and withdrew a small package. He followed her every move, his eyes glued to the peppermint stick she unwrapped.

"Here. Why don't you smell it?" She placed the striped sweet under his nose, pulling back when he attempted to snatch it. "You may have it if you'll sit quietly while your papa cleans up the mess you made." She indicated a chair at the kitchen table.

The boy's gaze was riveted on the red-and-white stick. He licked his lips. "I don't like you, and you can't make me."

"You don't have to like me, and I won't make you. You just have to do as I ask." She set him down but kept a firm grip on his shoulder.

His face scrunched in puzzlement. "You're not mad?"

Tess shook her head. "I understand. You want your mama, but she's gone now. I know you don't want me here, but you need someone to cook your food, wash your clothes and buy you candy, don't you?"

"You'll buy me candy?"

"I will." Provided Mr. Abbott hired her.

Luke studied her with the same intensity his father had. "Whenever I want?"

"No. Candy is a treat, but you'd get it sometimes." She released her hold on him.

He sidled over to the chair and stood beside it a moment before sitting down. Tess handed him the sweet, which he promptly stuck in his mouth.

Mr. Abbott hefted a pail in each hand and headed to the back door. She beat him there and held it open for him. His bright blue eyes held a hint of amusement—and something else. Attraction perhaps? Of course not. She must be seeing things.

"I didn't expect you to stoop to bribery."

"Oh, I wouldn't classify it as bribery. I prefer to think of it as a reward for making a good choice."

"Whatever you call it, it worked." She warmed at his approval and smiled at his retreating form.

When Mr. Abbott and Mrs. Carter returned, he got the story out of her.

"I kept my eyes peeled, Mr. Abbott, but you know how troublesome your young'un can be. Luke got into a scuffle with the baby. Both of 'em wanted to play with that canvas ball you brung 'em last week. Lila wouldn't let him have it, so he smacked her. I told him to stand in the corner, but he don't mind any better than I cook."

Judging by the deplorable state of the kitchen, cleaning wasn't one of Mrs. Carter's strengths, either. Dirty dishes were piled everywhere, chunks of dried food clinging to them. If the house hadn't been filled with the overpowering stench that had greeted her, Tess would have been able to follow her nose to the kitchen.

Mrs. Carter set Lila on a blanket with a pile of blocks. The little girl seemed content to play with them. "Sorry 'bout the trouble with the salve. I opened all the windows, but I don't think it done much good."

Tess wrinkled her nose. "What kind of salve would make it smell like some poor creature died in here?"

Mr. Abbott explained. "My dog has mange. I mixed lard and powdered sulfur, which I've been rubbing on him. It doesn't have much of an odor normally, but it stinks something fierce if it's burned."

She laughed. "I'll say. So, what do we do?"

"I got the stove cleared out. Now we wait for the smell to go away."

"And the dog?" she asked. "What about him?"

"I'm keeping him in the barn until I get the mange under control. Could be a week or more."

Mrs. Carter patted Tess's arm. "I'm awful glad you're here, young lady. You got a big job ahead of you. The place needs a bit of sprucin' up, but I done my best. Those young'uns need a firm hand. I spent most of my time cha-sin' after Luke. He's a real handful, that one. Mind you, don't let him out of your sight."

Mr. Abbott washed up and donned his frock coat with its row of shiny brass buttons and a black armband to show he was in mourning. How sad that such a handsome man wore a perpetual frown. Perhaps one day she'd be able to make him smile.

"Might I have a word, Miss Grimsby?"

"Yes, sir." She followed him onto the porch, doing her best to quell the queasiness his request had caused. Had she failed to please him already?

He cleared his throat and ran a finger under his collar. If she didn't know better, she'd say he was as uneasy as she. Surely, in his position, he was practiced in dismissing people.

"I understand you were governess to a number of girls before but only one boy—all of them considerably older than my children. Do you think you're up to dealing with my son? He can be a challenge at times."

Luke couldn't begin to compare with some of the boys at the orphanage. "I am. Does this mean…?"

"What it means is that I'm considering things. Show me what you can accomplish before I get home tonight, and we'll talk." He descended two steps, paused and inclined his head toward the house. "You might want to go back inside before Luke springs a surprise on you."

Tess maintained her composure until she was in the foyer. She lifted her hands to the heavens. *Thank You, Lord.*

She would set the place to rights, prepare a delicious meal and prove to Mr. Abbott she was the woman for the job. If all went well, she'd have a family to care for at last. It might not be her own, but it was the next best thing.

Chapter Three

A shrill whistle signaled the departure of an outbound freight train, relieved of its load and ready for the return trip to Sacramento City. Spencer checked his pocket watch. Right on time, just the way he liked it.

He crossed the platform and went in search of his freight traffic manager, notebook in hand. The sooner he got the statistics on the latest shipments from Peter, the sooner he could update his records and find out how the station was doing.

Processing the cargo quickly and keeping their customers happy would improve their chances of gaining more business and ensure that he could keep his position as long as possible. He'd known ever since taking the newly created Shingle Springs stationmaster position the summer before that the Transcontinental Route to the north would bring about the end of his company's monopoly, which was why he had a plan that didn't depend on the railroad.

He located Peter talking with one of his workers. He finished the conversation and ambled over. "Come for the numbers, have you?"

"Are they any good?"

Peter consulted a sheaf of papers. "You'll be happy

with them. But not as happy as when the Sutro Tunnel Act passes. Should be soon from what I hear."

Handling the many supply shipments needed to construct the six-mile tunnel connecting Nevada's Comstock's silver mines would give them plenty of work—for the time being. "Let's hope we get a fair amount of the business before it's siphoned off by the CP."

"Don't be such a killjoy. They haven't even reached the summit yet. It'll take some doing to blast through all that rock. We got us a few good years before our dreams of being rich railroaders die."

Peter didn't want to accept the bitter truth. Since Congress had granted the Central Pacific the right to lay track east of California, it wouldn't be long before they reached Reno. Word was the CP aimed to make it to Cisco high in the Sierras by year's end and bore tunnels in the mountain passes through the winter. When that happened and the CP met up with the Union Pacific, the Placerville & Sacramento Valley Railroad, now enjoying its heyday, would become a sleepy passenger line.

Unlike his father, who'd counted on selling cattle to the army indefinitely, despite the fact that the war wouldn't last forever, Spencer had a contingency plan. That's why he'd turned down the offer of a company house in town and invested in a place of his own instead. Some thought him crazy, but once his bull arrived and he could begin building a herd of cattle—

"Spence?"

"Yes?" What had he missed?

"I asked if you wanted to take a break and see what kind of pie Miss Minnie fixed today. Based on the mouth-watering smells coming from the café, I'm guessing it's peach."

"As tempting as that sounds, I have too much to do."

"When are you going to relax and have some fun, Cap'n? You can spare ten minutes, can't ya?"

Spencer fought the urge to grimace. He never knew whether the nickname had been bestowed on him out of respect or if his workers were poking fun at him. Sure, he checked up on the various departments, but he trusted his men. He just wanted to assure himself things were running smoothly. His father had spent his time holed up in his office oblivious to his ranch manager's shenanigans, and look where it had gotten him. He'd come close to losing everything.

"Take a whiff. If that hint of cinnamon in the air doesn't win you over, I don't know what will. Then again, perhaps you're saving your appetite for Mrs. Carter's latest culinary catastrophe." Peter gave Spencer a playful punch in the arm.

"She's done her best." The well-intentioned widow had ruined a perfectly good pot roast last night and made chicken as dry and tasteless as paper the night before that.

"Polly tells me Tess knows her way around a kitchen, so your troubles could be over."

"Perhaps." If the food on his table that evening wasn't scorched beyond recognition and he could swallow it without gulping water after each bite, he'd be happy.

"How about joining me, then? That way you know you won't starve."

Peter had a point. The simple dinner of bread and cheese Spencer had eaten at his desk left much to be desired. Supper was hours away, after all. This would give him an opportunity to show his men he wasn't as regimented as they seemed to think. "I'll drop this off—" he held up his notebook "—let Drake know where to find me and meet you there."

Fifteen minutes later Spencer chewed his last bite of pie, savoring the sweetness of the peach filling. "This was a good idea."

"At least you won't waste away if Tess's cooking doesn't pan out." Peter grinned at his pun. "And speaking of Tess, what do you think of her?"

"It's too soon to tell."

"She's tall. At least as tall as you, isn't she?"

Not quite, if his estimate was correct. "It's the hat."

Peter chuckled. "Quite something, isn't it? She could provide shade for half the town under that thing. Although her taste in bonnets might be questionable, she's easy on the eyes. Or didn't you notice?"

He'd noticed all right. Because of her, he'd had a hard time concentrating ever since he returned from running her to the ranch. Memories of her captivating smile kept resurfacing. "My mind was on the interview."

"Do you think you'll hire her?"

"Maybe. Maybe not. I offered to give her a one-week trial period, but she countered, claiming she could convince me of her suitability in a day. I accepted her challenge." Spencer stood, and Peter followed suit.

"Polly said she's got pluck."

She did indeed. Would her plucky ways keep his headstrong son in line? Or would she resort to mollycoddling to get Luke's cooperation, as several of the church women had? One stick of candy to win him over initially couldn't hurt, but a lack of consistent discipline could ruin him.

Since his son was almost guaranteed to act out at supper, he'd have Miss Grimsby handle the situation. If she didn't exert a firm hand, he'd have no choice but to give her a day's wages and put her on a train back to Sacramento City. He hoped it didn't come to that.

* * *

Tess surveyed the parlor. Mrs. Abbott had certainly loved red. At least she'd chosen burgundy furnishings rather than the cherry red on the house itself. The plush chairs and settee in the rich color coordinated with the blue flowers sprinkled amid sprays of wine-colored roses on the wallpaper's white background. Some slate-blue accents would bring out the secondary color and add a soothing element. Curtains, pillows and a rug, too.

She could imagine Mr. Abbott in the wingback armchair by the fireplace, a child on each knee. A sewing basket sat on the table beside the settee. His wife's favorite place to sit had likely been the end of it nearest him. The picture of domestic bliss.

A wistful sigh escaped, and Tess chided herself. Giving way to the longing for a family of her own would do no good. She mustn't fuel futile dreams. How many times had Mr. Grimsby told her she'd best prepare for a lifetime of service?

His words uttered on her tenth birthday came back as sharp and piercing as ever. *No man will look twice at you, Tess. You're going to tower over most of them. And those who are tall won't be interested in a woman who can look them in the eye. A man wants to feel superior in all respects. Take my word for it, and apply yourself to your studies, so you can earn a decent living.*

And then came the nickname. Of course Charlie had been the one who'd overheard that dreadful conversation. Charlie, who taunted anyone and everyone, from the youngest children all the way to the orphanage director himself.

Too-Tall Tess.

That's what Charlie had dubbed her, and nothing she

could say or do would silence him. So, she'd done the only thing she could—pretended it didn't matter.

From that day on she'd vowed never to let anyone see how much she detested being different. She'd stood tall, proud and unflinching as the other children singsonged the ditty Charlie had coined.

Oh, what a pity! Oh, what a mess!

When God said height, she shoulda asked for less.

She's Too-Tall, Too-Tall, Too-Tall Tess.

It didn't help that Tess wasn't her real name. Mr. Grimsby had given it to her when her father left her at the orphanage, despite the fact that she'd told the domineering director her name was Faith. Although Tess was a fine name, his insistence on using it and offering no reason why had rankled.

After shaking herself from her reverie, Tess smoothed the crisp white cloth covering the pedestal table in the center of the room, repositioned the antimacassar on the back of Spencer's armchair and pronounced the parlor ready for inspection.

Restoring the dining room to rights would take no time at all. The layer of dust coating everything gave evidence no one had eaten there since Mrs. Abbott's passing. Perhaps Mr. Abbott felt her absence in that room more deeply than other places. Replacing old memories with new would help.

Tess gathered the soiled shirts draped over the chairs and picked up the toys. She removed the petrified bouquet serving as the centerpiece. She'd send Mrs. Carter and the children in search of fresh flowers, thus gaining the time needed to scour the kitchen and plan her supper menu.

Discovering the whereabouts of the widow and the little ones was easy. Mrs. Carter must have asked Luke to do something he didn't want to do. His complaints coming from the backyard could be heard throughout the house. That boisterous boy would require a firm hand—and a full measure of compassion. He must miss his mama terribly.

Tess stepped through the back door onto the wrap-around porch. She called to the older woman, who had the baby propped on one hip. They stood beneath a sprawling oak with a rope swing suspended from one of its sturdy branches. "I'd like a fresh bouquet on the table tonight, Mrs. Carter. Might I ask you to pick some flowers? I saw a nice selection in the beds out front."

The widow appeared relieved by the request. Luke even ceased his whining. "The children and me would be happy to do that, wouldn't we, Luke?" She gave him an over-bright smile.

"I don't wanna, and I'm not gonna. I want her to push me on the swing. Right now!" He jabbed a stubby finger at Mrs. Carter.

Tess feigned indifference. "That's all right. I don't want your help, after all."

He eyed her with suspicion. "You don't?"

"No. This is a special job, and you're still quite young. I don't think you could pick flowers without breaking their stems or crushing their petals."

He rammed his fists against his sides and scrunched his face in a sour-pickle expression. "I could, too."

"What do you think, Mrs. Carter? Should we let him try or have him sit with Lila and watch while you pick the flowers?"

Luke snorted. "I'm not a baby. I'm a big boy. Papa says so, and he knows everything."

The snowy-headed woman looked from him to Tess and back again, understanding dawning. "I reckon we could let him try...if he promises to be careful."

"I won't hurt them. I'll show you." He raced around the

corner of the house. Lila bounced on Mrs. Carter's ample hip as she hurried after him.

With the children occupied, Tess had the house to herself once again. She donned her apron and plunged her hands into a tub of hot water. Determined to get the mountain of dirty dishes washed quickly, she attacked an encrusted dinner plate with such fervor that soap bubbles formed on the water's surface. Normally she didn't relish the scent of lye soap, but today she welcomed anything strong enough to cut the lingering stench of the sulfur.

What could she prepare for supper that would overpower the horrid smell and fill the air with tantalizing aromas? When she was out back, she'd noticed a garden with a healthy crop of weeds mounting a takeover. Perhaps she could find some ripe vegetables among those that had rotted on the vines. That would be a start.

"Lord, You know how much I need this position, so please show me what You'd like me to prepare." If He'd led her here, as she believed He had, surely He could provide her with inspiration.

She was eager to impress Mr. Abbott, so he'd hire her. Although he was a bit on the dour side, he struck her as a fair man. Working for the handsome stationmaster could prove to be a distraction, but she was more than willing to deal with that.

Twenty minutes later Tess dried the last bowl, put it in the cupboard and hung the damp dishtowel on its peg. She delivered lemonade to Mrs. Carter and Luke, who'd picked enough flowers to fill two vases.

He leaned back against the porch railing, his ankles and arms crossed, looking adorable despite his dirt-streaked face. "We picked whole bunches of flowers, and I didn't hurt none of them."

Tess smiled. "You did a fine job, Luke. I'll have to tell your papa what a big help you've been."

The little boy beamed, seemed to think better of it and assumed a stoic manner so like his father's it was all she could do not to laugh. She shifted her attention to Mrs. Carter, who sat in a rocking chair with Lila in her lap. "If you're content to enjoy the shade and the cool drink, I'll get to work on the meal."

"We're fine, dearie. Chasin' after these young'uns the past week plumb wore me out, so I'm happy to sit here and keep 'em out from under your petticoats."

Normally Tess would welcome the children's help. She had wonderful memories of working alongside Josette, the cook at the orphanage, when she was a girl. However, since this meal had to be exemplary in order for her to secure the position, she would leave Luke and Lila in Mrs. Carter's care.

Wending her way between the rows of the garden with basket in hand, Tess found what she needed to prepare a light but tasty soup to start the meal.

Luke raced around the house and hollered. "A wagon's coming, and it's not Papa."

She set her bounty by the back door and followed Luke to the front of the house. A wagon rumbled down the rutted road toward them. The young man beside the driver waved. "I wonder who they could be."

The rhythmic creaking of Mrs. Carter's rocking chair ceased. She joined Tess at the porch railing. "Looks like that German man and his son from over yonder." The widow waved her free hand toward the parcel of land to the east. "The young fellow speaks right fine English, but his father ain't learned it so good."

The wagon approached the house with a jangle of harnesses. The driver parked beside the porch. "*Guten Nach-*

mittag. Ve haf Lachs." The stocky older man reached in a pail and pulled out a fish large enough to feed Mr. Abbott, his children, Mrs. Carter and Tess with some left over. "Ve haf much. You must some take."

"See what I mean?" Mrs. Carter muttered.

Tess smiled. "I believe he said 'good afternoon.' It appears he's sharing his catch with us." She knew just what to make for supper. The Lord had evidently heard her prayers.

The driver's son, a young man about eighteen, jumped to the ground. He took the fish from his father, wrapped it in a cloth and held it out to her. "We didn't catch them. They came up on the train. When Vati saw them, he got this one for Mr. Abbott. A gift. Vati knows how difficult it is for a man to lose his wife and be left with children to raise on his own. He wanted to do something to help."

Tess took the fish and nodded at the older man. "That's kind of you, Herr..."

"Mueller," the young man offered. "He's Wolfgang—" he jabbed a thumb at his father "—and I'm Frank."

"Well, thank you both. This is a godsend."

"I've met Mrs. Carter—" Frank nodded in the widow's direction and shifted his attention to Tess "—and you must be Miss Grimsby."

"Yes, I am. I hope to become Mr. Abbott's housekeeper. How did you hear about me?"

"Mr. Flynn over at the railway station told us about you. It seems you stood out. There aren't too many women in Shingle Springs as tall as a *Hopfenpfosten*—a hop pole." He grinned. "I wish you well. I know from helping Vati build the large pen beyond Mr. Abbott's barn that he can be an exacting boss, but he's a fair one."

Mrs. Carter huffed. "If he's to be her boss, she'd best

not spend her day yammerin' with the likes of you. She's got a supper to fix."

Tess chuckled. "As much as I've enjoyed meeting you, Mrs. Carter has a point." She bid the Muellers farewell and headed for the kitchen, eager to fillet the fish.

Some time later Mrs. Carter and the children joined Tess.

"That supper of yours is smellin' mighty good, young lady. What're you fixin'?"

"We'll start with julienne soup. Then we'll have the salmon sprinkled with black butter, served with herbed potatoes and tomato slices. I found fresh peaches in the pantry, so I was able to whip up a pie for dessert."

Lila, who sat on a blanket in the corner, squealed.

Mrs. Carter smiled, proving she had a kind heart beneath her brusque manner. "Sounds like she's happy. Let's hope her papa is, too. I'm more'n ready to leave this place in your hands and get back to mine."

Tess stirred the soup. If Mr. Abbott didn't arrive soon, the vegetables would be mush.

As if on cue, a wagon pulled in.

"Papa!" Luke took off.

Mrs. Carter lifted Lila into her arms. "We'll go meet him, wash up and give you time to get the last of your supper rustled up. You'll find us waitin' in the dinin' room."

The next ten minutes flew by in a blur as Tess grilled the salmon and browned the butter. She removed her apron and said a silent prayer of thanks. Everything had turned out fine, after all. Savoring the sense of accomplishment, she poured the soup into the tureen, grabbed a ladle and headed to the dining room.

Mr. Abbott's deep voice carried, sending a shiver of excitement shimmying up her spine. "It certainly smells better in here. Do you know what we're having, son?"

Luke made a horrid sound like a cat trying to rid itself of a hairball. "I don't want any of it 'cept for the pie. She ruined the soup and burned the fish."

Tess came to an abrupt stop in the doorway, the soup she carried sloshing precariously. Luke's uncomplimentary proclamation was to be expected, but the welcome hint of merriment in Mr. Abbott's eyes had faded all too rapidly, leaving him looking as formidable as ever.

Well, he could frown all he liked. She was an excellent cook and would impress him with her culinary skills, or her name wasn't Tess Grimsby.

She marched into the room with her head held high.

Chapter Four

Spencer didn't know which amused him more, Luke's antics or Miss Grimsby's show of pique. He hid his twitching lips behind his napkin. "Luke, that's unkind. We must be grateful for what we're served."

She set a large bowl of soup on the table, performed an about-face and left the room without a word.

He cast a glance at Mrs. Carter, seated to his left on the other side of Luke with Lila in her lap. The widow appeared to be concealing a smile, too. "You got nothin' to fear, Mr. Abbott. I slurped a spoonful of the soup earlier, and it's delicious."

"I look forward to tasting it myself."

"But she said the soup was ruined, Papa. I heard her."

"I said no such thing." Miss Grimsby placed a platter of fish in front of Spencer that smelled so good his mouth watered. "It's julienne soup. Not *ruined* soup. I gather you've never had it before."

Luke shook his head so soundly his long hair flapped from side to side. "Mama didn't fix things with funny names. She made what Papa likes. Steak and baked potatoes. Not smelly old burned fish."

"I didn't burn the fish, Luke. What makes you think

that?" Miss Grimsby gazed at the ceiling for several moments.

All of a sudden she nodded. "I understand. You heard me tell Mrs. Carter I was going to make black butter to drizzle over the fish. The butter's not really black, though. It's just browned, and it tastes good. I'll bring in the rest of the food, and you can see for yourself."

She returned with a dish of small potatoes cut into chunks and sprinkled with herbs, along with a plate of artistically arranged tomato slices. Rather fancy fare for a family supper. Not that Spencer was complaining. Steak and baked potatoes were fine, but a man could do with a change on occasion.

And fresh fish? How had she managed that? This looked to be salmon. His favorite. Trudy couldn't stomach seafood, so he'd not had any in years.

His gut tightened. Trudy. He'd eat steak and potatoes every day for the rest of his life if that would give him one more hour with her. One more opportunity to take her in his arms, pull her to his chest and feel the silkiness of her hair against his chin. One more chance to tell her how sorry he was for—

"Mr. Abbott?"

"Hmm?"

Miss Grimsby sat at the opposite end of the rectangular table with Lila in her lap. "Did you want to say grace?"

"Yes. Of course."

She took Lila's hands in hers, pressed the baby's palms together and covered them with her own.

Spencer swallowed the boulder that lodged in his throat at the site of his little girl in another woman's arms, a capable and caring woman as different from Trudy as California was from Texas. A comely woman who'd filled his thoughts far too often since their trackside meeting.

"Thank You, Father, for the meal and for...the h-hands that prepared it."

He cast a furtive glance around the table to see if anyone had noticed his hesitation. Mrs. Carter and Luke's heads were bowed. Miss Grimsby, on the other hand, had something akin to sympathy on her face. When she realized he'd seen her, she blushed a pretty shade of pink and squeezed her eyes shut. He hastened to cover his halting start. "Thank You that we can gather around the table to enjoy this unexpected treat. Be with us as we partake. In Christ's name. Amen."

Miss Grimsby plopped some potatoes on her plate and averted her gaze, for which he was grateful. The only sound was the clink of silverware on porcelain as they filled their plates.

Spencer dipped his spoon into the soup. Despite the strange name, the little strips of vegetables swimming in broth were tastier than he'd expected. Crisp, not mushy—just the way he liked them.

How strange it was to be in the dining room. They hadn't eaten there since Trudy's dea— in months. The shirts he'd slung over the chairs were gone, the tabletop gleamed and his wife's cherished vase overflowed with a massive bouquet. "Those flowers. Where did they come from?"

"We picked them, Papa. Me and her." Luke pointed to Mrs. Carter.

"They're from the beds out front, aren't they?" He hadn't meant for his question to come out with such force, but—

"They are." Miss Grimsby eyed him warily. "I thought they would brighten the table and fill the air with a pleasant aroma. Is there a problem?"

"My wife planted them. They were her pride and joy."

"I'm sorry, sir. I didn't know."

There was no way she could have. The vase was so full of colorful blooms that there couldn't be many left out front. But there would be more. In time. "It's all right."

Miss Grimsby's fine features relaxed, although he detected pity in the glance she sent him. Sympathy was bad enough, but he wanted no part of pity.

Conversation had ceased following his heated question. Not that he could blame the others for being quiet. The same thing often happened at the rail station when his feelings got the better of him, which happened far too often these days. He must regain control.

His normally unobtrusive daughter wriggled and whimpered. His prospective housekeeper had her hands full holding Lila while trying to eat. The baby's flailing fist sent Miss Grimsby's spoon sailing. Then his little girl flung her arms open wide and said "Papa" as clear as you please. Her first word ever, and she'd said it for him.

"It would appear she wants you, sir."

"So it does. Would you mind bringing her to me?"

Miss Grimsby did so and promptly returned to her seat. He caressed Lila's cheek. She gave him a dimple-producing smile, showing off her first four teeth. It was hard to believe she was already ten months old and had been without a mother three of them.

It soon became clear he wouldn't be able to get much eating done with his squirming daughter in his lap. Trudy had always been the one to hold Lila during meals. A woman seemed to have a knack for juggling a baby while eating that he lacked.

"Would you mind bringing your plate down here, Miss Grimsby, and sitting beside me so you can help with Lila?" He inclined his head toward the chair on his right.

"Certainly." She quickly obliged.

"No!" Luke shrieked. "She can't sit there. That's Mama's chair."

"What do you think you're doing, son? You know better than to yell at the supper table."

"Make her get up."

"She's sitting there, and that's that." Spencer could understand how difficult it must be for Luke to see another woman in Trudy's place, but the sooner he accepted the new order of things, the better. Miss Grimsby had already managed to lift the gloom that had settled in on that dark April day when he'd lost Trudy after her unfortunate accident in the garden. The house wasn't just clean. It felt welcoming for the first time in months.

Lila fussed again, and Spencer turned to comfort her. Something cool and wet hit his cheek and fell to the floor. He hadn't even figured out what it was when another of the sticky projectiles pelted him in the chest, leaving a round, red spot on his white shirt before sliding beneath his waistcoat. Luke must be lobbing tomato slices at him.

Sure enough, a third slab sailed across the table and landed in his lap. "Lucas Mark Abbott, you stop that this minute, or I'll—"

"I can handle this, sir. Here." Miss Grimsby handed Lila to him once again, grabbed Luke by the hand and forced him to follow her. "You're coming with me, young man."

Taken unaware, Luke didn't have time to protest. He shot a pleading look at Spencer, who inclined his head toward Miss Grimsby. "Go."

Because the attack had taken him by surprise, he'd forgotten his plan to have Miss Grimsby handle any needed discipline and had been ready to take his son to task. She'd taken charge of the situation before Spencer had time to act—a bold but admirable choice. He was curious to see what she'd do.

As much as he detested the thought of leaving the care of his children to a virtual stranger, he had no choice. He'd know soon what type of disciplinarian she was and if she could be trusted with his children.

Mrs. Carter paused with her fork halfway to her mouth. "That young woman is just what you been needin', Mr. Abbott. You'd be a fool to let her get away." She went right on eating, which suited Spencer, since he couldn't think of a suitable response.

Lila poked his cheek with a pudgy finger. "Papa." That one word meant more to him than he'd thought possible. It seemed like only yesterday Luke had said it for the first time.

"Yes, my sweet. I'm your papa. And you're my little princess." He kissed her forehead, letting his lips linger a moment. Trudy used to say nothing was as soft or sweet as a baby's skin, and she was right.

But she was gone, and this precious girl would have no memories of her mother. The all-too-familiar ache squeezed his chest.

Spencer strained to hear what was taking place in the parlor, but other than the murmur of voices, he couldn't make out anything. No screaming. No crying. No spanking. The higher pitch indicated Miss Grimsby was doing most of the talking. He'd like to be privy to that conversation.

A good two minutes went by with Lila gnawing on a potato chunk, Mrs. Carter shoveling in her salmon and Spencer doing his best to clean up the aftermath of Luke's assault while balancing Lila on one knee. If Miss Grimsby and Luke didn't return soon, Spencer would have no choice but to intervene.

Moments later Miss Grimsby and Luke appeared in the dining room doorway. Rather than the defiant stance Spencer expected, Luke's shoulders slumped. He scuffed the toe of his shoe over the wooden floor, his eyes downcast, and mumbled something.

Miss Grimbsy leaned over and spoke softly beside Luke's ear. "Remember what I said. Look at your papa and say it loudly enough for him to hear."

"She said I gotta tell you I'm sorry. So, I'm sorry. I didn't mean to make you sad."

"I'm not sad, son. I'm disappointed. Throwing things is not the way a gentleman deals with his anger. You must be punished for this."

"He will be, sir." Miss Grimsby picked up Luke's plate. "Right now he's going to finish his meal at the kitchen table. Alone. And tomorrow he's going to scrub your shirt until the tomato stain is gone."

With Luke exiled and Lila back in Miss Grimsby's lap, Spencer was free to enjoy the meal, one of the best he'd been served in a long time. The food rivaled that prepared at the restaurants in Sacramento City's finest hotels.

Miss Grimsby chatted with Mrs. Carter about the town, the weather and numerous other topics. Spencer made no effort to join in. He was content to enjoy his supper and the fact that—should his conversation with Miss Grimsby afterward prove satisfactory—he'd be having many more like it in the days to come. The prospect of coming home and finding the good-looking woman in his kitchen lifted his spirits more than it should.

A glance at Luke proved that being forced to eat by himself was an effective punishment. The wistfulness in his eyes made Spencer consider overriding Miss Grimsby and allowing Luke to rejoin them. But only for the briefest moment.

If he did hire her, he couldn't undermine her authority. One didn't treat one's employees that way. She deserved respect, and he'd give it to her. In return she would brighten his world and make his days a bit more bearable.

Tess stood on the porch and watched the wagon grow smaller. With Luke accompanying his father on the trip to take Mrs. Carter home, she could clear the dining table quickly, make short work of the dishes and plan what she'd serve for breakfast.

"If there's time, lovely Lila, I'll give you a bath. It doesn't look like you've had one in ages." She kissed each of the baby's cheeks and held her close for a minute, savoring the incredible sweetness of having a little one to care for. At ten months, Lila was her youngest charge ever—and so pretty.

The baby had her father's striking eyes—the brilliant blue of an alpine lake—as well as his golden hair. Luke, on the other hand, must take after his mother, although the brown-haired, brown-eyed boy did have Mr. Abbott's broad forehead and strong jaw. If he ended up half as handsome as his father, he'd be a fine-looking man one day.

"What am I doing woolgathering when I have work to do?" She set Lila on a blanket in the corner of the kitchen. The little girl banged her blocks together while making sounds resembling speech. At this rate she'd be adding words to her vocabulary in no time.

Lila held out a block to Tess. "Papa."

"No, sweetheart. I'm not your papa, but he'll be home soon." She left the baby attempting to build a tower and attacked the dishes.

What would Mr. Abbott have to say when he talked with her after his return? Perhaps she'd been hasty in her handling of Luke, but if he was allowed to get away with bad behavior, he could turn out like Charlie. Although the boy from her orphanage days was bright, he'd become a bully and a troublemaker. She wouldn't let that happen to her young charge.

By the time Mr. Abbott and Luke returned, the kitchen was clean, the next day's breakfast was planned, and Lila was bathed and ready for bed. Tess didn't relish the tug-of-war sure to take place if Mr. Abbott expected her to put Luke down for the night. Something told her the boy would raise a ruckus. After her travel and hard work, along with the pressure to please, her bed at the hotel was calling her name. By the time she walked the mile back to town, she'd have to force herself to stay awake long enough to complete her toilette.

She went out front with Lila resting against her chest. "I'm glad you're back. She's about to nod off."

"He has." Mr. Abbott pointed to Luke, asleep on the wagon seat next to him, his head in his father's lap. "I'll see if I can get him upstairs without waking him."

With slow, steady movements, Mr. Abbott extricated himself, gathered Luke in his arms and mounted the stairs. "Come with me please, Miss Grimsby."

She complied.

Luke didn't stir as his father carried him to his room and put him to bed. Mr. Abbott rummaged under the rumpled bedding, pulled out a crib-size quilt and laid it next to his sleeping son. "Good night, my boy. May God bless your slumber." He placed a kiss on Luke's brow, a gesture so tender that Tess's lips trembled.

She couldn't remember anyone ever tucking her in or praying a blessing over her like that. Mr. Abbott might have a serious mien, but he was a caring father.

"Come to Papa, princess." He took his daughter from

Tess and, with a tilt of his head, beckoned her to follow him to Lila's room.

Mr. Abbott repeated the bedtime routine and launched into a lullaby, his beautiful baritone filling the room. Tess, who loved music but was about as melodic as a mule, marveled at the gift given him. If anyone had told her the stoic stationmaster sang to his children, she wouldn't have believed it. What a surprising man. She looked forward to learning more about him.

Lila was asleep before her father reached the last verse. He smoothed the sheet over her and placed a small quilt by her side, as he'd done with Luke.

"Your wife's handiwork I presume?"

"It was the last thing she made. She'd planned to make a quilt for us, too, but..." He released a ragged breath. Tess had a sudden urge to place a comforting hand on his shoulder as he gazed at his daughter but stopped herself just in time.

He cast a lingering look at the sleeping girl and turned to Tess, all business once again. "I'll see to the horses while you're still here to watch the children. Give me ten minutes, and meet me on the porch."

"Yes, sir." He left, and she sank into the cozy rocking chair where Mrs. Abbott had likely nursed the baby. Tess spent a good five minutes listening to the rhythm of the rockers on the wooden floor and drinking in the sight of Lila's cherubic lips parted as she drew in measured breaths. *Lord, if it's Your plan for me to care for these children, I'd be grateful.*

Tess forced herself to leave the nursery. She paused in the doorway of Luke's room. The sheet Mr. Abbott had spread over his son had become tangled in the short time he'd been in bed. Even in slumber the boy was active.

Luke's room was strewn with toys, whereas Lila's was

devoid of clutter. Tess would help him clean his, so it would be a pleasant place to play. Not that she could picture him spending much time indoors. He was a boy who needed to get outside and expend some of his abundant energy.

She heaved a wistful sigh, made her way downstairs and busied herself in the kitchen. The parlor clock chimed. A quarter to eight already.

The time had come. She must face Mr. Abbott and find out if her hard work had secured her the position. He'd appreciated the meal. That was clear. But was he willing to welcome another woman into his home and entrust his children to her care—even a competent one such as she?

Tess located him on the porch, his hands resting on the railing, his gaze fixed on some distant point. She'd seen that look on the face of every man she'd worked for, the look of a man surveying his territory, be it his business, his house or his land.

She stood beside him, got a glimpse of his face and fought a wave of nausea. If Mr. Abbott's scowl was an indication of his thoughts, she'd be on her way back to Sacramento City tomorrow. She didn't know which would hurt worse—being denied the opportunity to care for adventurous Luke and his adorable baby sister or saying goodbye to their intriguing father.

Chapter Five

Mr. Abbott spun to face Tess. He caught her staring at his soiled front, where Luke had splatted him with a tomato. "It looks like I'll be hauling out the washtub after you leave."

"You're going to wash your shirt now? Tonight?"

His intention to see to the task himself surprised Tess, but not as much as her desire to tend to it for him. If she did, she'd have another half hour's work before she could leave and would have to arrive early enough the next day to iron the shirt before he headed to the railway station.

He leaned against the porch railing with his arms and ankles crossed, looking quite appealing—aside from the red splotch in the middle of his chest. She couldn't keep from smiling.

"Since this was my last clean shirt, I don't have a choice." He swept a hand toward the unsightly spot and gave a hollow laugh, but his attempt to lighten the mood couldn't mask the embarrassment that had left his neck flushed.

The admission hadn't been an easy one for him. Somehow she'd have to summon the strength needed, because she wasn't about to let him struggle with a chore sure to be foreign to him. Not when she could make short work of it. "I'll wash one of your shirts, but not that one. Luke's going to help me with it."

Relief flooded his fine features. "I shouldn't accept your offer since it's getting late, but I can't stop myself. The past few weeks have been— Thank you."

Her heart swelled with sympathy. "You are in need of help, aren't you?"

"I've managed."

"Yes, but life would be easier if you had someone to see to such things." Not *someone*. Her.

"My wife...she made sure I had..." He pressed a fist to his mouth. "I never expected to be in this position."

"Things *will* be different, Mr. Abbott. There's no denying that, but I can ease your burden, provided you'll let me. You've seen that I can cook and clean—and that I won't let Luke drive the locomotive."

Her metaphor elicited a smile. A halfhearted one but a smile nonetheless. She'd pushed as hard as she dared. Now to wait for his response.

It came before she had time to take a breath. "You said you could prove your worth in a day, and you've done that. The job's yours—for now. We'll reevaluate in a month after we've had time to see if the situation is agreeable to both of us."

Relief washed over her. It took great restraint not to shout "Hallelujah!" She'd secured the position. Now to make a personal request. "I realize a housekeeper generally goes by her surname, but in the homes where I served as governess, I was called by my Christian name. I'd prefer that."

He raised an eyebrow. "You want me to use your first name?"

"I was thinking of the children. Tess would be easier

for them to say." And she wouldn't have to answer to Mr. Grimsby's last name on a daily basis. Every time she heard it she was reminded of the dictatorial orphanage director who'd given it to her when she'd shown up on his doorstep too young and too traumatized to recall hers.

"You make a valid point, so I'll allow it, provided you'll call me Spencer."

She hadn't expected him to agree so readily, but she was glad he had. Spencer was a fine name, and she would enjoy using it. "Really?" She adopted a playful tone. "I thought a man like you who's used to being in charge might prefer *master* or *your eminence*." She fought to keep a straight face but lost the battle and laughed.

His eyebrows shot all the way to the ceiling. Perhaps she'd gone too far. He was a grieving widower, after all.

"You certainly have some spice to you, Tess. I do believe you and Luke will get on just fine." He cast a glance to the west. "It'll be late before you get to town. I can't leave the children alone to drive you. Will you be all right walking by yourself?"

"Yes, sir. I mean Spencer." While she appreciated his concern, she wouldn't be alone. The Lord was always with her. She would spend the time in prayer. After all, she had much to thank Him for. She'd told Him the desire of her heart, and it seemed He'd heard her. She had a family to care for and looked forward to delightful days ahead as she made a difference in their lives.

Spencer bid her farewell and headed inside, slowly shaking his head and sporting an amused smile.

Was the taciturn gentleman actually laughing? *Lord, let it be so. He could use some levity in his life.*

Tess hung the hoe on its pegs in the garden shed and rubbed her lower back. Running a household was harder than she'd thought. Even though she'd been working for Spencer two weeks, she had yet to grow accustomed to the constant juggling required.

The amount of work itself was a challenge, but the isolation made her want to scream. Some adult company would be nice. She saw Spencer at breakfast and again at supper, but their interactions were focused on household matters and the children, which was as it should be. She was his housekeeper, not his friend.

At least she'd get to see Polly while she was in town today. In the meantime she would have to keep Luke from soiling his clothing before she could get the team hitched to the wagon. That boy attracted dirt like a garden attracted critters. The latter problem had been solved by a chicken wire fence. The former seemed a hopeless cause.

She'd had to do some talking before Mr. Abbott agreed to have the fence built. For some reason, he seemed concerned about her working in the garden. She'd had to assure him three times that she would be careful and never leave tools laying on the ground where someone could get hurt. As though she would.

Tess lifted Lila out of the tub she'd set at the side of the garden and headed to the house. Spencer's dog trotted across the yard. The poor creature was bare in spots, but the salve had done its job, arresting the mange. Once his coffee-colored fur grew back, he'd be a fine-looking fellow. He'd proven to be a good watchdog, alerting her when anything was amiss.

"I'm going to leave Luke in your care." She patted the dog's head. "You'll let me know if he starts to wander off again, won't you?" She went inside to get ready for the shopping trip.

An hour later Tess sat on the porch of Polly's small house in downtown Shingle Springs, a glass of lemonade in her hand. Luke darted around the yard in search of insects. Polly's two-year-old daughter, Abby, did her best to keep up. Lila slept on a blanket near Tess.

Polly rubbed her rounded belly. "I've never seen you looking more content. Being a housekeeper agrees with you."

Tess chuckled. "If you'd been privy to my thoughts earlier, you'd disagree. I've gained a whole new respect for mothers with no hired help. How *do* you fit everything into your days?"

"Caring for a house while keeping two little ones out of trouble is much different than supervising the cultured children of Sacramento City's elite as we did before, but it's what you've always wanted."

What she wanted was a family of her own—impossible dream though it might be—not to step into one in the throes of grief, with a woebegone widower and a headstrong four-year-old. But that's exactly what she'd done. Meeting their needs was proving more difficult than she'd anticipated. Despite her desire to help them heal, she'd made little progress. "I have the situation under control."

"So I hear. Peter told me he caught Spencer smiling yesterday. When he asked him why, Spencer said he was looking forward to seeing what you'd fixed for supper. Apparently he's a man who appreciates good food."

"He does tuck in hearty portions of whatever I put in front of him. The only thing I've found that he doesn't care for is cottage cheese. I asked him to let me know if there's anything else he doesn't like, but he just said 'everything's fine.'"

Polly shifted in the rocking chair, causing it to creak. "He's not one for making long speeches, is he?"

Tess laughed. "When I give Spencer a review of the day, I usually get one or two words in reply. If I manage to get five sentences out of him in an evening, I feel like I've achieved quite a feat. I can understand his brooding silence, but he seldom interacts with the children, except when he tucks them in at night. That's so sad. I know fathers have to deal with the demands of their jobs, but their children crave a connection with them." She couldn't keep the wistfulness out of her voice.

Polly patted her arm. "Oh, Tessie, I'm sorry. Whenever I think of your father leaving you at the orphanage, my blood boils. I'll never understand how a parent could walk away from a child like that, especially one as bright and beautiful as you. What *was* he thinking?"

"A man can't raise a child alone." How many times had she told herself that? But her father hadn't even attempted it, giving her up the very day her mother had gone to be with the Lord. She'd never heard from him again.

"I know, but he could have found you a home with a family who would love you. Or gotten help like Spencer has."

Her father didn't want her. No man did. Not that she could blame them. Even if she wasn't taller than most of them, she lacked the beauty or charm that attracted men. It seemed her height was the only thing people noticed. Granted, she had six to ten inches on most women, but she wasn't a circus sideshow freak, although there were days she felt like one.

A sharp cry rang out. Luke had pinned his playmate's arm behind her.

"Abby!" Polly struggled to stand, but her bulging middle made the task difficult.

Tess leaped to her feet, her long strides carrying her across the yard in no time. "Let go of her this minute, Luke."

"It's my ladybug. I saw it first."

She pried his hands from Abby's arm, spun him around and dropped to one knee in front of him. "That may be, but you can't hold her like that. You could hurt her."

"I didn't."

That was true. Abby had flitted away unharmed and was back on the hunt. "You're right, but you could have. Since you're older than she is, you can make good choices—like your papa does."

"What kind of choices does he make?"

"Well, he chose where to live. Where to work. Who to have look after you."

Luke's eyes filled with tears, and he swiped a dirty sleeve across them. "I don't want anyone to look after me. Just my mama. I want her to come back."

"I know, sweetheart. But she's gone. You do have your papa, and he loves you very much." It took all her self-restraint not to pull the brokenhearted boy into her arms. She contented herself by caressing his cheek.

He swatted her hand away. "Don't touch me!"

"It's not polite to hit people. You need to sit on the top step until you calm down."

He sat but bounced right back up and clomped down the stairs.

"Luke," Tess called.

The rebellious boy spun around. "I'm calm. See?" He gave her a toothy grin.

She hid her answering smile behind her hand. "Very well."

Polly waited until he was out of earshot. "He's always been a strong-willed little fellow, but he began acting out after Trudy's death. You're good with him, though."

Tess warmed at the compliment. "I want to show him I care, but he's built a wall. It will take time to bring it down, but I've thought of a way to remove a brick."

She launched into an explanation of her plan, not stopping until she was done, despite the skepticism on Polly's face. "What do you think?"

"I think you're asking for trouble. Spencer isn't one to embrace change on a good day."

"I have a valid argument."

Polly swirled her glass of lemonade. "That may be, but you'd better brace yourself for some resistance."

She could deal with resistance. She'd overcome it a number of times when approaching her previous employers. They'd come to see things her way—eventually. Spencer was a reasonable man, so surely he'd be willing to consider her proposal.

Chapter Six

"Absolutely not." Spencer couldn't believe what Tess had suggested. She'd been here all of two weeks, and yet she had the audacity to barge into his office and stick that aristocratic nose of hers where it didn't belong. He'd come to value her opinions, but she'd gone too far this time.

"If you would allow me to explain…"

He stood behind his desk. She faced him, unflinching. Because of the high heels on her boots, the thick brown braid wound around her crown and that monstrosity of a hat, she had several inches on him. It was too bad he couldn't wear his top hat indoors.

Although he had no intention of changing his mind, he would hear her out. "Kindly take a seat, and we can discuss this."

She sat tall and proud. Spencer remained standing and tapped the toe of his boot. The sooner she got to the point, the sooner he could get back to work.

The forthright woman wasted no time stating her case. "I don't want to leave the children with Polly any longer than necessary, so I'll be direct. Parting with a loved one's possessions can be difficult, but it's a necessary step in the grieving process. I can't begin to imagine how difficult it must be for you to see your late wife's things every time you open your clothes cupboard."

"I'm fine."

"I felt sure you'd say that, but there's another factor to take into consideration—Luke's feelings."

Feelings? Why did women put so much stock in them? He had no desire to discuss his or his son's. "Leave him out of this."

She forged ahead as though she hadn't heard him. "I believe much of his misbehavior stems from the fact that he's grieving the loss of his mother. If you were to allow him to help me pack up her things and face his loss head on, I feel certain you'd see a change."

"I'll have a talk with him and tell him he must regain control of himself."

Tess had the audacity to laugh in his face, a musical sound he usually enjoyed. But not today. "This is Luke we're taking about. A mere boy. He's too young to master his emotions." She sobered at his frown. "Oh, dear. I've angered you."

"You presume to know my feelings now?" She had no idea what he was dealing with. How waking each morning alone in the room he and Trudy had shared brought back the stabbing pain that had pierced his heart when she'd drawn her last breath. How dragging himself to the railway station day after day required Herculean effort.

She persisted. "You're clenching your hands."

He unfurled the fists he hadn't realized he'd formed. "I'm not angry. I'm...frustrated. You waltz in here with no warning, interrupt my work and expect me to make a decision on the spot." He placed his palms on his desktop and leaned forward. "Let me make myself clear. I want things left as they are. I know what's best for my family, and you will abide by my wishes."

"I would if I could, but I can't keep quiet, not when one of your children is hurting. Luke let it slip that he misses his mother. Please give me permission. If not for your sake, for his." She lifted pleading eyes to him. Warm cocoa-brown eyes with the longest lashes he'd ever seen.

"He told *you* he's missing her? He hasn't said anything to me."

"Boys don't like to admit weakness—even sadness— to their fathers."

She was right. He would never think of telling his father how much he missed his mother. "Fine. You've made your point. You may remove all her things."

"What would you like me to do with them? Store them in the attic? Donate them to the missionary barrels? Or...?"

He spread the next day's train schedules on his desk. "Do whatever you'd like. I don't care. Just don't bring this up again. *Please.*" He had a job to do and didn't have time to think about such matters.

Tess stood. Her every word was clothed with compassion. "I'm sorry this is such a difficult time for you. I wish I could do more to help."

"Do your job. That's all I ask."

Sadness filled her eyes. She quickly blinked it away, sent him a polite smile and left, giving him the impression he'd disappointed her.

So be it. He didn't need her sympathy. All he wanted was to be left alone.

Red. Every one of Trudy Abbott's tiny dresses boasted a different shade. A petite woman, such as she'd been, could wear the vibrant color and look stunning. Tess preferred her understated blues. People made enough fuss about her height as it was without drawing more attention by looking like a red-hot poker.

The massive wardrobe in Spencer's room held few of his items but brimmed with his late wife's clothing. Tess pulled out a gown and laid the stunning creation on the four-poster bed. Luke sat cross-legged in the middle. He grabbed the dress and plunged his face into the folds. Was the dear boy crying?

He lowered the glossy fabric, his lips downturned in a pronounced pout. "I can't smell her anymore. She used to smell like roses."

"She must have worn rosewater. I do sometimes, but the scent doesn't last long."

He shoved the dress aside, scooted up to the headboard and leaned against it, his arms folded. He narrowed his eyes and shot daggers at Tess. "I don't wanna help."

"Hush now. I don't want you to wake your sister. You can just watch, but I would like your help with one thing. I don't know which of these dresses were your mama's favorites. Do you?"

He shook his head, but the telltale twitch around his mouth was a clear indication he wasn't being truthful. She held up the crimson silk, a gown so exquisite she wondered where the woman would have worn it. "Do you remember her wearing this one?"

Luke's expression didn't change, so Tess set the dress aside. She worked her way through a burgundy brocade, a scarlet satin and a vermillion velvet. Not one of the ornately trimmed garments—none of which showed wear—evoked a response. She reached for a calico the color of cherries generously kissed by the sun that had obviously seen a season or two, and Luke jerked his head. Three more calicos, two lawns and a red-and-white checked gingham elicited similar responses. Tess added the dresses to the growing pile.

Trudy Abbott had owned far more clothing than a

small-town housewife needed. If Tess were to venture a guess, she'd say the woman had come from a family of means. If that was the case, how had she ended up married to Spencer and living in a remote community like Shingle Springs? Someone of her tastes generally gravitated to Sacramento City or San Francisco.

Luke inched forward, casting surreptitious glances at Tess. She averted her gaze but kept him in her peripheral vision. When he reached the pile of his mother's everyday dresses, he leaned over and sniffed one as he'd done earlier. He beamed. "I can smell her!"

Tess didn't have the heart to tell the dear boy she'd dabbed herself with rosewater before leaving her room at the boardinghouse and that some of the scent must have come off on the clothing. "How nice."

He clamored off the bed and darted out of the room, making little sound in his stocking-clad state, for which Tess was grateful. Moments later he returned clutching his crib-size quilt. He rubbed a corner of it against his mother's dress, put the fabric to his nose and drew in a deep breath. Seemingly satisfied, he lay on his side, silent but watchful. And still.

By the time Tess had folded the dresses and stowed them in some crates she'd found in the barn, Luke had fallen asleep with the quilt pressed to his cheek. She'd never seen him as relaxed, even in slumber. She leaned over and pressed a kiss to his brow.

An idea struck her. She located the bottle of rosewater that had belonged to Luke's mother and flicked several drops of the floral-scented liquid on Luke's quilt. The fragrance, although strong now, would fade quickly, but perhaps smelling it again would help lock the scent in his memory.

Now to make good use of the unexpected hour while

both children slept. She could spare them the pain of witnessing the removal of their mother's things from the house.

Working quickly, Tess stowed the items from the dressing table in a crate. She opened the bureau drawers Spencer's wife had used and removed an impressive selection of nightwear and unmentionables, including several pair of expensive silk stockings.

She picked up a stack of corsets, and a bundle of letters tied with a red ribbon fell at her feet. Letters exchanged between Mr. Spencer Abbott in California and Miss Trudy Endicott of Houston, Texas. Love letters most likely.

Unsure what to do, Tess added them to the crate. Spencer had said he didn't want to talk about his late wife's things, but she had no choice. Surely he'd want to save something so special. He might not be up to reading the letters now, but in time they could serve to bring him comforting reminders of his courtship.

Letters were important. Those she'd taken to writing to her someday fiancé on her birthday each year brought her solace in the midst of her loneliness. She used her real name, Faith, when she penned them. Somehow it seemed fitting that the man she hoped to marry would be the only person to know the name—along with the sensitive side of her that she kept hidden. She certainly wouldn't want to lose those letters.

She carted the crates downstairs and added Trudy's hats and cloak from the foyer, her aprons from the kitchen and her sewing basket from the parlor. Tess didn't have the heart to remove anything more than the most obvious personal items. She stowed the crates in the attic, where they would available should Spencer or the children want to see Trudy's things again someday.

Her task complete, she moved from room to room. Although the changes were subtle, the removal of the everpresent reminders of his late wife might lessen Spencer's pain. Would he notice the difference?

Chapter Seven

Spencer's steps slowed as he neared the house. Trudy used to have their son watch for him each evening and alert her when he approached so she could greet him, but Tess involved Luke in the supper preparations. Spencer missed the warm welcome.

He entered, reached up to set his top hat on the shelf above the coat hooks and froze. Trudy's cloak was gone, as was her profusion of fancy bonnets. His slouch hat and Tess's monstrosity were the only hats remaining. His hat rested on its crown to keep the brim from losing its shape, whereas hers, with its frothy fabric and feathers, sat right side up. It was a wonder the massive thing didn't fall off.

Apparently Tess had wasted no time clearing out Trudy's things. Considering her belief that doing so would help Luke, her haste made sense. Clearly she cared about his son.

Spencer marched upstairs to his room, threw open the wardrobe doors and stared at the empty space. True to her word, Tess had removed every last one of Trudy's dresses. His few items looked lost in the large clothes cupboard. He yanked open the drawers on Trudy's side of the bu-

reau and found gaping caverns. Tess was not only fast.
She was thorough.

But why, if she'd whisked away all of Trudy's things,
did the room smell so strongly of roses, as though his wife
had been there moments before? He had to do something
to clear his head. Now.

As quickly as he could, he changed from his work
clothes to ranch wear. He shut the doors of the wardrobe
with more force than he'd intended and stormed down
the stairs, not stopping until he reached the barn. Inhaling deeply of the scents of his childhood—horses, straw
and leather—his senses were restored.

Spying his ropes, he knew what to do. He grabbed
his favorite one and entered the pen. With the coils of
his lariat in his left hand, he spun the loop with his right
and let it fly.

Tess wiped her hands on a kitchen towel and stepped
out the back door. What was Spencer doing? She'd worked
hard to have supper ready when he got home, but he'd
raised a ruckus in his room overhead, with doors and
drawers slamming, and stomped out of the house a good
ten minutes ago. Evidently he was angry about the changes
she'd made, even though he'd given her permission.

Regret settled in her stomach like a rock. In her desire
to help Luke, she'd neglected to take Spencer's feelings
into consideration. What was done was done, but perhaps
she could find a way to show that she understood his pain
and assure him she was only trying to ease it.

She followed the wraparound porch to the north side
of the house where she could see the barn and stopped,
her chin dropping. Never had she seen a man work off his
anger by lassoing things. She stood transfixed as Spencer
spun his loop and threw it.

He roped fence post after fence post, not missing a single one. His form and prowess were awe-inspiring. She could watch him for hours. If only he hadn't started his roping before supper.

Supper! She dashed inside to rescue her meal, moving pots and pans to the side of the stove where the dishes would stay warm. "Please play with your sister, Luke, while I get your papa."

He grunted a reply.

Tess left the children rolling their canvas ball back and forth. She stepped off the back porch and rounded the corner. To her disappointment, Spencer stood outside the pen with one foot resting on the lowest slat of the fence, gazing into the distance.

Loath to disturb him and yet having no choice, she crossed the yard, her boots making little sound on the hard-packed earth. She reached him and rested a hand on his shoulder.

He started.

"Forgive me. I didn't mean to surprise you, but supper's ready."

His eyes widened, and he shook his head as though clearing it. "The smell. It's you. I wasn't imagining it. I thought…"

"Luke noticed it, too. I didn't know your wife wore rosewater. My intention was to help, not to stir up memories."

"It's fine. The job needed to be done. I was just… surprised."

"I know it's hard. I'm sorry for that, truly I am, but you'll be happy to know that Luke fell asleep on your bed with the quilt his mother made him, breathing in her scent. He rested peacefully. No tossing and turning. When he woke he was more amiable than I've ever seen him. Not that I'm expecting the change to last, but this was a start. He can begin his healing."

Spencer stretched a section of the rope taut and snapped it. She resisted the urge to jump.

"He's a strong boy. He'll be fine."

Eventually yes, but now wasn't the time to delve into the merits of dealing with one's grief instead of acting as though nothing was wrong. She had a more pressing matter to discuss. "I found some letters hidden among your wife's things. I felt sure you'd want to keep them."

Concern creased his brow. "Those are personal. You didn't—"

"Read them? Of course not. I just wanted to know what you'd like me to do with them."

The silence hung heavy until he broke it. "Hide them somewhere. I couldn't bear to see them again."

"I understand. I'll do that." She started for the house but turned when he called her name.

"I'm expecting a shipment soon. A bull. I thought you should know."

"A bull?" She wouldn't have expected Spencer to send for one, although she shouldn't be surprised. He was a rugged, manly man who had quite a way with a rope, so it made sense he knew about raising cattle.

Without realizing it, he'd given her a way to gain a foothold as she attempted to scale the walls the Abbott males had erected—and have fun at the same time. "Would you teach me how to lasso something?"

"You were watching me?" His impassive expression gave no indication of his thoughts.

Heat sped to Tess's cheeks. Since she'd already blurted her request, she might as well make it sound like a reasonable one. "I'd like you to teach me, so I can show Luke how. Or better yet, you could teach us both. He'd love it if you were to spend time with him."

"Would he?"

Although they were talking about Luke, Tess got the distinct impression Spencer was challenging her. Well, she hadn't backed down before, and she wouldn't now. "Your son is much like you. He needs an active outlet for his emo—his energy. I'd love to see him use it for something as impressive as r-roping."

If he'd stop staring at her with that quirked eyebrow, she might be able to complete a sentence without stumbling over her words and saying more than she'd intended. *Impressive* indeed! What would he think of her now? She sounded like a smitten schoolgirl instead of the levelheaded housekeeper she was. "If you'll give it some thought, I'd appreciate it. Now, I must go inside and get supper on the table. I do hope you'll be joining us soon."

She'd taken a total of ten steps when a rope encircled her, tightened around her waist and pinned her arms to her sides. The force jerked her back, causing her to stumble as if she'd run full tilt into a clothesline.

Before she could turn, a tug on the rope spun her to face him. A flash of anger sent a renewed rush of warmth to her face. She struggled to free her hands. "You *lassoed* me?"

The shocked look on his face showed he was as surprised by his out-of-character behavior as she. "I'm sorry. I don't know what came over me. I didn't want you to leave, and then—" he shrugged "—it just happened."

Although the leather rope was smooth and the binding not uncomfortably tight, she didn't cotton to the idea of being bound. "I'm not a cow. I'm a woman."

"You are. And a fine one, too. Here, let me take it off." He rushed to help her. His gaze locked with hers as he gently loosened the rope and slipped it over her head.

The warmth in his eyes melted much of her anger and ignited a different emotion. Her heart was racing so wildly she felt lightheaded. "I could have fallen."

"I wouldn't have let you. I had a solid grip on the rope." He gave her a sheepish smile. "I am sorry. Mostly." Mischief glinted in his brilliant blue eyes, and a corner of his mouth twitched.

"Is this what cattle ranchers do for sport?"

He shook his head, his earnest expression reminding her of Luke when he explained his actions following one of his antics. "I like roping. Always have. I've roped a lot of things, but never a pretty woman—until now."

Pretty? Even if he was teasing, the possibility that he might mean it chased away the remnants of her anger. She smiled. "Thank you for the compliment. I'm flattered."

"You're different from any woman I've ever known. You have a ready laugh, and you don't make a fuss when I—" He averted his gaze and kicked at the ground. "I don't know why I'm rambling. It's not important."

It was to her, but she knew from experience Spencer wouldn't say any more. Once he put the stopper in the bottle, she couldn't get another word out of him.

He turned away and coiled the rope. "Thank you, Tess."

For what? For packing up his late wife's things so he didn't have to? For making inroads with his son? For finding a way for father and son to spend some time together?

Once again he left her guessing what he'd meant. But one thing was clear. He'd reached out to her. Not in an ordinary way, but in his own extraordinary way.

A tingling sensation stole over her, unexpected but not unpleasant. Perhaps she could help this family travel the path from their pain-filled past to a promising future, after all.

Chapter Eight

Tess sat at the tiny dressing table in the room Spencer rented for her at the boardinghouse in town. She had to tuck her feet under the stool to keep from banging her knees into the tabletop. Why must they make furniture so small?

She shook her head, reveling in the feel of her chestnut tresses cascading over her shoulders. She'd loosened her braid just to watch the waves ripple as she swung her head from side to side. Her hair was her one beauty, but she'd best plait it forthwith or risk being late getting to the ranch.

In First Peter, the apostle warned a woman not to take pride in her physical appearance, but Tess appreciated the fact that the Lord had blessed her with nice hair, even if He hadn't seen fit to give her fine features. Good looks could actually prove detrimental to a housekeeper or governess. No mistress wanted a staff member who turned heads and could draw the attention away from her. Tess had never had to worry on that account. Her height was the only thing men noticed.

She wound her braid atop her head, secured it with hairpins and lifted the plaited hair switch she'd purchase— one of her rare splurges—into place securing the added coil with more pins until the switch was firmly anchored. Surveying the results in the mirror, she smiled. The extra loop added a good inch to her height.

Now for the final touch. She reached for her rosewater, and the scene outside the pen with Spencer the night before came back to her. On second thought, she'd go without.

She had just enough time to add a few words to her journal before departing. Capturing her thoughts and impressions on the page helped her make sense of them. After Spencer's unusual way of getting her attention the night before—and her surprising response to him—she had much to sort out. She'd been certain she'd seen attraction on his part, but perhaps it was only wishful thinking on hers. No matter what it was, she was eager to see him again.

Minutes later she donned her hat and gloves and set out for the ranch, enjoying the coolness of the early morning hours. Nothing cheered her like the start of a new day ripe with promise. And this day would be unlike any other. She and Luke would get their first roping lesson.

She reached the house just as the sun crested the horizon, splashing the sky over the Sierras with vivid yellows and oranges on a brilliant blue canvas, and drank in the Lord's handiwork. A profound sense of peace filled her soul. She felt like singing praises. If she had a pleasing voice, she would. Instead, she lifted her face to the heavens and uttered a silent prayer of thanks.

"Tess? Are you all right?"

She wheeled around to face Spencer. "Very much so. I was thanking the Lord. It's a lovely day, isn't it?"

He brushed some straw from his chambray shirt. "Not much different than yesterday."

"Oh, but it is. I can feel it in the air."

He moistened the tip of his finger and held it up, turning it every which way. "No breeze. Hot and dry. Again."

She chuckled and mounted the stairs with him right behind her. "I cooked bacon and eggs yesterday. Today you're getting a ham and cheese omelet served with peach slices—" the urge to tease him was too strong to resist "—on a bed of cottage cheese. That's different."

"Cottage cheese?"

"Yes. You said it was fine."

"For some people it is, I suppose, but it's not my favorite."

She removed her hat and set it on the shelf in the foyer, turning it just so to keep it from falling to the floor. "So, you do have preferences, after all. If you'll apprise me of them, I'll take them into consideration when I plan my menus."

"I'll make a list."

"Good." She was making progress. First with Luke and now with his father. Small steps, true, but it was a start.

She headed into the kitchen. Rather than going upstairs to change as he normally did, Spencer leaned against the doorjamb watching her. Dressed in his ranch wear, he was quite appealing. She could feast on the sight for hours. "Did you need something?"

He shook his head.

Fine. Let him watch. She appreciated the company—and the view. She donned her apron, pulled out a mixing bowl and set it on the counter.

"It's too low for you, isn't it?"

It was, but she'd grown used to that. Kitchens weren't designed with tall women in mind. "I manage."

"I'll raise the kitchen table, and you can use it instead."

She spun around. "You'd do that for me?"

"How high would you need it?"

"I'm not sure." She started for the table, came to a stop and smiled. Two coils of rope lay on its well-worn surface. He must have planned the gift of her very own lariat as a surprise. The thought warmed her clear through. "Ropes. For Luke and me?"

"Yes. I'll show you how to make the slip noose now, so you can teach him."

Tess watched intently while Spencer formed a loop in one end of her rawhide rope, sneaking peeks at his arresting profile. He handed her the lariat and talked her through the process until she'd produced a loop of her own. She longed to step out back and try to lasso something. "What's next?"

"Breakfast, I hope. That is if you can tear your eyes off me long enough to fix it." He grinned.

"What?"

"You were staring at me."

He was right, but she hadn't meant to be so obvious. Clapping a hand to her chest, she feigned innocence. "What do you mean? I was merely hanging on your every word, so you'd know how eager I am to learn."

"Is that so?" If his wry smile was any indication, he'd seen right through her ploy. "Well, that bodes well for our lesson, then. I'm looking forward to it."

So was she. That evening couldn't come quickly enough to suit her.

Spencer stood on the platform as the final train of the day prepared for its return trip to Sacramento City. The L. L. Robinson sat poised to devour the track, the shrill whistle warning everyone of the sleek black locomotive's imminent departure.

The freight handlers had made short work of offloading the freight and getting it into the waiting wagons. A steady stream of drivers shouted commands to their teams as they left the station with supplies bound for the Comstock and other points east.

Another day done. A good day.

Peter clapped Spencer on the shoulder. "Is that a smile I see?"

"You and your men did a fine job today."

"A smile *and* a compliment? You feeling all right, Cap'n?"

Spencer chuckled. "Remind me not to be so lavish with my praise next time."

"In all seriousness, Spence, it's good to see you smiling again. I'm thinking Tess and her fine fare may have something to do with that. What's she fixing tonight?"

"I never know what to expect, but it's sure to be tasty."

Peter narrowed his eyes. "I'm thinking you won't be sending her packing when the month's up. That true?"

"I'm happy with her work." The woman herself posed a problem. He couldn't shake the image of her caught in his lasso, her big brown eyes wide. She'd taken her capture well, but he'd have to be careful not to have another lapse of judgment like that. He was a widower in mourning who had no business thinking about a woman, especially his housekeeper with the engaging smile.

"Polly's going to be mighty glad to hear that. She's been looking forward to having Tess nearby again. I'm glad, too. Polly gets chattier and chattier the closer she gets to her time. A feller can only take so much yammering about names, baby clothes and such, but Tess will listen for hours."

"Enjoy it while you can."

Peter smacked his forehead. "Sorry. I didn't mean to make you think about Trudy again."

"It's not a problem. I listened to her, so I don't have regrets." At least not about that.

"Speaking of Polly, I should finish up. She'll be waiting for me." Peter strode toward the main warehouse.

Spencer returned to his office, checked to make sure he had the next day's schedule ready and left the depot, his step lighter than it had been in weeks. For the first time since Trudy's death, he couldn't wait to get home. He might not know what he'd be having for dinner, but he knew what was coming afterward.

Any excuse to do some roping was welcome, and Tess had given him a good one. He'd soon know if her interest in learning to throw a lariat was genuine. It wasn't like her to stumble over her words, but she had last night. Then she'd gawked at him that morning and blushed when he'd pointed it out to her. He wasn't a dandy, but having an attractive woman take notice of him was…nice.

As soon as he reached the ranch, Woof bounded up to Spencer. He scratched his dog behind the ears. "It's good to see you, boy."

A combination of childish and feminine laughter rang out on the north side of the house. "Faster!" Luke shouted.

Spencer rounded the corner and smiled at the spectacle that greeted him. Lila sat on a bale of hay, Luke straddled a stack of two bales and Tess was atop a tower three high. They had saddle blankets beneath them and held ropes that encircled upturned buckets in front of them—makeshift horses from the look of things. He laughed.

Luke spied him first and waved. "Lookee, Papa. I'm winning the race." He used the ends of his rope to flick the side of his so-called steed.

"Oh! Are you home already?" Tess, who'd been "riding" sidesaddle, leaped to the ground and held out the "reins" to him. "That's wonderful. You can take my place. I'm sure you're a much better horse racer than I am."

Did she honestly expect him to engage in a game of

make-believe? She might be willing to mount a horse made of hay, but he wasn't about to do something so foolish. He could imagine his father having laughed at his mother if she'd suggested such a thing. *A grown man has better things to do,* he would have said. The man had no patience for childish games, even though Spencer and his brother had begged him to join in the fun.

Truth struck Spencer with the force of a speeding locomotive. Luke longed to spend time with him just as he had with his father. "That's a great idea, Tess, but Luke had better watch out because I'm fast."

Spencer strode to the stack of bales she'd been sitting on, straddled them and grabbed the rope serving as reins, allowing his hand to brush hers and linger a moment.

Her chin hung to her knees before she snapped her mouth shut. "You're going to do it?"

"You don't have to look so surprised. I used to race my older brother all the time when we were kids—and beat him, too."

"You won't beat me, Papa." Luke kicked the sides of his "horse" and encouraged it to run faster.

Tess pulled her hand away and gazed at it with wonder. She caught him watching her, smiled shyly and hid her hand in the folds of her skirt. "I hope you'll give your son a chance." Her voice was unsteady. "He's not as experienced a rider as you are, although I doubt you've ridden many hay bale horses."

"I'm not as buttoned-up as you might think." Spencer grinned.

"Really?" Disbelief filled those expressive eyes of hers.

"Really." He'd given his mother fits with his adventure-seeking nature—until his father had squashed it with his ironfisted control and cutting remarks. Spencer wouldn't do that to his children. He flicked the rope reins, dug his knees into the hay bales and urged his steed into a gallop.

The broad smile on Tess's face disarmed him. She looked lovely when she beamed like that.

"I'm happy to see there's not as much starch in your collars as I thought." She started for the house.

He couldn't let her have the last word. "What possessed you to do this?" He waved a hand at the hay bales. "And how did you move them? They're heavy."

"I did it because it's fun, and I used that to move the bales." She pointed at the wheelbarrow nearby, her usual self-assurance restored. "I'm more capable than many give me credit for." She shot him an impish grin and disappeared around the back of the house before he could say anything else.

She was capable all right. Capable of surprising him at every turn. What would she come up with next?

Tess flung the dirty dishwater into the yard and put the washtub away. At last she'd get the roping lesson she'd looked forward to all day. Forcing herself not to skip, she crossed the yard to where Spencer and the children waited. Luke held his rope, his slip noose formed like she'd taught him. Lila sat on a blanket in the shade of the barn, with Spencer's loyal watchdog nearby.

Spencer eyed Tess skeptically. "Are you sure you want to do this?"

Surely he wasn't going to change his mind. Luke would be devastated. "Yes."

"Let's get started, then." He demonstrated how to wind the coils and grasp them in the left hand while holding the loop in the right.

Once Tess mastered that, she knelt to help Luke and nearly bumped heads with Spencer, who'd done the same.

With both of them on their knees, his eyes were level with hers. A flicker of something indistinguishable filled his before he focused on the rope in his son's hands.

She stood and backed away, startled by the flood of emotion that swept over her—a surge of something she'd never felt before. If she were forced to name the feeling, she'd say attraction.

No. That couldn't be it. Or could it? A man who showed interest in his child was attractive. That's all it was. She turned away and fanned her warm cheeks.

Spencer's dog padded over to her. She stooped to scratch him, and he wagged his tail. "You like that, don't you, Wolf?"

"Did you say Wolf?" Spencer asked.

She straightened. "Yes."

"His name isn't Wolf. It's Woof."

"I beg your pardon?"

Luke chimed in. "I told her it was Woof."

She enunciated carefully. "Woof?"

Spencer nodded. "As in *woof woof.* Luke called him that when he wasn't much older than Lila. Trudy thought it was cute, and the name stuck."

Tess couldn't keep from smiling. "It is cute." What was even cuter was hearing him say it.

Spencer cleared his throat. "Shall we move on?"

Half an hour flew by as he showed her and Luke how to spin a loop and toss it at just the right moment. He continued to work with Luke while Tess practiced by herself.

Despite doing her utmost to follow his directions, she couldn't get the rope to sail more than a few feet, where it fell as quickly as her spirits. She blew out a breath, her lips vibrating as though imitating a horse.

Spencer laughed. Loudly. At her.

She jammed a hand onto her hip. "It's not funny."

"Oh, but it is. My son has more patience than you do."
He inclined his head toward Luke, who coiled the tail end
of his rope, spun a wobbly loop and tried unsuccessfully
to lasso the bag of oats Spencer had set in front of him.

Luke shrugged and smiled. "I'll get it next time."

Spencer leaned so close to Tess she could smell the
sooty scent she'd come to associate with him and spoke
softly, his breath warm against her face. "Looks like my
boy could teach you a thing or two."

Her breath froze in her throat as she waited to see what
he'd do next. She didn't dare move, or his lips would graze
her cheek, and she couldn't let that happen. Shouldn't let
it happen, even though the possibility was appealing. She
was his housekeeper. As such it was her duty to remain
professional—although her thoughts at the moment were
anything but.

"Some things can't be rushed, Tess." He strode over
to Luke, rested a hand on his son's shoulder and offered
an encouraging word.

She stood in stunned silence, not trusting her voice to
work properly. Had Spencer read her thoughts? Was he
letting her know that he found her attractive but could do
nothing about it when his loss was so fresh?

The idea was preposterous. She'd let her active imagination get the best of her, which she mustn't do. She would
keep things professional and not think about how warm,
witty and wonderful her new employer was.

At least she'd try.

Chapter Nine

Spencer stared at the date he'd written in his ledger earlier that day—August 16, 1866. Four months.

It seemed like yesterday he'd held Trudy's slender hand in his, bathed her flushed face and done everything Doc suggested in an effort to bring her some relief—to no avail.

If only he'd gotten Trudy the help she wanted, she wouldn't have been working in the garden that warm spring day, wouldn't have fallen on the rake and wouldn't have developed the raging infection that had robbed him of his wife and the children of their mother. But, no. He'd told her he couldn't afford to hire someone to take over her chores. That he needed to save money to build up the ranch while the rail line was enjoying its soon-to-end period of prosperity.

And yet here he was paying for a housekeeper, after all. A stubborn housekeeper who'd waved away his warnings about the dangers of working in a garden. At least Tess promised to be careful with the tools.

He leaned back and rested his head in his clasped hands. A fly flitted around his office, reminding him of Luke and his boundless energy. Tess channeled it in clever ways.

Spencer had a hard time believing she'd been with them a month already. While the first two weeks had been a rough ride at times, things had settled into a manageable routine the past two. She served delicious meals, saw to it that his clothes were in excellent condition and managed to keep his son under control.

While Luke still tested his limits on a regular basis, he hadn't been as prone to outbursts since Tess removed Trudy's things. Spencer had to admit that his forthright housekeeper knew what she was doing, even if her methods were unorthodox at times. He never would have believed that hay bale horse rides and roping lessons could make such a difference, but Luke couldn't get enough of either.

His son's willingness to practice roping was impressive. He had a real knack for it.

Spencer smiled. That wasn't the case with Tess. While her tenacity was inspiring, her aim was anything but. She had yet to lasso a single thing. If she didn't bristle whenever he offered a suggestion, he could help her, but she'd been pricklier than a pincushion cactus the few times he'd tried.

When she'd first come, he hadn't known what to make of her, but she'd carved a place for herself. He no longer dreaded going home at night because she'd be there, adding spice to his meals as well as his life. Having her beside him at the table each evening filling the chair that had been empty all those months made things not only bearable but pleasant, too.

A knock at the door roused him from his musings. "Enter."

His ticket agent held out a telegram. "For you, sir. From Mr. Walker."

At last some news about his bull. "Thanks, Drake." He left, and Spencer scanned the few lines. Delayed again. He wadded the telegram and hurled it across the room.

How frustrating to be forced to wait three more weeks for the delivery when everything in him cried out to move forward. Trudy was gone, but he didn't have to abandon his plan. He'd take the next step. Now.

He shoved his arms into his frock coat, donned his top hat and found Peter.

"It's no trouble for me to see to things, Spence, but it's not like you to leave early. There's nothing wrong, is there?"

"Everything's fine. I just need to tend to something."

Peter removed his well-worn derby and mopped his brow with a bandanna. "Go on, then."

Spencer covered the mile to the Mueller's place in no time.

"*Hallo*, Herr Abbott. Ve haf you since long time not see. *Wie geht's?*"

Frank had taught Spencer the phrase, so he knew how to answer. "It goes well."

Herr Mueller shook his head. "*Nein, mein Freund.* Your heart is not well. I see in your eyes. You miss your Frau much. *Ja?* Come."

Spencer followed him inside, where Herr Mueller pointed to a painting of a dimple-cheeked woman. "Katrin. She was my *alles.* How you say it?"

"All? Everything?"

"*Ja.* My everything."

Frank burst into the cabin. "Vati, I finished the— Mr. Abbott. I didn't know you were here. It's good to see you."

Spencer appreciated the interruption. While Herr Mueller was a hard worker, talking to him could be a challenge.

Spencer waited while the older man spoke to his son in rapid German.

Frank translated. "Vati wants you to know how sorry he is about the loss of your wife and that he understands how difficult it must be for you now. He wants to know if he can do anything to help."

"As a matter of fact, that's why I've come. I'd like to hire the two of you to build a bunkhouse. If you're available that is." Spencer explained what he had in mind.

Frank filled his father in, and Herr Mueller nodded. "*Ja*. Ve can a bunkhouse build."

"Good. When can you start?"

Frank conferred with his father. "The day after tomorrow. He thinks it will take us about four weeks to complete the job. We'll come before you leave for the station, so you can show us where you'd like it."

Spencer left feeling more optimistic than he had in a long time. One month from now he'd have a bunkhouse and a bull. It was a beginning.

Woof greeted him as he neared the house, his dog's tail wagging wildly. Lila's charming chatter came from the backyard.

"Higher," Luke hollered.

Tess laughed. "I'm going as high as I can."

"You gotta move your legs like I showed you."

Curiosity drove Spencer forward. He skirted the house and stopped, leaning against the porch railing. Tess and Luke didn't notice his arrival.

She was in the swing. It was easy to see why Luke was giving her directions. She was barely moving. From what he knew of her, she was letting his son teach her—or think he was—in order to make him feel important.

"No!" Luke bellowed. "Not like that. You gotta run and jump on the seat to get going like I done. Then you pump."

"I'll try." She did, landing on the plank with a thud and moving her legs forward and back. Because of the proliferation of petticoats Spencer couldn't be sure, but it didn't look like she had the proper rhythm to gather momentum.

"You're not doing it right." Luke threw his hands in the air and stormed off.

"I'm sorry. Come back." He didn't stop. "All right. Fine." She hopped out of the swing and caught up to him.

"Go 'way."

"Not until you listen to me. I want to learn, Luke. Really I do."

"You're dumb."

She recoiled and spoke more sharply than normal. "That's unkind and uncalled for. I didn't have a swi— I didn't get to play much when I was young."

Spencer had heard enough. "She's right, son. That's no way to talk to her."

"Papa!" Luke flew at him full tilt and grabbed him around the waist.

"Whoa there, my boy. You about bowled me over."

Luke tugged on Spencer's arm. "C'mon. I wanna show you something."

Tess stopped at a blanket spread in the shade to pick up Lila, who held her arms out to Spencer and whimpered. "You're home early, but as you can see, your children are delighted. Here's your darling girl." She handed Lila to him, and he had no choice but to take her.

"I have things to tend to." He had plans to draw and a lumber order to calculate.

Tess nodded excitedly. "Yes. Very important things. Wait until you see what Luke can do."

That wasn't what he meant, and he was sure Tess knew it. The sooner he got this over with, the better.

Spencer trooped after her and ended up in front of the

barn. Luke held his lariat. He stepped back, got into position, swung and missed. Undaunted, he tried again and dropped his loop over the sack.

Fatherly pride filled Spencer. "Why, look at that. You did it."

"I been practicing. She has, too—" Luke aimed a smug smile at Tess "—but she can't rope nothing."

"Not yet, but I will," Tess countered. "You'll see."

Luke wouldn't give up. "You can't even swing, and anybody can do that."

"What did I tell you about talking to Tess like that, son? Say you're sorry."

He mumbled an apology.

Tess took her time responding. When she did, sadness tinged her reply. "I didn't have a fine family like yours, Luke." She rested a hand on his shoulder, but he shrugged it off. "You're doing a good job roping. Why don't you show your papa how many times you can get the loop over the sack while I see to supper?"

Spencer almost stopped her but thought better of it. Although he was curious about her comment, it wasn't his place to pry into her past. For some reason, though, he wanted to ease her pain. He knew just what to do.

Tess changed Lila into her nightclothes and prepared to cajole Luke into putting on his, as well. He'd been having such a good time doing some more roping with his father after supper that he'd made a fuss when she said it was time to come inside.

She entered his room, but he wasn't there. A quick check under the bed and in his wardrobe and toy chest showed he hadn't hidden from her. When her search of the rest of the house proved fruitless, she laid Lila in her crib and headed outside. The sun hung low on the horizon, preparing to bid the day farewell.

Luke wasn't on their makeshift horses, on the swing or in front of the barn where he practiced his roping. Perhaps he was inside. She slipped though the open door. The scents of animals, straw and leather mingled with the sounds of the horses shifting in their stalls to create an earthy atmosphere that might tempt Luke, since he was enamored of the outdoors.

Tess scoured the barn, even climbing into the loft, and yet she found no sign of the wayward boy. For that matter, Spencer was missing, too. If they were together, he should have told her he was taking his son.

She stepped into the yard, scanned the area, spied Spencer kneeling on the far side of the pen and tromped through the dried bunchgrass. "Have you seen Luke?"

Spencer stood, folded a hastily drawn diagram and stuffed it in his waistcoat pocket. "I thought he was in the house with you."

"He's not there, in the yard or in the barn. I'm getting a little concerned."

A dog barked in the distance, and they turned their heads simultaneously. Luke was far afield trotting after Woof and swinging his rope.

Tess shook her head. "Well, grease my griddle. He's trying to lasso the poor dog."

Spencer chuckled.

He was enjoying this? While the sight was amusing, he didn't have to keep the adventurous lad out of harm's way day after day. "You mustn't laugh. We can't encourage him. We have to be firm."

"So we do." He stuck two fingers in his mouth and produced a loud whistle. Woof bounded over to Spencer with Luke right behind.

Tess opened her mouth to scold the fun-loving boy, but Spencer spoke before she could.

"I'll handle this." He leaned over, placed his hands on his knees and addressed his son in a commanding but controlled manner. "You know better than to run off like that, Luke. You're to do as Tess says, and you're not to try roping Woof again. Do you understand?"

Luke nodded. "Yes, Papa. I'm sorry."

"Good. Now go with Tess. She'll put you to bed."

"But you'll be in to sing, right?"

Tess rested a hand on Luke's shoulder. "Of course he will."

Spencer shook his head. "Not tonight. Since Luke disobeyed, I won't be singing to him."

"But, Papa—"

"You heard me, son. Go on. I've got work to do." He returned his attention to his project.

Tess accompanied the disappointed boy, as was her duty, but what she really wanted was to question Spencer's decision. When someone let a child down, they didn't forget. Ever. She'd have to make that clear to Spencer.

She tucked Luke in and offered to sing in place of his father, but as expected, the sullen boy refused. "I don't want nobody but him. You can go 'way."

The sight of his sorrow-filled eyes and trembling chin, which he attempted to hide by facing the wall, squeezed her chest. She'd spent many nights as a young girl quelling her loneliness as thoughts of her father swirled in her head. She used to lie in the dark making up stories in an attempt to block her persistent longings. Only when she accepted the fact that he wasn't coming back for her had she been able to regain control.

Control was what she needed now, or she was likely to snap at Spencer. How could he hurt this precious, precocious boy? Luke hadn't meant to misbehave. His curiosity had just gotten the best of him.

He yawned. Within minutes he nodded off.

Tess returned to the site where Spencer was working. He'd marked off three sides of a good-size rectangle using stakes and twine. "The children are asleep, and we need to talk. I don't believe I made myself clear earlier. I asked you to be firm, but I didn't mean for you to deny Luke his bedtime ritual."

"He'll be fine." He stooped and stretched twine along the final side of the figure.

She chose her words with care. "A child counts on certain things and has every right to do so. You hurt Luke."

Spencer straightened. "He has to learn that there are consequences for his actions. Sometimes denying him what he wants is an effective deterrent. My housekeeper taught me that." He smiled.

How could he use her words against her? "This isn't the same. Not allowing him to eat at the table is one thing, but not singing to him seems a bit…harsh."

"One night without his song won't hurt him that much, but it might make him think twice about running off next time."

She had to make him understand. "You didn't see his tear-stained cheeks or hear his muffled sobs."

Spencer studied his string-framed figure. "I've witnessed them before and will again, but knowing Luke, he'll greet us with his impish grin at breakfast."

"Perhaps." What he said made sense, but she couldn't drop the matter without a final attempt to make her point. "I feel it's my duty to tell you when your child is…is aching. If you prefer not to be told such things, it's best I know now."

He continued staring at the marked-off plot of land but said nothing.

She counted to ten under her breath, and yet he'd still not spoken. "Fine. The month's trial is up today. I'll get my things and go—as soon as you give me my pay packet."

Spencer spun around. "Go? No! I need you. I mean, I need a housekeeper, and you're doing a fine job. I have no complaints."

Hope planted itself deep inside and grew until she couldn't stop herself from smiling. "You want me to stay? Permanently? But what about my concern?"

"You're right, Tess. It is your job to tell me how my children are doing, but you can trust me to do right by them. I would never let any harm come to Luke or Lila."

His assurances rang true and calmed her fears. Spencer was a good father, the kind every child deserved.

"Even though their mother is gone, I'll do my utmost to let them know they're loved." He winced at his mention of his late wife.

Tess placed a hand on his arm and pulled it back, aghast. "I'm sorry."

He rubbed his arm where her hand had been and gazed at a lone hill on the back of his property. "Today was a trying day. It's been four months since I lost her. I thought it was supposed to get easier."

She ached to see him in such pain but was certain he wouldn't appreciate her sympathy any more than he had her touch. A matter-of-fact approach seemed a wiser choice. "It does, but it takes time."

He tossed the spool of twine in his toolbox. "You sound like someone who's experienced loss."

More than he could ever imagine. "I have. That's why I want to help. I know what Luke's going through."

"A parent perhaps?"

His perceptiveness surprised her. "How did you know?"

He scuffed the toe of his boot in the dirt, looking so boyish she had the urge to hug him. "I saw you on the swing earlier and heard some of what you told Luke."

"Oh, yes. You did, didn't you? I'm sure I looked anything but ladylike."

"I won't tell anyone." His radiant smile turned her knees to applesauce. Not the response a housekeeper was supposed to have, but no matter how hard she tried not to take notice of her employer, she couldn't help herself. If only he weren't so handsome or so endearing. She stooped and picked up Luke's rope to keep Spencer from seeing the color sure to be staining her cheeks.

"If you'd like to learn how to swing, I can teach you."

She spun around. "Really? I mean, yes, I'd like that." Very much.

He grabbed the pail filled with his supplies, led the way to the backyard and had her sit on the swing. "I'm going to give you a push to get you started. Get a good grip on the ropes."

She did. He grabbed the wooden seat, pulled it back toward him and let her go, sending her soaring. The swing reversed course, returning her to where he stood. He placed his hands on the small of her back, shoving her forward again. The wind whipped her skirts and fluttered the loose tendrils at her temples.

When the swing was out of his reach, he stopped pushing and stood to the side in her line of vision. "Now lean back a little and extend your legs toward the house when you go forward. Lean forward and tuck them under the seat when you go back."

By following his instructions, she got the swing to go higher and higher until she could see the barn over the roof of the house. She ceased pumping her legs and reveled in the sensation of flying through the air as free as a bird.

As much as she'd like to stay longer and enjoy Spencer's company, she let the swing slow. "I can see why Luke likes swinging so much. It's fun. But I should be going. I've stayed later than usual, and it'll be dark soon."

"Allow me." He grabbed the ropes, brought the swing to a stop and helped her to her feet. His gaze roamed over her face. There was no sign of a frown on his.

She said nothing, unwilling to shatter the mood. He'd actually alluded to his grief for the first time. And he'd taught her to swing.

At the moment he was looking at her as though he saw her as a person—not just a domestic fulfilling her duties—and seemed pleased with what he saw. She was certainly aware of him. Decidedly so. She should do something. But she couldn't move if she tried, content to savor the sweetness of the moment.

He released the swing, and it bounced behind her. "I almost forgot to tell you. The Muellers will be over in the morning to start work on a bunkhouse. That's what I was marking. I'll need you to fix enough to feed them while they're here."

So much for the mood. He'd smashed it to smithereens, but that was a good thing. She had no right thinking fanciful thoughts about him anyhow. She'd passed his test, and she would do her best to ensure that he had no reason to regret hiring her.

Chapter Ten

"You may pick out ten gumdrops, Luke." Tess reread her list while the owner of the general store assisted him. Mr. Hawkes had added all the household items on it to the crates. He carried them to the waiting wagon and returned.

Now to see to her special purchase. Since her position with Spencer was secure, she could afford to treat herself. She shifted Lila from one hip to the other. "I'm interested in getting a new fragrance, but I don't want anything smelling remotely like roses. What might you have?"

"Let me see." The kindly proprietor reached into a display case and withdrew three stoppered bottles. He opened the first and invited her to inhale.

She wrinkled her nose at the musky fragrance. "I'm not partial to heavy scents."

"See what you think of these." He held the other bottles for her one by one so she could sniff the contents, but neither scent suited her.

"I'm not after anything woody or spicy, either. I'd like something fresh and light."

Mr. Hawkes smiled. "I have just the thing, but I must warn you. It costs a pretty penny." He withdrew a dome-shaped bottle covered with gold-painted bees and an emblem bearing crossed swords. Placing one hand beneath the stunning creation and the other behind, he presented it with flair. "This is *Eau de Cologne Imperial* by Guerlain, imported directly from France and used by Empress Eugénie as well as Queen Victoria and Queen Isabella—or so the vendor told me."

"It's beautiful." The bottle itself was a work of art, but she wasn't one to be taken in by fancy packaging. "What does it smell like?"

"You can be the judge." He removed the stopper.

Tess took a whiff. She had to have the citrus cologne, one so gloriously sparkling and bright she couldn't resist, no matter the cost. "How much is it?"

Mr. Hawkes lowered his voice and said the price almost apologetically. She did her best not to flinch. Never in her life had she spent the better part of a month's salary on a single luxury item, but this would be her present to herself. A woman deserved something special for her twenty-fifth birthday—especially when she didn't have a husband to buy her fine things. "I'll take it."

The cologne would provide a sharp contrast to the rosewater she'd worn before. Its crisp, clean scent was suitable for a housekeeper and shouldn't raise any eyebrows—as long as no one knew how much she'd paid for it.

Luke tromped over and tugged on Tess's skirt. "I got all black gumdrops. Know why?"

"Because you like the taste of licorice?"

He gave his head a sound shake. "Because they turn my tongue black."

"That they will."

The proprietor completed the sale. Tess took the children—and her precious package—to the wagon.

"Wuke!"

The childish squeal drew her attention. Abby pointed

at Luke and tugged on her mother's hand, urging Polly forward. Tess's friend plodded along, looking fatigued. The hot August days would be hard on a woman in her condition.

Polly reached Tess, grasped the side of the wagon and blew out a breath. "While I prefer the dry heat of California to the humid summers back in Baltimore, this is not the time of year to be great with child."

"I'd be happy to carry a child anytime, but I agree with you about the humidity. I don't miss it one bit."

"You don't miss anything from those days, do you? I still remember your excitement on our final Sunday in Maryland when we sat in our favorite pew at church and you told me you'd found a job out west, too. You were so excited. By the time we boarded the ship the following Wednesday you were downright giddy. I dreaded leaving my friends and relatives, but you couldn't wait to get underway."

Tess didn't care to revisit her dismal childhood. "I had an opportunity to make a life for myself, and I embraced it. Things have worked out well for me."

"And for me, too. You're here in Shingle Springs now, and I can wish you a happy birthday in person. I have a little something for you." Polly held out a package.

She removed the tissue paper and smiled when she saw the embroidered handkerchief bearing the verse from Proverbs she and Polly had chosen as theirs years ago, "A friend loveth at all times." Tess hugged Polly. "It's lovely. Thank you."

"If I weren't as big as a barn and slow as an ox, I'd have done more to make the day special for you. You should have a birthday cake at the very least."

Tess grinned. "I made myself one. Chocolate with chocolate frosting."

"Mmm. Chocolate cake. The best kind."

Luke clamored for Tess's attention. She sat him beside Abby on one of two benches in front of the shop and gave each of them three gumdrops—along with a challenge to see how long they could make the candies last, thus buying her some time with her friend. She had to know what Polly thought of her latest idea.

The women settled on the other bench. Polly didn't give Tess a chance to say a thing before she peppered her with questions. "I know you, Tessie. You've got something on your mind. Does it involve a certain stationmaster? Is Spencer in for another surprise?

"When I cleared out Trudy's things, I found some letters the two of them had exchanged. It appears they were written when he was courting her."

Polly eyed Tess with curiosity. "Does he know?"

"I told him. He said he didn't want to see them ever again and that I could hide them somewhere."

"Did you read them?"

"I was tempted to, but that would be wrong. I didn't know what to do with them—until now."

"Go on." Polly's enthusiasm was encouraging.

"He told me his wife had intended to make a quilt for their bed. But she was taken from him before she'd even begun. Since I love to sew, I can make that quilt for him myself. Not just any quilt. One to honor Trudy. I'll use the Double *T* pattern. I plan to make the *T*s out of red fabric from her dresses and mount them on a white background."

"I'm sure he'd be thrilled to have such a special remembrance, but what's that got to do with the letters?"

"I've heard women sometimes use paper as batting material when fabric's scare. Newspapers, catalogs and… letters. Although I would only have enough sheets of stationery to add two or three to each of the blocks, their words would be preserved this way, but he wouldn't have to see them."

Polly's round face creased in confusion. "But if you put the letters inside the quilt, you'd have to take them out of the envelopes."

"I'd turn the pages over, so I wouldn't see the words." Tess heaved a wistful sigh. Trudy had been blessed to find a man who enjoyed writing. "The letters he wrote to her are nice and thick. He must be a prolific writer."

Polly laughed. "Spencer? The man who won't use two words if one will do?"

Tess recalled the conversation they'd had the evening he taught her to swing. "He does talk when he has something to say, but it seems putting things on paper comes more easily to him. If only I could get him to tell me about his loss..."

Eagerness lit Polly's green eyes. "I have an idea."

"Do tell."

"I learned the hard way when Peter was courting me that a woman can't force a man to discuss his feelings, but I think you could get Spencer talking if you try. You need to find something he's interested in and start with that. In time he'll feel more comfortable opening up to you."

Tess bounced Lila on her knees and enjoyed the resulting smiles. "Do you think that would work?"

"It did with Peter. Once I wised up, I asked him what it was like to work at the depot in Sacramento City. He loves the railroad and spent hours telling me everything he knew. Although he was only a baggage handler in those days, he got permission to give me a tour of the railway station."

"That must have been exciting."

Polly sighed dreamily. "It was. Peter introduced me to everyone. To hear him talk, you would have thought I was a princess and not a lowly governess. I knew then that if he asked for my hand, I'd say yes. But enough about me. If you were to ask Spencer what it's like to be stationmaster, you might be able get the words flowing."

"Perhaps." Tess couldn't wait to give it a try, although she wouldn't ask him about his job. He didn't seem all that interested in it, but she knew what made him come to life.

Where were they? Tess held her journal over the bed in her room at the boardinghouse that night and shook it. A shower of ticket stubs, theater programs and other memorabilia rained on the coverlet. She rummaged through the pile of papers, but the letters she'd written to her imaginary fiancé weren't there.

That was odd. She distinctly remembered seeing them shortly before boarding the train bound for Shingle Springs. The ribbon around them had slipped off. She'd tied it again, reached into her satchel and tucked the packet inside the back cover of her journal. At least she thought she had.

Perhaps she'd misjudged and the letters had gotten wedged between her magazines and Bible. Considering how many times she'd swapped her reading material while waiting to board, she might have pulled out the packet by mistake and dropped it. No doubt someone had found the letters and tossed them in the dustbin.

Oh, well. They'd been fanciful musings anyhow. She was better off without them. Penning sentimental missives was for poets and romantics, not levelheaded housekeepers.

Although she couldn't perform her annual ritual of rereading the letters she'd written on her previous birthdays, this birthday had been memorable. She'd enjoyed her visit with Polly, even if it was brief. Sharing her cake with Spencer and the children had been fun, too. Not that she'd told them it was her birthday. It was hard enough reaching her twenty-fifth year and knowing that, unless the Lord decided to answer her prayers for a family of her own, she was destined to spinsterhood.

The best part of the day was the time she'd spent with Spencer after they'd put the children to bed. Due to the long summer days, she could leave later than usual and have plenty of daylight for her walk back to the board-inghouse, so she'd taken advantage of that. By following Polly's advice, Tess had been able to get him talking.

She'd asked him to tell her about his earliest roping lessons. Watching his face light up as he'd leaned against the column at the top of the front steps and recalled a memorable time from his childhood had been an unexpected gift. He'd given her one of his too-rare smiles, the kind that transformed him from attractive to breathtakingly handsome, and launched into a tale of good-natured rivalry as his three-year-old self had attempted to best his older brother. He'd actually laughed—a genuine laugh that really got air into his lungs—as he recounted the day when he, at the tender age of five, had succeeded in roping a calf on his father's cattle ranch before his brother, who had two years on him.

Although Spencer had stopped after ten short but delightful minutes, saying he shouldn't keep her, it was a start. If she bided her time and waited for other such openings, perhaps he would grow more comfortable and move beyond childhood recollections. She could hope.

Yes. She *could* hope. Even though she'd marked another birthday, she didn't have to give up on her dream of having a family of her own to love and care for. Not every woman was wed by the time she was twenty-five.

The Lord knew how much love was inside her ready to be poured out, so surely He had someone in mind for her.

Diving into her trunk, she found her writing supplies. She squeezed herself under the tiny dressing table and dipped her pen in the inkwell. The nib scratched across the blue-bordered stationery as she poured her heart on the page.

Monday, August 20, 1866

To the man I look forward to marrying…

Chapter Eleven

Tess left the general store, her shopping complete, and set out for Polly's place.

"Papa." Lila pointed at her father, who was headed straight for them.

Spencer dashed between two wagons rumbling past and doffed his top hat to Tess. "Where's Luke?"

"He's with Polly. She offered to watch him so I could get the grocery order filled more quickly."

"That's good, since the Muellers will be expecting their dinner shortly."

He didn't really think she'd forgotten, did he? Frank and his father had spent the past week working on the new bunkhouse Spencer had staked out, and she'd been feeding the two of them three meals a day right on schedule. "I got everything ready for dinner before I left the house and will return in plenty of time to serve it."

"Of course you will. How are things going? Did they get started on the west wall as expected?"

"Yes. Why? Is there a problem?"

He ran a finger under the stand-up wing collar of his white shirt. "Just keeping tabs on things."

"You seem a bit restless. Is there something you wanted to tell me?"

Leaning toward her, he sniffed. "You're wearing a new perfume. It's lemony. I like it."

He'd noticed. How nice. That eased her regrets regarding her impulsive purchase. "I appreciate the compliment, but surely you didn't leave your job and rush across the street to discuss my choice of fragrance."

"I, um…" He closed his eyes and scrunched his face in a gesture so like Luke's she couldn't keep from chuckling. His eyes flew open, a flash of something akin to hurt in them.

"I'm sorry I laughed. I—"

"How are you at giving haircuts?"

"What? You want *me* to cut your hair?" He could use a trim in the worst way, but why had he asked her?

"I received an unexpected summons to a meeting at the rail station down in Folsom tomorrow, and I can't go looking like a scarecrow. I thought, with all your skills, you might have given a cut or two."

"I have, but…" She'd trimmed more heads of hair at the orphanage than she cared to remember, but they'd belonged to young boys and to Mr. Grimsby, who was old enough to be her father. Not to her golden-haired twenty-eight-year-old employer. How could she perform such an intimate service for Spencer? She'd have to touch him, and she wasn't sure he was ready for that—or if she was.

He held up his hands in the surrender pose and took a step back. "I can see by the shocked look on your face that I've asked too much."

She swallowed and hoped her voice wouldn't come out of her constricted throat as a squeak. "Couldn't you go to a barber?"

"I suppose so. It's just that Tru— that I always had it cut at home. Forget I asked."

He spun around and left without another word, but not before Tess spotted sadness in his eyes.

"Spencer, wait." She was sure to regret her hasty decision, but she couldn't let him think she didn't care. Not when she did, far more than she should. "I'll do it."

His stop was so abrupt it was a wonder he didn't stumble. He returned and stood before her, relief apparent in every line of his handsome face. "If you're sure."

She was anything but. "Quite sure."

"Will you charge me?"

Was he serious? She tilted her head. Lila mirrored the motion, giving Tess an idea how she could lighten the mood. "Did you hear your papa, Lila? He thinks he has to pay me extra for a haircut, something that will take all of ten minutes—provided he sits still and does what I tell him."

"Papa." Lila twisted in Tess's arms and reached out to him.

He brushed his daughter's cheek with the back of his hand. "I have to go to work, princess, but I'll see you tonight." He shifted his gaze to Tess. "And I'll see you, too, with your shears at the ready. Yes?"

She nodded.

"That's settled, then." The lingering look he gave her, filled with gratitude he couldn't put into words, eased her earlier misgivings. Spencer had given her an opening. While asking her to cut his hair wasn't the same as sharing his feelings with her, he had come to her with his request. That was promising.

Tess dried the last of the supper dishes and put them away. She hadn't been thinking straight when she'd agreed to this. Caring for Spencer's children and his house was one thing. Cutting his hair was another. If only she didn't have such a soft spot for hurting souls. One look into his sorrow-filled eyes was all it had taken to override her usual good sense.

Luke burst into the room. "Papa's waiting out front for his haircut."

She was all too aware of that fact. "Please tell him I'll be there soon."

The energetic boy raced out of the kitchen. She gave it a final look, making sure everything was ready for the following morning. The bowl, wooden spoon and dry ingredients for the flapjacks she'd planned sat on the table Spencer had raised for her. Satisfied, she hung her apron on its peg and went upstairs.

She collected the shears, comb and hand mirror from Spencer's bureau and a sheet from the cedar chest. With steps slower than a gout-riddled old woman's, she descended the stairs. "You can do this. It's just a haircut like any other."

Who was she fooling? Although Spencer was her employer, he was also a man. A handsome man with a head of beautiful blond hair she'd soon be snipping.

She stopped on the bottom landing, clutched the things she carried in her left arm and held out her right hand. Trembling, as she'd expected.

By flexing and straightening her fingers several times, she brought an end to the shaking. If only she could calm her quaking nerves as easily.

She crossed the foyer and stood in the doorway.

Lila saw her and scampered across the porch. The baby hadn't been crawling long, but she could cover ground. Craning her neck, she looked up at Tess. "Eff."

Tess wanted to believe the darling girl had attempted to say her name, so she pointed at herself and said it.

"Eff."

Yes. Lila *was* trying to say *Tess*. How wonderful.

Tess set the items in one of the rocking chairs, hugged Lila to her and kissed each of the baby's cheeks. The little girl patted Tess's face and said her name one more time.

Luke laughed. "*F?* That's not right, Lila. You gotta start with *A, B, C.*"

"She's not old enough to say the alphabet, Luke. She's trying to say my name, but she can't make the *T* or *S* sounds yet, so it sounds like *F.*"

"That's dumb."

Spencer leaned back against the porch railing, his characteristic frown in place. "What did I tell you about using that word, son?"

"Not to say it."

Tess decided to see if she could get Luke to use her name. "You could help your sister by saying my name for her."

The hardheaded boy acted as though he hadn't heard her. He ran down the steps and threw a stick for Woof to chase instead, which was not surprising. Whenever Luke referred to her, he used *she* or *her*. She tried not to let it bother her, but it would be nice if he called her by name on occasion.

"If I can pry my lovely daughter out of your hands, Tess, I'd like you to begin, so you can finish before the sun goes down."

Clearly Spencer wasn't going to echo her suggestion. He probably hadn't even noticed Luke's obstinate refusal to call her by name. Oh, well. She had more important things to deal with. Such as giving Spencer his haircut. "By all means." She handed him his little girl.

Spencer set Lila in a large washtub with her blocks. They would have to put up with her banging them against the side from time to time, but at least the now-mobile toddler wouldn't be in danger of tumbling down the stairs.

"If you'll take a seat, I'll get started." Tess pointed to the dining room chair she'd carried out earlier.

She stood behind him, took a deep breath and prepared to tuck his collar inside his chambray shirt. No sooner had she touched his neck than he shuddered. She jerked her hands back.

"I'm s-s-sorry," he spluttered. "It's all right. Go on."

Evidently he was as jumpy as she, if not more so. Perhaps if she focused on making him comfortable, her uneasiness would lessen. "I just need to get your collar out of the way, and then I'll cover you with the sheet."

Those tasks completed, she braced herself for the next one. "I'm going to, um, run my fingers through your hair to gauge its thickness."

"Do what you need to." He sat as rigid as a broom handle.

Tess lifted her gaze heavenward. *Lord, help me through this.*

The sooner she began, the sooner the ordeal would be over. She dove her hand into his hair and lifted a hank of it between her fingers. Habit took over, and her nervousness eased. "It looks like you need a good two inches taken off if you want it up over your ears."

"Fine."

His blond hair was thick and healthy. The only things she had to watch out for were the cowlick on top and that lovely wave over his right eye. The rest would be easy. She set to work.

Birds joined in a jubilant chorus as the sun sank lower. Luke shouted to Woof, while Lila occupied herself clapping blocks together. Spencer maintained his customary silence.

As the cut progressed, the tension in his neck and shoulders eased, and his breathing grew slow and deep. Something resembling a sigh escaped him. Tess leaned to the side to get a glimpse of his face. His eyes were closed, and his features relaxed. He'd never looked as at peace as he did at that moment.

He turned toward her. "You're not finished already, are you?"

How interesting. He sounded disappointed. She was almost done, but it wouldn't hurt to make sure she hadn't missed anything.

A profound sense of pleasure enveloped her as she lifted one section of his satiny hair after another between her fingers and clipped the few strands that were longer than the others. She'd found a way to minister to him. Surely the Lord wouldn't mind if her act of service brought her enjoyment, would He?

Moving to the front, she prepared to trim the portion at Spencer's temples and urged him to keep his eyes closed. Looking into the brilliant blue depths would be her undoing.

When the cut was nearly complete, she squatted so they were face-to-face and examined the sections over his ears to check for uniformity. Just right. She brushed loose hairs off his forehead with her fingertips.

His eyes flew open, his gaze locking with hers. Pleased with her efforts, she smiled, receiving a subtle lifting of his lips in return.

A flush rushed up his neck and flooded his cheeks with color. Oh, bother. Things had been going so well. How sad to have embarrassed him right at the end.

Doing her utmost to maintain a professional demeanor,

she handed him the mirror, not realizing her mistake until it was too late. He wouldn't want to see his face so red. Apparently she was right because he laid the mirror in his lap, reached behind his head and fiddled with the knot she'd tied in the sheet. Rather than rushing to help, she busied herself sweeping up the golden locks littering the porch, allowing time for his blush to subside.

Once he'd freed himself, he gathered the sheet by the corners, flung the contents into the yard and returned to the porch, where he examined the cut in the mirror. "It looks good. Thank you."

Coming from him, that was glowing praise. Tess schooled her features. "If you'd prefer to visit the barber in the future, I understand."

"That won't be necessary. I'm happy with the cut."

"I thought… It seemed you were…" Why was talking to him so difficult? Words didn't usually fail her.

"I like having my hair cut. I was used to Trudy doing it. That's all." He folded the sheet in a perfect square, set it on the chair he'd vacated, lifted Lila into his arms and strode out to where Luke romped with Woof.

Tess bit back a sigh. Evidently Spencer was eager to get away for her. She gathered the supplies, took a lingering look at the heartwarming scene and went inside.

God knew the desires of her heart. Although it did no good to dwell on hers, she couldn't deny her dream of having a family. If only she had one like Spencer's, she'd be a very happy woman.

Chapter Twelve

As soon as Spencer arrived at his place, he went directly to the bunkhouse. The invigorating scent of freshly cut pine greeted him. Although the Muellers had only been working on the project two weeks, the structure itself was finished and the roof on. The bunks and kitchen area were all that remained. As hard and fast as the father-son team worked, they'd be done in another day or two.

Spencer stooped to pick up a claw hammer and placed it in the Muellers' wooden toolbox beside its twin. He'd better hurry and get washed up for supper. The tantalizing aromas he'd smelled when walking past the house promised that he'd soon be enjoying another of Tess's mouthwatering meals.

She could certainly cook. And she gave a mighty fine haircut. Unlike Trudy, who'd hurried through the task, Tess had taken her time. Having her touch him had been awkward at first, but once he'd gotten used to it, he was able to relax—until the end.

Opening his eyes to find her looking into his had startled him. He'd been so busy thinking about his plans for turning his place into a successful cattle ranch that he'd forgotten Tess was the one cutting his hair.

She had a way of making him forget the past and believe in the future again. Perhaps it was her willingness to listen. She'd encouraged him to tell her stories from the early years he'd spent working on his father's cattle ranch, before his father had become such a strict disciplinarian. Spencer couldn't forget the way she'd chuckled when he told her how determined he'd been to best his brother at roping or the smile she'd sent his way when he'd boasted about his first takedown.

He shouldn't have taken such pleasure in another woman's company, let alone her touch. He'd loved Trudy and missed her something fierce. So much so that the emptiness seemed overwhelming at times. He was lonely, which was understandable, but that didn't excuse his traitorous thoughts.

Spencer passed Elmore Dodge's carriage. His neighbor to the west must have arrived shortly after he had. He doffed his hat to the shifty fellow on the driver's seat and went in the house. Animated voices floated into the foyer from the kitchen, a combination of English and German. He set his hat on the shelf and joined the group.

Tess was the first to see him. "Oh, good. You're home. Frank and his father have been occupying the children while I put the finishing touches on supper. Then Mr. Dodge arrived, so we've got quite a houseful tonight. You needn't worry, though. I've made plenty."

Spencer wasn't worried about that. What did concern him was Dodge's unannounced visit. The ruthless cattle rancher didn't come by unless he wanted something. Spencer extended a hand, which Dodge shook far too enthusiastically. "What can I do for you?"

The lanky man bared his gums in an overly wide smile, his top two gold teeth gleaming. Word was he'd lost his real ones in a barroom brawl some years back, but no one knew for sure. All Spencer knew was that a visit from Dodge wasn't a friendly social call.

"Heard in town you've got a bull on the way, and now the Germans are putting up a bunkhouse for you. That true?"

It was none of his business. "The Muellers have been doing some construction work. And a fine job of it, too."

Frank acknowledged the compliment with a nod and leaned over to translate for his father.

Wolfgang's tanned face bore a smile filled with all the warmth Dodge's had lacked. "*Danke schön*. Ve like for you to work."

His son was quick to reword the sentence so it made sense. "Vati's right. We like working for you. You're a fair boss and pay good wages."

"Better watch it, Abbott, or word will get out that you're an easy mark." Dodge thumped Spencer on the back in an overly familiar gesture so unexpected that he had to tamp down his temper. "You wouldn't want all the sauerkraut set heading your way, now would you?"

Tess caught Lila as she scooted past her, propped the baby on her hip and pulled Luke to her side in a protective gesture that stoked Spencer's ire toward Dodge. Evidently she was uncomfortable around the overbearing man. "I'll not have you speaking ill of my guests. State your business, Dodge, and then you can be on your way."

"My business, as you well know, is cattle ranching. I've been in Shingle Springs building my herd for six years, and no greenhorn is going to cut in on my profits. If you know what's good for you, you'll stick to railroading and leave the raising of beef to those of us who know what we're doing."

Frank chimed in. "But Mr. Abbott does know—"

"I know a threat when I hear one." Spencer regretted

having to cut the young man off, but the less Dodge knew, the better. "I don't take kindly to them. There's room for all of us, and I have no intention of stopping."

Hours later Spencer stood on the porch after putting Luke and Lila to bed. He gripped the railing and gazed at his land. Tess's footfalls sounded on the foyer floor. She was at his side in seconds. What would she think of his display earlier? Trudy would have been appalled, reminding him that a gentleman didn't give way to his anger and he certainly didn't openly challenge another.

"Your show of force earlier was impressive."

Tess had surprised him once more. Unsure how best to respond, he said nothing.

"Do you think Mr. Dodge will make good on his threat? I wouldn't want anything to happen to the children."

He looked into her eyes. Apprehension filled their brown depths. "In my experience, those who issue threats rarely follow through on them. It's the ones who don't divulge their evil intentions I watch out for. Dodge is all talk."

"I hope that's the case." She perched on the top rail and leaned back against a support column, with one foot on the floor steadying her, the other swinging like a pendulum. She must not realize she was giving him glimpses of her ankle. He dragged his gaze from the alluring sight.

"He has a surprise coming when he finds out you're not a greenhorn. I'm curious. If you enjoy cattle ranching so much, why did you leave Texas and come to California?"

A desire to put as much distance between himself and his father as possible. "The same things that bring most people I suppose. A chance for a fresh start, the abundant land, the climate."

She laughed. "You left out the opportunity to make

one's fortune. Isn't that what the Golden State is known for?"

"Many came expecting to get rich, but a man has to work as hard here as anywhere."

"I know. I was teasing you, although I gather you have grand plans for this place. Frank said the bunkhouse could hold twelve men. But how can you run a ranch if you're working at the station? Will you have a foreman handle things?"

"You're full of questions tonight, aren't you?"

She stood, and he followed suit. "Apparently I've asked too many. It's getting late. I'll get my things and be on my way."

"Wait a minute, please."

She stopped. "Yes?"

He would have to broach his plan in a way that would meet with her approval. "I'll be staying in the bunkhouse once it's finished. After I've cleared out my things, you can have my—the extra bedroom."

Her mouth gaped, but she quickly composed herself. "Are you asking if I want to move out here...or telling me I will?"

"I'm offering you a room so you don't have to walk to and from town once it starts getting dark earlier."

She held herself flagpole straight. It seemed she was trying to appear as tall as possible. "Am I to be on duty all day and all night, too?"

He hadn't thought about that, but if she was living in the house, she would be the one to see to the children if they woke in the night. "I could hang an iron triangle out here, and you could ring it if you needed me."

"Give me a moment, please."

She went inside and returned shortly. Her enormous hat added to her height. Determination radiated from her, almost palpable in its intensity. What an impressive woman she was, not to mention attractive. Peter was right. She would turn any man's head. Spencer didn't like to admit it, but she'd turned his.

"I'll consent to live here if you'll agree to my terms. I will prepare dinner on Saturdays and have the rest of those afternoons and evenings off—in addition to my Sundays—but you will not reduce my pay. In fact, since you will no longer have the expense of my room at the boardinghouse, you will increase my salary by one dollar a week to compensate me for the added duty time."

Her requests were reasonable, but perhaps he could get her to accept some other benefits in lieu of increasing her pay. He needed his funds to build his herd. "That's a tall order. Too tall, Tess. Perhaps we could—"

She inhaled sharply.

"What's wrong?"

"I'm sorry. I know what you meant, but hearing those words again…"

He went back over them. "Oh, you mean…?" Someone must've teased her about being tall. That explained a lot of things.

"I thought I was over it, but I can still hear the other children chanting that awful name."

"There's nothing wrong with being tall."

She toyed with a button on her bodice. "Not for you. You're a man. In your case, height is an advantage. It's different for tall women. We're seen as odd or ungainly or even intimidating."

He started to contradict her but stopped. She was right. He'd thought those very things when he first met her. But that was before he knew her. Despite her height, she was a woman like any other. She could be somewhat formidable at times, but she was remarkably agile—except when it came to throwing a rope. He recalled her awkward attempts and smiled.

"You find it funny?"

"I was thinking about how determined you are. The truth is, you stand head and shoulders over other women in many respects, but that's not necessarily a bad thing. Come with me, and I'll show you what I mean."

She eyed him dubiously but followed him into the foyer. He pointed at his Henry repeating rifle resting on its pegs above the front door. "Not that I expect it to happen, but if anyone were to make trouble, you'd be able to reach the gun without having to drag a chair over. That could make a difference at a time when every second counts."

"You expect me to fire that thing? I don't even know how to load it. And look how long it is."

"I keep it loaded, which is why it's mounted well out of reach of the children. Your height would be another advantage when it came to firing it. Holding on to it would be easier for you than for a shorter woman." Trudy had balked at the idea of using his rifle. When he'd forced her to fire it once, she'd ended up on her backside.

Tess wouldn't have a problem. She'd be the master of the gun, not the other way around. He was tempted to ask her to hold it just to see how she'd look.

He didn't have to. She removed the gun, stepped through the open door and sighted down the lengthy barrel, keeping her finger away from the trigger. What a sight she made, both amusing and admirable. It seemed she would attempt just about anything.

She ran a hand over the gleaming stock before passing the gun to him. "This a beautiful piece of workmanship. I certainly hope I never have cause to fire it, although if the children were in danger, I wouldn't hesitate."

"I'm counting on that." He placed the rifle on its pegs

and joined her on the porch. They stood side by side, a chorus of crickets and bullfrogs filling the silence that hung heavy between them.

At length she spoke. "Thank you, Spencer."

"For what?"

"For not laughing about the name. For giving up your room for my sake. Most of all, for entrusting me with your children. Does this mean you accept my terms?"

"I do." He never knew what to expect from Tess, but this was a welcome change. He wouldn't have to deal with the children alone night after night. Perhaps they'd sleep better knowing she was there for them. He certainly would. "You'll be moving out here, then?"

"I will, so if you'll drive your wagon into town tomorrow, I'll have my trunks packed and ready for you to pick up." She descended the stairs and tossed her parting words over her shoulder. "I'll enjoy that extra afternoon off— and the larger pay packet, too."

So much for negotiating with her. Tess was Tess, and she knew how to get her way. Not that he minded as much as he should.

Chapter Thirteen

A rap on his office door rescued Spencer from his search for the error in his tallies.

Peter poked his head inside. "Got a minute?"

"Sure. What do you need?"

"Help solving a mystery." Peter plopped down on the bentwood chair and slapped a packet of papers on Spencer's desk.

"What are those?"

"Letters that were lost on one of the trains a couple months back and made a reappearance today."

"Why bring them to me? Drake's in charge of the lost and found office. Just have him drop them in the mail."

"Can't do that. There are no envelopes and no address."

Spencer shrugged. "Then I guess you'll have to toss them in the burn barrel."

"Can't do that, either. I gave the woman who turned them in my word. Said we'd do what we can to return them to their rightful owner."

"Why would you do that? We're not detectives."

"See for yourself. I took a quick look. These aren't just any letters, as the woman pointed out." Peter shoved the packet toward Spencer.

Curiosity propelled him to slip the top sheaf of stationery out of the blue ribbon binding three sheaves together. He unfolded the crisp white sheets, read the salutation and met Peter's expectant gaze. "They're love letters."

"Sure enough. I reckon the fellow who lost them would like to get them back."

"I agree, but how are we supposed to get them to him without a name or address?" Spencer pinched the bridge of his nose. "Did the woman who gave them to you say anything that might help us find him?"

Peter leaned back in the chair, raising the front legs off the floor. "Not much. She found the letters inside one of her children's picture books that hadn't been opened since their trip to Shingle Springs in July. Her parents gave her children the copy of *Little Bo Peep* to read on their way up the hill. She figures the letters must have accidentally ended up in her basket en route and gotten lodged between the book's pages."

"Do you know where the mother and her children first boarded the train?"

"Sacramento City."

Spencer groaned. "That means the gentleman could have lost his fiancée's letters anywhere along the line. Finding him would be highly unlikely."

"Maybe, but we can't just throw 'em out. They might be all he has to remember her by."

Peter had a point. Letters were often the only ties a fellow had to his lady back home. The fact that this man had still been carrying a letter his intended had written him three years before showed how important it was to him.

If Spencer had lost the letters Trudy sent him during their long-distance courtship, he would have wanted them back. As it was, he'd asked Tess to hide the letters he and Trudy had exchanged. And he had no regrets. A man couldn't cling to the past. He had to go on. "How do you propose we find him?"

"The way I see it, you'll have to read the letters. There might be some clues in them."

"Why me? You're the one who gave your word."

Peter grinned. "You're the one in charge, Cap'n." He grew serious. "The truth is, I don't have time to do any sleuthing. I oversee freight shipments all day. At night I go home to a pregnant wife who's mighty uncomfortable in this heat and needs my help."

Spencer couldn't argue with Peter's logic. He did have more free time than his friend. "I can't read them. They're private."

"What choice do you have? That's the only way to find out who they belong to. I figure the fellow will be so happy to get them back he won't care that you saw them."

Spencer chuckled. "I didn't know you were such a romantic, Peter." He wasn't. His friend would no sooner write a love letter than he would jump in front of a speeding train.

"I'll have you know, I am too romantic," he said with mock indignation. "Polly's been whirling through our place like a tumbleweed in the wind lately, cleaning every nook and cranny, so I gave her a new feather duster. Might not have been the best choice, though, since she went to smack me with it—after rolling her eyes that is." Peter returned the chair legs to the floor with a thump and grinned. He stood and tilted his head toward the letters. "Let me know what you find out."

The sound of Peter's boot heels thudding down the hallway soon ceased. Spencer set the letters aside and studied the numbers that wouldn't balance. He added the columns again but got the same sums as before. He closed the ledger and stared at the beribboned packet.

Somewhere out there a man could be mourning the loss of those letters. Spencer couldn't do anything to change his own situation, but perhaps he could brighten another man's day.

He took the first of the three letters in hand, unfolded the sheets of fine stationery and admired the elegant handwriting of the woman who'd filled several blue-bordered pages. She must be a lady of refinement.

Spencer began reading.

Thursday, August 20, 1863

To the beloved gentleman I look forward to marrying,

As I think of you on this most glorious of summer days, a delightful sense of anticipation envelops me. I'm eager to gaze into your eyes and see my love for you reflected in their depths. After years of dreaming dreams and lifting prayers, I can only imagine how wonderful it will be to have your arms around me, to feel your lips pressed against mine, to become the wife of the man the Lord handpicked for me.

I hope that wherever you find yourself things are going well for you. God has given you many gifts and talents, and I trust Him to direct your steps as you go about your business. May He bless your endeavors, help you through the dark days we all face at times and draw you ever closer to Him.

The more Spencer read, the more his admiration for this godly woman grew. Her fiancé—or perhaps he was her husband by now—must thank the Lord repeatedly for having brought her into his life. What a gift it would be for a man to have a supportive wife like her who had such unrelenting faith in him and his abilities.

Trudy had tried her best not to complain, but she'd longed for a life of leisure like the one her cattle baron father had provided, which was understandable. She'd spent countless hours in Sacramento City's most highly respected dressmakers' shops.

Memories of those outings assaulted Spencer. Although he'd given his wife all he could afford—and then some— he hadn't succeeded in sating her appetite for fine things or lightening her workload. His failure to put her desires ahead of his own ambitions had cost him dearly.

He shoved his self-recriminating thoughts aside and read the final paragraph of the letter.

> As difficult as the waiting can be at times, I cling to the promise in Psalm 37. The Lord knows the desires of our hearts. Mine is to be the wife you deserve, giving my utmost to the task of loving you and any children He grants us the privilege of parenting. Until that glorious day arrives when I take the long-awaited journey down the aisle and we say our vows, know that you are ever in my thoughts and prayers.

> With love from Faith

A sense of awe enveloped Spencer. This woman— Faith—was a woman among women. Her kindness, compassion and loyalty leaped from the page. A man with her at his side could accomplish great things. No matter how slim the chances of finding the recipient of this letter after so much time had elapsed, Spencer had to try.

As tempting as it was to read the remaining letters, he had enough information to begin his search, and that's what he'd do. Reading any further would be dishonorable. If and when he met the man this remarkable woman loved, Spencer wanted to be able to look him in the eye.

Minutes later Spencer stood behind Drake and listened to the clicking of his ticket agent's telegraph key. The carefully composed message Spencer had written was on its way to all the stationmasters from Latrobe to Sacramento City.

Please post the following: Seeking male passenger who lost items given him by woman named Faith. Must describe to claim. Direct inquiries to Spencer Abbott, Stationmaster, Shingle Springs.

Drake's tapping ceased. "Deed's done, boss."

"Thanks. Let me know if I get any replies."

Spencer returned to his office and stowed the letters in the back of his deepest, darkest desk drawer. Flipping open the ledger, he prepared to find the erroneous number that had eluded him. If only he could find the recipient of the letters as easily...

Tess slipped into the pew next to Polly and leaned over to whisper to her friend. The prelude covered their hushed conversation. "How are you feeling?"

Polly shifted on the wooden bench. "Pretty good considering how big I've gotten. My back's been bothering me a bit, though."

"At least you don't have to wait much longer."

"Two weeks if Doc's estimate is correct."

The minister entered, and a hush descended on the room. Reverend Josephs opened the service in prayer. An enthusiastic quartet led the congregation in the singing of two hymns. Tess stood, reveling in the wealth of voices lifted in praise.

One in particular stood out—the rich baritone belonging to Spencer, who occupied the pew behind her with Luke and Lila. Tess closed her eyes and concentrated on Spencer's voice, isolating it, savoring it. What she'd give to be able to sing like that.

The final chord faded, and Reverend Josephs bid them be seated. Even though he was a mouse of a man with round-rimmed spectacles, a transformation took place when he preached. Emboldened by his passion for the Word of God, he seemed taller, larger and more compelling. He was such a dynamic speaker that she hung on his every word, eager to learn all she could about how to live out her faith day by day.

"Brothers and sisters, members of the flock, our great Shepherd has given me a message for you today from the Twenty-third Psalm. A message of hope and healing. A message sure to fill your hearts with a hunger to know Him more deeply and live more fully for Him."

Tess's skin tingled with anticipation. She loved that psalm. She'd spent time in the valley of the shadow of death craving comfort, and the Lord had been there for her. No matter how difficult life at the orphanage had been, she'd clung to the One who would never leave or forsake her. Ever since she'd first learned about God from the French cook, Josette, at the age of seven, Tess had sought solace in His arms, faithfully visiting His house every Sunday morning.

Those precious times of worship had filled her soul and equipped her to endure the endless toil as she tackled the many chores Mr. Grimsby assigned her. Why he'd required more of her than he had the other children was a question she'd never been able to answer. The one time she asked him about the inequity, he'd merely stated that he had her best interests at heart.

If equipping her for a life of service had been his goal, he'd succeeded. Her abundant skills had enabled her to secure employment. Until now, she'd been unable to put all of them to work. These days she was governess and teacher, housekeeper and cook, stable hand and gardener, laundress and seamstress. A wonderful blend that kept life interesting and fulfilling.

Reverend Josephs raised his voice to make a point, rousing Tess from her musings. So powerful was his message about the care given His flock by a loving Shepherd that she was drawn in deeply, her surroundings fading as she focused on the minister's every word.

All too soon the sermon ended. The leader of the quartet that led the singing addressed the congregation. "We have a treat for you today. Our pianist, Mrs. Brubaker, received a piece of sheet music from her sister in Boston. It's a new hymn that embodies the spirit of our good reverend's sermon called 'He Leadeth Me.' I think you'll blessed by it. We'll sing the first verse and chorus for you once. Then we'll start again, going through all the verses, and you can join us on the refrain if you'd like."

The moving words soaked into Tess's soul. How she longed to let the Lord lead her. If only His plans included a family of her own with a warmhearted husband and precious children to love and care for, she would thank Him every day for the rest of her life. She wouldn't complain if that husband happened to be handsome, too.

The final verse mentioned "death's cold wave," jerking her back to reality. Spencer's wife had been taken from him. How was he feeling, having been reminded of that, first with the talk about death in the sermon and again in the hymn? She couldn't turn around and gawk at him, but the closing prayer was coming.

The final note of the chorus rang out. She waited for the prayer with bated breath. *Forgive me, Lord, but I must know how he's doing.*

As soon as all heads were bowed, Tess grasped her locket with its filigree front and smooth back. She'd bought it years ago on a whim, dreaming of the day it would hold photographs of her children. Today she hoped it could serve as a mirror. If she angled the shiny back just so—

An elbow jabbed her in the side. Polly cast her a questioning look.

Tess smiled and pretended to polish the locket by rubbing it against her bodice. Polly shook her head and bowed it.

Hoping the minister was as generous with his prayer as he'd been the past seven Sundays, Tess held the locket above her shoulder and tilted it to and fro. A ripple of satisfaction shimmied up her spine when Spencer's face came into view. As she'd suspected, his frown was in full force.

Compassion squeezed her heart. He wasn't morose, as she'd first thought. He was just a man in mourning.

Reverend Josephs followed his closing prayer with an impassioned benediction. The congregation filed out of the stuffy sanctuary. Tess stood in a cluster with Peter, Polly and Spencer, who held Lila in his arms. Luke and Abby searched for ladybugs nearby.

Polly cast a longing look at a bench in the shade. "If you gentlemen will give me a few minutes with Tess now, I'll see that you get an extra slice of pie later. I feel the urge to talk about baby booties coming on."

Peter grinned and backed away. "Take all the time you

want. Spence and I will watch the children, so you ladies can gab to your hearts' content."

The men moved out of earshot. Polly gazed at her husband with adoration. "He teases me about what he calls 'baby talk,' but he's as excited about the little one as I am. I hope it's a boy. I'd love to give Peter a son who's a red-haired replica of him."

Tess hoped her smile didn't look as halfhearted as it felt. She loved Polly dearly, but witnessing her friend's happiness gave Tess a twinge of jealousy.

Polly rubbed her swollen abdomen and frowned.

"What is it?"

"Peter Junior is usually moving around this time of day. Perhaps he's resting after his antics yesterday. He was so active I was convinced he was turning somersaults."

"How do you sleep with all that going on inside you?"

Polly chuckled. "It's not easy, but sometimes fatigue takes over."

"I've always been curious what a birthing is like. How do you feel when you see your child for the first time?"

"Hmm. How can I describe the indescribable?" Polly gazed at the cloudless sky a moment before returning her attention to Tess. "I won't do you any favors if I glamorize things, so I'll be truthful. A birthing is some of the hardest work a woman ever does, but the rewards are far sweeter than any piece of pie. Somehow the memory of the pain fades the instant you gaze into the face of that beautiful baby the Lord's entrusted to your care, replaced by a love so intense it threatens to steal your breath away."

"It sounds wonderful. Not the pain part, but the rest." Tess fidgeted with the fan hanging from her wrist. "Does it matter if a woman's older when she has her first child? Would that make things more difficult?"

"I've known women who didn't wed until they were

thirty, and they went on to have children with no trouble at all."

"I have at least five years, then." Although she'd attempted to sound lighthearted, the sympathy filling Polly's eyes told Tess she'd failed.

"My dear Tessie, the Lord has a plan for you. Your job is to trust Him. As it says in that new hymn we sang, He'll lead you. And who knows? Maybe you'll end up with a family right here in Shingle Springs."

Tess shook her head. "I don't see that happening."

"I saw you peeking at Spencer. You obviously care for him."

"Of course I care *about* him, but that doesn't mean I'm harboring foolish notions." She hadn't intended for her voice to have such a sharp edge and softened her tone to match Polly's. "He's my employer—and a grieving widower."

"That gives you a unique opportunity to minister to him. Did you take my advice about engaging him in conversation?"

"I did."

Polly leaned forward expectantly. "And?"

"We've had some good talks about his childhood back in Texas. I've enjoyed them, but…" Her gaze rested on Spencer, who held his adorable daughter in his arms.

"But you're impatient. I understand. You want him to unlock the door to his feelings and let you in. If you take your time, it will happen. Have faith."

"I do."

Polly shifted and rubbed her back. "Spencer might not give you the key to that door as soon as you'd like, but the way I see it, you've made progress. I never expected him to move you out to the ranch. He must trust you wholeheartedly, and that isn't something he does easily. How are things working out? Do you two sit in the parlor after the children are in bed, or does he head to the bunkhouse?"

Tess smiled. Leave it to inquisitive Polly to pepper her with questions. "I don't know what he does. As soon as we tuck them in, I go to my room."

"Why? Since you want him to open up to you, I thought you'd welcome the opportunity to be alone with him. Or could it be that you're afraid to spend too much time in his company because you care *about* him?"

"I'm not afraid." Tess toyed with the button on her glove. "Although I would enjoy talking with him, I need time to work on the quilt. I can't when Luke's around. He'd be too apt to tell his papa what I'm doing and spoil my surprise. I want to present the quilt to Spencer on the anniversary of his wife's passing. If I'm to have it ready by then, I mustn't tarry."

"If you continue to slip off the minute the day's work is done, he won't see you as anything but a housekeeper. If you want him to confide in you, I suggest you spend a few minutes together before you head to your room. Show him you're interested in him. You *are* interested in him, aren't you? Or at least in helping him?"

"Well, yes, but I—"

Polly gasped and clutched her middle.

"What is it?"

"My water just broke!"

Chapter Fourteen

Concern sent tremors through Tess. "The baby's coming? But it's not time yet."

"Obviously the Lord has other plans." Polly winced and drew in a series of shallow breaths.

Tess leaped to her feet. "I'll get Peter."

"Wait!" Polly grabbed Tess's hand. "I believe this is the Lord's timing. It's your day off, so you can stay with me and witness a birth for yourself."

"I couldn't. It's not my place."

"Please, Tessie. I could use a friend to help me through it. I do my best to appear as strong as you are, but inside I'm a quivering mass of jelly."

Tess couldn't resist the plea in Polly's eyes. "I wouldn't be much help, I'm afraid. I don't know the first thing about birthing babies."

"Doc will see to all that. You could bathe my forehead and give me something to focus on besides the pai— besides the work ahead of me."

Compassion and curiosity combined, making it impossible for Tess to decline. "I'll stay, but right now I'm getting Peter."

Twenty minutes later Tess eased Polly's head onto her

pillow following a contraction. "It won't be long, and Peter will be back with the doctor."

"I hope so. Things are happening much faster than they did with Abby."

"That's good. It means the work will be over quickly, and then you can see your baby."

Another contraction overtook Polly a minute later, causing her to groan. Tess offered her hand. "Hold on."

Polly did, squeezing so hard Tess gritted her teeth to keep from protesting. She was grateful when the pressure eased and Polly fell back against the mound of pillows.

"Talk to me, Tessie. Tell me something. Anything. How's the quilt coming along?"

"I've cut out the pieces for the *T*s. I decided to use blue fabric from my rag bag for half of them so there's part of me in the quilt. But before I begin sewing the squares, I'm going to make a gown for your baby."

"That's nice."

Tess dabbed Polly's flushed face with a cool cloth. "I know you're convinced you're having a boy, but what if it's a girl? Do you have a name picked out?"

"Peter likes Elizabeth. It was his sister's name. They called her Beth, so we would use Lizzie. Oh!" Polly breathed her way through another contraction, her mouth open and her rigid body hunched forward. The pain subsided, and she relaxed her hold on Tess's hand. "Doc had better get here soon."

Tess did her best to sound convincing. "I'm sure it won't be much longer." *Please, Lord, let that be true.*

Four more contractions seized Polly, the intensity of each increasing and the time between them decreasing, making conversation difficult. As she rested during the brief interval following the latest one, she patted Tess's arm. "I hope I'm not scaring you. It is worth it. You'll see that when the baby arrives."

"Don't worry about me. I'm fine." Tess needed no convincing. She would do anything to have a child of her own, would endure any amount of pain.

The thundering of hooves out front sent waves of relief rippling through her. Peter shouted something indistinguishable to Spencer, who was on the porch watching the children.

"They're here!" Tess's exclamation was drowned out by Polly's sharp cry as another contraction overtook her.

The doctor entered the room, black bag in hand, an air of competence and calm about him. He greeted them warmly, rolled up his shirtsleeves, rinsed his hands in the basin Tess had filled and took his place at the end of the bed. "Let's see what's happening."

Tess sat with her back to him, her attention focused on Polly, murmuring words of comfort while he completed his initial examination.

"I got here just in time, Mrs. Flynn. This baby's ready to join your family."

Tess tingled from head to foot. She was about to behold a newborn baby, one of God's greatest marvels.

The following five minutes passed in a blur as Polly followed the doctor's instructions, clinging to Tess as though she were a lifeline. Never had Tess felt as needed—or as privileged.

"One more push, Mrs. Flynn, and it will all be over," the doctor assured Polly. "You can do it."

Polly bore down, her cheeks turning the color of ripe cherries, and let out a keening wail like that of a wounded animal. She fell back into the pillows, spent.

Tess turned in time to see the doctor swat the baby's bottom. The little fellow gave a single lusty cry. She inhaled sharply. "You were right, Polly. It's a boy! A strong, healthy boy."

"I knew it." Polly gave a weak smile. "Can I see him?"

"Momentarily." The doctor cut the cord, held out the tiny baby to Tess and inclined his head toward the blanket nearby.

"Me?" Tess pressed a hand to her chest.

"Yes. I need to see to your friend now. Wrap the little fellow and let her hold him while I finish up."

Tess took the squirming newborn in her hands, exercising the utmost care as she followed the doctor's instructions. A profound sense of awe consumed her. The baby was so much smaller than Lila, but he had plenty of hair that was every bit as red as his father's. Polly would be so happy.

"Here's your son." She placed the bundle of wide-eyed boy in his mother's arms.

Tears of joy streamed down Polly's cheeks. "He does look like Peter. Please, get him for me. He needs to see his namesake."

Tess opened the bedroom door and nearly crashed into Peter. He lifted his ashen face. "I heard the baby cry and then nothing."

"Everything's fine. She's asking to see you."

He flew past her. "Poll, are you all right?"

"Very much so. Come see your son."

The happy couple kissed, and Tess sighed. Oh, to be loved like that.

She closed the door behind her and stepped onto the porch, eager to escape the confines of the small house. Standing at the railing, she watched Luke and Abby ride pretend ponies and reveled in the hint of a breeze.

Spencer crossed the yard with Lila in his arms, his little girl busy exploring his features. He dodged a finger aimed at his eye. "How did it go?"

"Polly and her son are both doing well. She's exhausted, but he's alert, looking at everything."

"And how are you?"

"I'm fine."

He raised a brow. "Just fine? You witnessed the wonder of birth, and that's all you have to say?"

"Everything went so quickly. Polly didn't have to suffer very long."

The color drained from Spencer's face. He sank onto the top step and planted a kiss on top of Lila's head. "I—" His voice came out raspy. He cleared his throat. "I'm happy for them. It doesn't always go as well. Sometimes a delivery takes an eternity—and an enormous toll on the mother."

Tess plunked down beside him and rested a hand on his forearm. "You're thinking about your wife, aren't you?"

He glanced at her hand, his expression unreadable, and she removed it. "Lila's birthing went on forever, but that's not something I like to talk about."

She ached for him. "It must have been difficult for you."

Several seconds passed in silence as Spencer stared at his daughter standing in his lap, her tiny hands grasping his fingers. Tess didn't say a word. Didn't move. Didn't even breathe. *Lord, please help him open up. It's clear he's in pain. Talking about it might make things easier for him.*

When at last they came, his words were halting, as though forcing each one out required considerable effort. "Trudy was a small woman and lacked Polly's strength. She labored long and hard with Luke, but that was nothing compared to what she went through with Lila. She came early, and Doc was out of town. I'd helped birth many animals, but this was different. This was my wife and child.

If I made a mistake, I knew I'd never be able to live with myself. But I had no choice."

Spencer pulled his daughter toward him and placed a kiss on each cheek. Tess blinked to clear the sudden moisture in her eyes.

He released an audible breath and continued. "Trudy labored eighteen long hours. There was little I could do for her. I'd never felt as helpless or prayed as earnestly as I did then. When Lila finally made her appearance, I saw a foot. She was breech. Fear had me in a chokehold, but I couldn't give way to it. Her life depended on me getting her out quickly."

"And you succeeded."

"Yes, but I came so close to losing them both that day. Trudy lost a great deal of blood during the delivery, which left her weak." He swallowed, his Adam's apple bobbing. "At least she was with me seven more months before she fell on the tines of a rake and developed an infection she wasn't strong enough to fight. I'm grateful for that."

His concern about using garden tools finally made sense. She felt his pain, but as much as she longed to wrap an arm around him and offer words of comfort, she restrained herself. A man who fought to keep his feelings in check wouldn't welcome an effusive show of sympathy. She focused on Lila instead, tugging the hem of her dress into place. "You saved this precious girl's life, and look how much she loves you."

"Come here, princess." He cradled her to his chest and nuzzled his face in her golden hair.

Sensing his need to be alone, Tess stood and rested a hand on Spencer's shoulder. Not the wisest choice perhaps, but she couldn't help herself. He tensed. She removed her hand and turned to leave. "I should go inside and see what Polly had planned for her Sunday dinner. I'm sure everyone's getting hungry."

"Wait." Spencer should let Tess go, but he couldn't. Not yet.

She spun around. Uncertainty and curiosity waged a battle on her lovely face.

Lovely? Where had that come from? She was attractive, to be sure, but he was still in mourning. He had no right to be admiring another woman.

"Did you want something?"

He cleared his throat. "Forgive me. I didn't mean to blather."

"You didn't. You just gave me some history that helps me better understand your situation." She returned and sat beside him but didn't press him for a response.

How considerate of her not to shower him with sympathy and platitudes. He'd seen the caring and concern in her chocolate-brown eyes, but she wasn't one to let her emotions get the better of her. He admired her self-control, but there were times he wished she wasn't quite as restrained.

Ever since reading the letter Faith had written to her intended, he'd found himself wondering what it would be like to have such a woman in his life. Her way with words spoke to the brokenness that had him in its clutches. He felt certain someone like her would understand and appreciate him.

At times he thought Tess did, but lately she seemed to be holding back. She'd moved into the house eight days back, but every evening since she'd headed to her room the instant the children were in bed. Sitting alone in the parlor with nothing but his memories for company wasn't how he liked to spend his evenings. Despite her previous attempts to get him talking, it seemed she preferred keeping to herself of late when what he'd really like was for her to unleash her laughter and chase away the shadows that hovered in the corners.

Even though he missed their conversations, keeping things professional was probably wise. It was one thing to imagine life with a woman he'd never met but quite another to entertain thoughts about a woman who could take his thoughts down a track he wasn't ready to travel. Especially the woman living in his house.

He forced himself to come up with a suitable response. "I don't make a habit of talking about such things."

Her matter-of-fact manner gave way to one of the sweetest smiles she'd ever sent his way. It had the power to turn darkness into sunshine. "I understand. It can be difficult to recount painful experiences." Her voice conveyed compassion but not an ounce of pity. "Perhaps you could write about them. I keep a journal, and I've found writing in it beneficial."

Was that what she was doing in her room at night? It would explain why her lamp burned for an hour or two after she'd gone upstairs. Not that he made a point of noticing. "I'll have to give that some thought." His stomach rumbled. "Pardon me."

"That's quite all right." She stood. "I'll get a meal on the table right away."

Three of her lengthy strides carried her across the porch. She paused in the open doorway and studied him for a moment before smiling once more, an understanding smile that eased the dull ache in his chest. "I'll continue to pray for you."

Tess didn't have Faith's way with words, but her simple statement meant a great deal to him nonetheless. It came from a pure heart and a genuine desire to serve others. Look at her now, giving up her day off to care for Polly and her family without a second thought. She'd been there for him, too, when the memories had become too much to bear. And he hadn't even— "Thank you, Tess. I appreciate that."

Surprise at his gratitude parted her lips before she shook herself and entered the kitchen. He had the unexpected urge to chase after her and plant a kiss on those rosy lips.

What had come over him? He'd given way to his feelings, sensed a bond and come far too close to telling her how he'd failed his late wife, that's what. Well, he wouldn't do that again.

Chapter Fifteen

As soon as she'd completed her chores the next morning, Tess hitched the team to the wagon. She'd not been able to get a moment alone with Polly after Petey's earlier-than-expected arrival.

Although Tess was eager to prepare enough food to last a couple of days so her friend could devote herself to her infant son, she would have arranged to pay Polly a visit no matter what. Tess couldn't wait to tell her friend about the conversation she'd had with Spencer after the baby's birth.

When Spencer had stopped her as she'd headed inside to fix dinner after having told her about one of the most difficult days of his life, she hadn't known what to expect. Although entirely unnecessary as far as she was concerned, his apology made sense. He wasn't one to openly address his past or his pain.

While she'd felt a connection to him born of concern, everything had changed when she'd assured him he hadn't "blathered." He'd gazed at her with such admiration that her cheeks had warmed. No man had looked at her that way before.

He'd gone on to thank her for offering to pray for him and given her a smile so disarming the heat had intensified, fueled by her wayward thoughts. Thoughts an upstanding Christian woman had no right thinking—especially about her employer.

What had possessed her to wonder what his lips would feel like on hers? Perhaps the fact that she was twenty-five and had never been kissed. Or perhaps it was witnessing a birth and seeing Peter kiss Polly afterward, dredging up the dream of having a husband and children of her own that she fought to keep at bay. Whatever the reason, she'd forced herself to focus on Spencer's eyes after that, although her gaze had continually strayed to his mouth.

"Why are you smiling?"

Luke's question roused her. "Because we get to see little Petey again. Won't that be fun?"

"No. He didn't look too good. He was all red and wrinkly."

True, but Tess had never seen anything that moved her as deeply as her glimpse of Petey in the first seconds of his life. Arguing with Luke was pointless, though. "Climb on up. We're ready to go."

He scaled the side of the wagon in no time, plopped himself in the driver's seat and grabbed the reins.

"Be careful, Luke. You'd be sorry if the team took off on you." She took control of the reins, set Lila in the crate she'd wedged between the seat and the wagon's front gate and sat beside the overeager boy.

"I wanna drive."

"All right."

He fixed eyes as big as wagon wheels on her. "Are you telling the truth?"

"I am. You may sit next to me and hold the reins."

Luke grinned from ear to ear as the docile horses plodded along. Tess took over when they reached town and parked the wagon in the Flynn's barn. She carried Lila inside, unloaded the crates filled with supplies and saw to the horses. Luke raced off to find Abby.

Tess set to work preparing fried chicken, coleslaw and other easy-to-serve fare for the Flynn's upcoming meals. The older children played in the yard while Polly and her infant son dozed in the bedroom.

When Peter arrived at noon, Tess dished up pork chops, mashed potatoes and green beans. Polly joined them for the meal, which passed quickly.

Peter returned to the depot, and Tess made short work of the dishes. She went outside to sit on the porch with Polly. Luke and Abby piled rocks into a mound, and Lila napped on a blanket nearby.

The creaking of Polly's rocking chair ceased. She adjusted the thin blanket over her infant son, who nursed beneath it. She resumed her rocking. "I know why you came. Something happened with Spencer yesterday."

"I came to see you and do a little cooking so you can get a good rest before you have to resume your duties. I saw how hard you worked bringing that little fellow into the world."

Polly snickered. "That's a fine excuse—and a much appreciated gesture—but I saw the way your face glowed when you came inside after talking with him. No more stalling. Tell me."

Tess ran her hands over the arms of the ladder-backed rocking chair. "I'm probably making more of it than I should, but he talked to me. Really talked."

"Go on."

"He told me about Lila's birthing, how difficult it was for his wife and how close he came to losing them both."

"I didn't know him as well then. We hadn't been here long, but I remember Peter telling me how haggard Spencer looked. Did he say anything else?"

Tess shook her head. "He mentioned how weak Trudy was afterward and how grateful he was to have had a few more months with her before the accident and resulting infection took her from him. It's sad that he's suffered so, but I'm glad he told me. It helps me understand him better."

"I knew he'd open up to you in time. Maybe now you'll feel better about sitting with him in the parlor after the children are in bed. The more he gets to know you, the easier it will be for him to see you as a young, attractive, *unattached* woman instead of a housekeeper."

"Why would he? I'm not young or attractive."

Polly huffed. "Oh, Tessie, how many times must I tell you how beautiful you are before you'll believe it?"

"I'm tall."

"And lithe, and you have striking features many a woman would give her eyeteeth for. Me included."

"You? But you're short and have the prettiest face ever. Peter couldn't keep his eyes off you at dinner." His admiration had been so evident as to be almost embarrassing.

"He's just happy because I've given him a son. If you want to talk about a man whose gaze wanders to a certain woman, look no further than Spencer. He steals glances at you quite often."

Tess stopped rocking and sat bolt upright. "No! That's not true."

"'The lady doth protest too much, methinks.' He's a man, Tessie, and he's bound to be lonely. If he sees a beautiful woman, he's going to take notice. Especially when that woman is capable and caring…and close at hand."

Polly meant well, but Spencer was a widower in mourning, not a man looking to find a wife.

"No, Wuke! Bad boy."

Tess snapped to attention. She expected to find him pestering Abby again, but the little girl had called to him from where she sat at the rock pile. Luke stood inside the picket fence holding a large stone over his head while facing three school-aged boys on the outside.

She approached them, and the older boys took off running. "Put the rock down and come over here, young man." She pointed to the spot in front of her.

Luke threw the stone, narrowly missing her. She had half a mind to take him over her knee and give him a swat, but he sniffed, sending a tear trickling down his dirt-streaked face. Her irritation fled. "What did those boys say to you?"

He stood with his feet apart, his arms crossed and his face scrunched in a fierce scowl. "Nothin'."

"All right. You don't have to tell me. I can just punish you for throwing rocks."

He relaxed his stance. "If tell you, will I still get in trouble?"

"Throwing rocks is wrong. But if I know why you were going to do it, you wouldn't get in as much trouble."

He wiggled his mouth back and forth as he considered his options, looking so cute Tess tamped down a smile. "I'll tell you, but you can't laugh at me like they done."

After hearing his sad tale, she had half a mind to hunt down those boys and give them a tongue-lashing. Why did children have to be so cruel to one another? "I'm sorry they said those mean things, sweetheart. Would a hug help you feel better?"

He swung his head from side to side, his long brown hair slapping against his cheeks.

His resistance came as no surprise, but the plea for help in his watery eyes did.

She needed to make another change—one Spencer might balk at—and the sooner the better.

* * *

Spencer checked his watch again, shoved it into his waistcoat pocket and resumed pacing the platform. Only five minutes until his bull arrived. He whistled a few measures of Handel's "Hallelujah Chorus."

Drake approached and fell in step beside him. "I couldn't quite make out your note, boss. Was this how you wanted the telegram to Boston worded?"

Spencer scanned Drake's block letters and returned the slip of paper. "That works." A number of times he'd caught Tess singing that new hymn introduced in church last week, although she stopped as soon as she realized he was there. He'd decided to surprise her by getting a copy of the sheet music from the pianist's sister back east.

"Papa!"

"Luke?" Spencer spun around, spotted his son barreling toward him and braced himself for the impact. Luke flung his arms around Spencer's waist in an exuberant display of childish affection. He tousled his son's hair. "Where's Tess?"

"She's a slowpoke." Luke pointed at the far end of the platform. Tess clutched Lila with both arms and weaved her way between baggage handlers awaiting the arrival of the incoming freight train.

When she reached Spencer and his son, her chest was heaving. "You're faster than a lizard outrunning a cat, Luke. Even with my long legs, I didn't stand a chance of winning our race." She finger-combed his long hair. For once he didn't bat her hand away.

"I am fast, aren't I, Papa? I got to you first."

"That you did, my boy."

Tess handed her fan to a squirming Lila, who quieted and examined it. "Might I have a word with you, Spencer?"

This wasn't the best time for a discussion. "Could we talk tonight? I've got to check with Peter before my bull arrives. I want to be sure he and his crew have everything ready."

"It'll only take a minute. I'd like your answer before the children and I head back to the ranch because I might need to make a stop at the general store."

"All right, but you'll need to make it quick."

"Thank you." She gave him a smile as sweet as the slice of apple pie she'd put in his lunch pail that day. He'd have offered to give her more than a minute if he'd known he would receive such a nice reward.

She shifted her attention to Luke. "I'll let you drive again…*if* you'll sit over there while I'll talk with your papa." She held out her free hand toward a bench in the shade of the depot.

Luke took off without a word and planted himself on the spot she'd indicated.

Spencer couldn't believe what he'd heard. "You let my four-year-old son drive the wagon?"

"Right. Just like I let him play on the barn roof this morning." She smirked and gave her head such a sound shake that the three peacock feathers atop her hat did a dance.

"So he didn't drive?"

"I let him sit beside me and hold the reins, but I kept my hands on them, too. And don't you dare tell him. It'll be our secret." She winked—an action so unexpected that a cross between a cough and a chortle escaped him. My, but Tess was bold. He didn't care. He liked seeing her playful side.

Her gaze roved over his slouch hat, ranch wear and boots, and returned to his face again. The admiration in her beautiful brown eyes surprised him. She'd never looked at him that way before. As though she was seeing him as a man and not just her employer. "While you look nice in your stationmaster attire, the more relaxed look suits you."

A shrill whistle in the distance announced the incoming train—and kept him from having to come up with a response. He studied the sky to the west, looking for the plume of gray smoke that signaled the approach of an inbound train.

She cleared her throat in an obvious attempt to get his attention. "About my request?"

He divided his attention between her and the locomotive barreling toward the station. "What was it you wanted?"

"Since Luke's been growing, he could use a new wardrobe. I'd like to purchase fabric and trim so I can get to work on some outfits right away."

He pulled out his money clip and withdrew several bills. "Buy whatever you need."

She took the proffered banknotes and stuffed them in her handbag but didn't leave. He'd given her enough to buy an entire bolt of material. What more could she want?

"I want to be sure you understand my intentions. Luke's tall for his age, so rather than wasting your money on more of the loose-fitting little-boy outfits, I'd like to—"

"Put him in short pants? Yes. I understand. Do it."

Tess stared at him, her lips parted, looking entirely too attractive for her own good. He tore his gaze from her and listened to the rhythmic clacking of the wheels on the rails as the train covered the final half mile, a welcome sound any day, but never more so than today.

"I didn't think you'd agree, at least not so readily."

"I'm glad to know I can surprise you." He headed toward the edge of the platform, keeping his face forward so she couldn't see his grin.

She matched his pace stride for stride. "About the outfits. Do you have any preferences?"

The train pulled into the station, coming to a stop with a screech of metal on metal and the hiss of steam. "Do whatever you want, Tess. I trust your judgment."

Spencer jumped off the platform, jogged around the last rail car and disappeared. Tess smiled. He'd not only agreed with her plan to update Luke's wardrobe. He seemed eager for her to do so.

She couldn't wait to get started making Luke's first tunic and pair of short pants. He'd be so happy when he was found out he'd be wearing big-boy clothes that he might begin to trust her. If she could break down his walls, she'd be better able to help him heal.

He sat on the bench swinging his legs as he watched the flurry of activity on the platform. Tess balanced Lila on her hip and sidestepped a stack of crates on her way to him. "How would you like to watch the men unload your papa's bull, Luke?"

"It's here?" He jumped off the bench, his head swiveling.

"In one of those cars, yes. It looks as if they'll be unloading it on the north side of the tracks. Come on. Let's go."

They rounded the end of the train. Tess kept the children at a safe distance.

Several men strained to push a heavy wooden ramp up to the doors of a boxcar with holes drilled in the sides. The ripe smell of animal leavings caused Tess to wrinkle her nose.

Peter cupped his hands and called to Spencer, who'd

mounted his big black horse. "They've got the ramp in place, Cap'n. You ready for us to open the doors?"

Apparently the shouting had upset the bull. The sudden bellowing and stamping from the angry animal inside the car made the hairs at Tess's nape stand on end.

"Yes—" Spencer hollered "—but be on your guard. Sounds like he's madder than a miner facing down a claim jumper."

Peter clambered onto the ramp. "Don't worry," he yelled over the commotion. "The freight traffic manager in Sacramento City telegraphed. Said they've got the big guy tied to the sides of the car. We'll bring him out nice and slow."

Luke hopped from one foot to the other in his excitement, creating a cloud of dust. "Papa said he's real big and I gotta stay away from him."

Spencer had cautioned Tess, as well, but he'd assured her the animal wouldn't pose a threat. "He'll be in his pen. As long as we keep our distance, we'll be safe." She'd walked the perimeter the day before to assure herself of that fact. The Muellers had built a sturdy fence.

Peter beckoned to one of his men, who joined him on the ramp. They each held a handle and slid the doors aside.

"Watch out!" Spencer shouted. "He got loose."

The men jumped back.

The largest animal Tess had ever seen charged down the ramp. She'd heard of longhorns and seen sketches in the newspaper, but she'd never expected to see one for herself.

The behemoth pawed the ground, used his horns to throw up dirt and took off running in the direction of the ranch, trailing broken pieces of rope behind him.

Spencer grabbed his lariat, formed a loop, set it to spinning and gave chase. My, but he sat a horse well. "Be careful!"

"Get 'im, Spence!" Peter yelled.

Luke chased after his father. "Go, Papa! Go."

"No, Luke. Stop," Tess called. "He'll be all right." *Please, God, let it be so.*

Spencer caught up to the bull in no time and let his rope fly.

He missed.

The bull changed directions. He was barreling straight at them.

Tess's mouth went dry.

Chapter Sixteen

The pounding of Tess's heart rivaled the pounding of the bull's hooves as it raced toward the station. What would happen if Spencer couldn't stop the huge animal in time? She'd heard of men who'd been killed by raging bulls.

She grabbed Luke by the hand and rushed the children to safety behind a nearby freight wagon.

Spencer recoiled his rope, formed a larger loop than Tess had ever seen him throw and spun it as he raced after the bull.

Lord, help him stop that brute.

When Spencer was within a few feet of the charging creature, he sent his lasso sailing.

Tess held her breath.

The loop caught not one, but both horns.

Spencer whipped the end of his lariat around his saddle horn, grabbed the rope and, with a series of clever maneuvers, steered the rampaging bull away from town and back toward the ranch. At the speed they were traveling, it would be some time before their pace slowed.

Peter loped over to Tess and the children. "Are you all right?"

She drew in a shaky breath. "We're fine, but thank you for checking on us."

"Spence sure knows his way around a rope, doesn't he? I've never seen anything like it."

Luke chimed in. "Papa's the best roper ever. He's teaching me."

"So I hear. Heard tell he's been teaching you, too, Tess."

"She's no good," Luke scoffed. "She can't get her loop around anything."

Peter quirked an eyebrow. "Hasn't your papa taught you it's not nice to talk about a lady that way?"

"She's not a lady. She's just Te—" Luke slammed his mouth shut and stormed off, kicking a stone.

"Polly said the boy's got it in for you. What do you aim to do about it?"

"Bide my time. And pray."

Peter removed his sweat-stained derby and passed a sleeve over his damp forehead. "I'd best do some praying myself. Don't think Spence is going to take too kindly to having his bull bust out of the car like that after I told him we had things under control. He's counting on the big fellow to launch his cattle-ranching empire. Can't see what the draw is myself. I'd take railroading over ranching any day." One of his men hollered for him, and he returned to his work.

"Come on, Luke," Tess called. "I have an errand to run before we head back to the ranch."

Minutes later she entered the general store. The friendly owner greeted her. "Afternoon, Miss Grimsby. What can I do for you?"

Tess shifted Lila from one hip to the other. "I'd like some sturdy fabric in colors suitable for an active young boy."

"Master Luke's getting some new togs, is he?"

She glanced at Luke, who was engrossed in the toy display, and lowered her voice. "He doesn't know what I have in mind, and I'd prefer to keep it that way. If he were to find out, he'd pester me endlessly."

Mr. Hawkes chuckled. "I didn't have a whole lot of patience when I was his age, either. Let's see how soon we can get you out of here then, shall we?" The proprietor cut and wrapped her selections quickly.

Since Spencer had been so generous, she had more than enough money to buy everything his son needed. A quick glance revealed that Luke was enraptured by a brightly colored Noah's ark set.

She returned her attention to Mr. Hawkes and kept her voice low. "I'd like to get him a new pair of boots, too."

He rubbed his chin. "I can't help you with that. Since I don't have much of a demand for children's shoes, I don't carry them. The shoemaker in Folsom would be able to help you, though."

"It appears I'll have to plan a trip down the hill. In the meantime, I'd like you to set aside a couple of items for me—some early Christmas shopping. I could get them a week from today." She would receive her second month's pay packet that coming Monday.

"Certainly."

Tess tucked the brown paper package under her free arm and lured Luke away from the store with an invitation to drive the wagon again. She couldn't wait until that evening when she could start working on his first big-boy outfit.

The wagon lumbered into the yard with Luke driving, assisted by Tess. He jumped to the ground as soon as they came to a stop and ran toward Spencer. He caught his son in a hug.

"Oh, Papa, you were so brave. You chased after that big ol' bull and caught him. I wanna see him." He slipped out of the embrace and raced toward the pen.

"Hold up there, son. We need to go slow and easy." Spencer was comfortable around cattle, but Tess would have his hide if he didn't impress upon Luke the need to exercise caution.

The bull's escape had probably confirmed her fears. Although the longhorn had given up the fight well before reaching the ranch, she'd seen him fresh out of the rail car, some sixteen hundred pounds of angry, ornery, seemingly out-of-control animal. Now that the big fellow no longer felt threatened, he stood contentedly munching hay in the pen.

If things went according to plan, this bull would be as calm as the sires Spencer had helped raise on his father's ranch and would do his job as well as they had. The future of the ranch rested on this fellow. Two ranchers eager to incorporate the admirable characteristics of a longhorn into their herds had agreed to give Spencer a heifer in exchange for every four calves his stud sired.

Tess held Lila out to Spencer. "Would you please hold her so I can get these crates inside?"

"I'll carry them for you." He completed the task, took Lila and strode toward the pen.

Tess fell in step beside him. "I thought you'd want to care for the team right away since that's what you've asked me to do each time I drive them."

He had, but a man could change his mind once in a while. "The horses won't care if they have to wait a few more minutes. I want you to—"

"Take a look at your new addition?" She sent him a smile so bright it rivaled the September sun slanting from the west. "Oh, Spencer, I can't begin to tell you how scared I was when that bull burst from the rail car. And when you charged after him, my heart was pounding something fierce. But then you roped the beast by both horns. I've never seen anything quite as—" she spun her hands in small circles as though willing the words to come "—awe-inspiring."

He'd never seen Tess as animated—or as full of compliments. She was gushing like a schoolgirl. Not that he minded. He hadn't set out to impress her, merely to capture the bull before it harmed someone, but he liked having his skills admired.

"Well, grease my griddle. What am I doing carrying on like that when you want me to see your latest acquisition? Let's go, so you can introduce us to the king of the pen." She took Luke by the hand before he had a chance to protest. "Let's skip, shall we, like I taught you this morning?"

Spencer followed with Lila. Tess was acting strangely. While she'd ridden a hay bale horse and spent many an evening practicing her roping, she hadn't dropped her guard to this extent before. Something must have happened while she was in town.

Of course. She'd seen Polly and little Petey. That had to be it. Nothing caused a normally controlled woman to turn to mush quite like a baby. Even his stiff-as-a-starched-shirt grandmother had gone misty-eyed whenever she saw a newborn.

Tess neared the pen, ground to a halt and released Luke's hand. "I could tell your bull was huge, but he's even bigger than I thought. How close can we get and still be safe?"

Spencer stood beside them. "As you can, see he's settled down. He let me go right up to the fence."

Her eyes widened. She inclined her head toward Luke,

who stood slack-jawed. "Surely you don't want *us* to get that close?"

"It's best to stand back a ways, since we don't know him yet."

"What's his name, Papa?"

"I haven't picked one yet. Do you have any ideas, son?"

Luke tilted his head from side to side, studying the bull. Before he could answer, Tess did, merriment dancing in her dark brown eyes. "Moo." She dragged out the vowel sound.

Spencer laughed. "I'm not about to call him that."

She feigned surprise. "This, coming from a man who calls his dog *Woof*?"

Luke crossed his arms and scowled. "*I* called him Woof."

Tess managed to look genuinely apologetic, a feat Spencer admired. She rested a hand on Luke's shoulder, removing it when he shrugged. "Yes, you did, and it's a fine name. But I think your Papa's prized pet needs a different kind of name. Something that sounds big and powerful."

Prized pet? This bull was a working animal. Spencer would have to set Tess straight. But wait. Her lips twitched. She was teasing him, and he'd almost taken the bait. "Since he is king of the pen, what about King?"

"Yes, Papa. King David. Like they talked about in church. He was big and powerful."

Tess nodded. "That's a good idea, Luke. But who was even bigger than David?"

His face lit when he remembered. "The giant man, Goliath. We could call him that."

Spencer nodded. "That's a fine choice. Goliath it is."

The bull looked up from the mound of hay he was munching and grunted. Lila let out with a good imitation, causing the rest of them to laugh.

Spencer's gaze met Tess's. Something flickered in her eyes before she broke the connection. Perhaps it was attraction. No. She wasn't interested in him. Sure, she'd admired his rope work, but that was as far as it went. His loneliness was fueling his imagination.

"Papa!" Luke tugged on Spencer's sleeve, dragging him back to the present. "Tell her I can rope Goliath if I want." He jabbed a finger at Tess.

"Not until you're older, son."

Tess beckoned to Luke. "Let's go meet Goliath. I'm sure your Papa will be happy to introduce us."

Spencer followed them to the slat fence surrounding the pen. Tess stood back a good three feet as she watched the bull enjoy his meal. She kept hold of Luke, although he was none too happy about that.

She studied the bull intently. "Just how big are those horns?"

"I haven't been able to measure them yet. My guess is they're over four feet from tip to tip, but he's only three years old. They'll continue to grow as he ages. My father had one old fellow whose tip-to-tip measurement was a hair over six feet."

She turned to Spencer, her mouth agape. "Amazing. That means his horns were as wide as I am tall."

He resisted the urge to smile at her unbridled surprise. "Would you like to touch him?"

Luke broke free of Tess and rushed to Spencer's side. "I would, Papa."

"Um, Spencer. Do you think that's a good idea? I'm not so sure we should encourage him. I don't want him to think he can approach Goliath on his own."

"He won't go near him, will you, son? Not without one of us close by?"

Luke shook his head.

"Then if you'll hold this little lady, Tess, I'll let Luke have a closer look."

She took Lila from him. He hefted Luke onto the fence, planted his son's feet on the middle slat and stood beside him. The bull lifted his head. Luke stroked Goliath's muzzle. The longhorn studied the curious boy. Without warning, the bull stuck out his tongue and swiped Luke's hand.

"Lookee, Papa. He likes being petted. He licked me. Like Woof does."

"Seems that way, doesn't it? I'm going to put you down so I can take Lila and let Tess have a turn."

She shied away. "Oh, no. I'm fine."

"I can understand your hesitation, but he's settled down now. You two should make friends."

Luke laughed. "She's scared."

"It's not polite to laugh at people, son."

She lifted her chin. "I'm not scared. I'm…cautious."

Spencer dipped his chin behind Lila's head so Tess couldn't see his smile. He could understand her fear, but when she assumed her "I've been affronted" pose, she looked cute.

Cute? Tess was many things, but cute wasn't one of them. Striking, perhaps. Even beautiful. But not cute. "Caution can be a good thing, but you're usually more adventurous. Perhaps you'd feel more comfortable if I were to help you the way I did Luke."

She caught her lower lip between her teeth and looked from him to the pen and back again. "I don't think that would be wise."

"You're right. It's probably a bad idea. It takes a brave woman to contend with a massive longhorn and a rugged cattle rancher at the same time." He grinned and turned to leave. If he knew Tess, she wouldn't back down.

"Please, don't go. I'll do it—if you'll stay right beside me."

Gladly. "If you're sure. I wouldn't want to rush you."

She nodded and handed Lila to him. Tess held herself poker straight and approached the fence with halting steps. Spencer stood beside her, so close he could hear her rapid breathing as she mustered her courage.

"Now what?" She faced him.

Her eyes held such warmth he could do nothing but gaze into them, his resolve to remain impassive melting. Seeing Tess's uncertainty had brought out an unexpected desire to protect her.

"I suppose—" Her voice broke, and a becoming flush spread over her cheeks. "I suppose I should get on with it." She clutched the top slat with her left hand and held out her right. Several tense moments passed before the bull raised his head. She grimaced but stroked him—once— and jerked her arm back. "H-how was that?"

"It's a start. It'll be easier next time."

"I'm not so sure there will be a next time. I plan to give Goliath a wide berth." She took two steps away from Spencer, sending the message that she'd be keeping her distance from him, as well. Not that he could blame her after the way he'd stared at her.

Luke bounded up to them. "Someone's coming, Papa."

Sure enough, a rider approached from the east. Frank Mueller. He'd recognize the young man's pinto anywhere.

Frank reined in his mount and doffed his hat to Tess. "Afternoon, Miss Grimsby. Mr. Abbott. I came to see if either of you found— What is *that*?" He stared at Goliath. "I know it's a bull, but I've never seen one like it. Look at the size of those horns. When did he get here?"

"Today," Luke announced. "He ran off the train, and Papa had to throw his rope and catch him. He done it, too, and it only took him two throws. He's real good. I got to pet Goliath. That's his name."

Spencer warmed at his son's praise. "Thanks to the work you and your father did on the fence, I've got a sturdy pen to hold him. What brings you out here today?"

Frank dragged his gaze from the bull and shifted in his saddle, the leather creaking. "Vati was wondering if you'd seen his hammer. The last time he remembers seeing it was when we were working on the bunkhouse. I thought maybe he'd left it here."

"I haven't seen it," Tess volunteered.

Spencer handed Lila to her. "I found one a couple of days before you finished the job and put in your toolbox next to the other."

"I figure he's misplaced it in our shop, but if you see it, would you give us a holler?"

"Will do."

Frank left. Luke darted off to play with Woof, and Spencer started for the barn.

"Spencer." Tess caught up to him. "May I take the children to Folsom?"

"What for?"

"Luke's outgrown his shoes. I'd like to get him a pair of boots, but Mr. Hawkes doesn't carry his size. He suggested I see the shoemaker down the hill."

Woof barked and raced after the stick Luke had thrown. The familiar pain gripped Spencer, squeezing his chest so hard that drawing a breath was an effort. "Luke's growing up so fast, and his mother's not here to see it."

"I'm sorry it's so difficult. I wish I could ease your burden." Compassion filled her eyes.

"I'm fine."

"Papa." Lila reached out to him.

He took her from Tess, kissed each of his daughter's round cheeks and inhaled her fresh, clean fragrance. No. That hint of citrus wasn't Lila's scent. It was Tess's.

Tess. The woman who cared for his children, fed him delicious meals and continued to offer solace even though he'd done precious little to thank her. He must do something to show her how much he appreciated her. "I'll take you."

"I beg your pardon?" Confusion creased Tess's brow.

"You said you want to go to Folsom. I'll take you there. Luke's only ridden the train once. He'd be delighted to do so again. I could arrange for him to ride in the locomotive. We could do the shopping and have a picnic down at the river."

"A picnic on the riverbank would be wonderful. I love being near the water. When shall we go?"

"A week from today. I'll ask Peter and Drake to see to things at the station while I'm gone."

She gave him one of her radiant smiles, the kind that made him feel like a king. "I look forward to it."

So did he. More than he would have expected.

Chapter Seventeen

Like Luke, Tess was enjoying her second train ride immensely. She sat beside the open window as the scenery raced past. Sprawling oak trees. Sun-bleached bunchgrass. An occasional glimpse of the rock fences being built by the Chinese. She inhaled deeply, breathing in the sooty scent that would always remind her of Spencer.

Stealing glances at him on the seat opposite her, she was pleased to see him with his head bent over Luke's, answering his son's incessant questions while he bounced his daughter on one knee. What made her even happier was the smile on his face. He still wore his customary frown much of the time, but this morning he was enjoying himself. She tore her gaze from him, lest he catch her staring, and let it rove over the rail car's paneled walls and plush seats.

Had it really been just two months ago that she'd taken her first train ride? She'd hoped to have Luke's first outfit ready for their outing, but she hadn't been able to spend much time sewing. Lila had been miserable due to teething pain. Tess had lost count of the hours she'd spent rocking the poor girl and rubbing her inflamed gums with a fingertip.

When Lila's teeth had finally broken through the previous afternoon, she'd returned to her contented self. Tess had gotten her first good night's sleep in a week and awakened that morning eager for their adventure.

"But she said you were gonna get me a ride in the engine, Papa." Luke jabbed an accusatory finger at Tess.

Spencer pushed Luke's arm down and mouthed the word *sorry* to Tess. "You'll have to be patient, son. The engineer on this train won't let anyone but his fireman ride in the cab, but the one on our way home will. He likes showing little boys what he does."

Luke scowled. "I'm not a little boy. I'm a big boy. You said so."

"You are. That's why you're getting a pair of big-boy boots today."

Tess smiled behind her fan. Wait until Luke saw the outfit she was working on—navy short pants and a matching tunic trimmed with gold braid. She hadn't expected to be so excited about making the clothes, but this was her first time to transition a boy into short pants.

The train pulled into the Folsom station. Tess grabbed the wicker picnic basket. Luke disembarked, followed by Spencer, who held his daughter in his arms.

Tess grabbed the handrail, placed her right foot on the top stop and prepared to put her left on the second. Her boot skimmed the slick surface. She fell forward, came down hard on her heel and crashed into Spencer.

"Lila!" she cried.

He grasped her by the elbow. "She's all right. How are you?"

A bit dazed and thoroughly mortified. "Fine…I think."

She took a tentative step. Her ankle wasn't sprained, but her boot didn't feel right. She stepped aside, out of the flow of traffic. As inconspicuously as possible she lifted her skirts to survey the damage. "Oh, no."

Luke squatted and examined her boot. "The heel's coming off," he announced at an embarrassing volume.

While he was right, that was the least of her troubles. The heel could be reattached, but the jagged tear in the leather side where it had scraped against the corner of the step was another matter. At least they were in Folsom where there was a shoemaker. He ought to be able to repair the boot.

"Son, please lower your voice. Tess doesn't want everyone to know her business."

How kind of Spencer to show her such consideration. She flashed him a smile. "If you don't mind, I'd like to visit the shoemaker first."

"A wonderful idea."

After peeking in the basket and assuring herself their lunch was all right, she headed up to the main street. She'd taken a total of two steps when she stopped.

Spencer followed suit. "Is something wrong?"

Her heel flapped every time she lifted her foot. If she set her foot down wrong, she could end up with a twisted ankle, after all. "I'll have to walk slowly, so you might want to go on without me."

"Why don't you sit over there and let me have a look?" He inclined his head toward a bench.

She managed to reach it without injuring herself, but with her unsteady gait, it must have looked as though she'd spent the morning in a saloon.

"Would you take Lila for a minute please?" He handed his daughter to Tess, lifted her foot and examined the boot.

She did her best to ignore the shocked looks on the faces of several ladies passing by.

"I see the problem. The heel's hanging by a single nail. I could remove it if you'd like."

Without the heel she would walk with a list, but that would be better than staggering. "Please do."

He tugged, and the heel broke free. He handed it to her, took Lila and propped her on his hip. "You'll be lopsided now. Why don't you take my arm?"

Take his arm? The idea sent a delicious shiver up her spine. *Control yourself, Tess.* "Thank you." She tucked her hand around his elbow and hoped he didn't look her way because she couldn't keep from grinning. They reached Sutter Street, and she reluctantly let go.

Luke raced up the stairs onto the raised boardwalk. Spencer held out his free hand to help Tess. She stared at it. Few men had shown her such courtesies. Granted, he was just doing his duty as a gentleman. Even so, she couldn't keep from imagining what it would be like to have him—to have a man care for her on a regular basis.

"Tess?"

"Hmm?"

"Don't worry. I won't let you fall."

She slipped her gloved hand into his strong, masculine one. When she was a girl at the orphanage, Charlie had teased her about having "giant paws." Compared to Spencer's hand, hers looked small and ladylike.

Luke led the way down the wooden walkway. He stopped in front of a plate glass window filled with shoes, boots and fancy slippers suitable for a ballroom. "Is this it, Papa?"

"Yes, son, but you'll have to wait for Tess to—"

"Please. Let him go first. He's been looking forward to this." Although Spencer was clearly torn, he agreed.

The shop smelled of leather, neat's-foot oil and stitching wax. Father and son conferred with the shoemaker, who set to work taking Luke's measurements. Tess sat on one of the varnished benches watching Lila as she held on to it and sidestepped her way up and down the entire length on wobbly legs. At this rate it wouldn't be long before she attempted to stand on her own.

Luke bounded up to Tess a few minutes later. "I don't get my boots now. I gotta wait two whole weeks before the package comes on the train. How many days is that?"

"Can you show me how old you are?"

He held up four fingers, and Tess held up all of hers. "It's that many. Fourteen."

His chin quivered. She resisted the urge to pull him into her arms. If only she'd thought to prepare Luke for the wait, but she did have a way to cheer him up. She could complete his first outfit in half that time. "You only have to wait this many days for a different surprise. How many is that?" She held up seven fingers and waited while he counted them.

"What's the surprise?"

"I can't tell you what it is, or it won't be a surprise."

"Can I guess?"

"You may try." No doubt he'd spend the entire week peppering her with guesses, but that would help keep his mind off the boots.

Spencer finished his talk with the shoemaker and joined them. "I'll take the children to the mercantile, so you can see about your boot—alone."

"Are you sure? I'd be happy to watch Lila for you."

He took his daughter in his arms. "You deserve a break after the challenging week you've had caring for this little one."

"Thank you, Spencer. Where shall we meet, and when?"

"How about the bench at the rail station at noon?"

Luke tugged on Spencer's sleeve. "C'mon, Papa. Let's go. I wanna see if the store has toys."

They left, with Luke skipping alongside his father and Lila clapping as though she was equally excited.

The shoemaker crossed the small shop and eased himself to a kneeling position in front of Tess. "I hear you lost a heel. Shall I have a look?"

"I'm afraid there's more to it than that." She held out her foot.

The stoop-shouldered older man studied her boot, making a series of discouraging grunts. "This pair of boots has served you well, but there's not much life left in them."

"I know they're old and not the best workmanship, but they're all I have." For years what little she'd earned over and above her room and board had gone into her wardrobe. Because she'd escorted the children of Sacramento's elite to a variety of functions, she was expected to represent the families well and had amassed a trunk full of fine dresses. Since her boots didn't show, she'd made do with an inexpensive pair. "Can you fix the damaged one?"

"I can put the heel back on, but the other..." He rubbed his chin. "If you'd ripped out the side welt, I could stitch it back up, but that tear in the back quarter poses a problem. I could sew a piece of leather under it, but it wouldn't be pretty."

Pretty didn't matter at this point. She just needed something to wear. "That sounds fine."

"I have an idea. Would you mind taking off your boots?"

She did and tucked her stocking-clad feet under the bench. The shoemaker took her boots and disappeared behind a curtain at the rear of his shop.

He reappeared shortly carrying a dust-covered pasteboard box. "I didn't want to say anything until I was sure, but I have a pair of boots that might be your size."

"My size? How can that be?" Her feet were larger than most women's, so it was unlikely he would have made a pair of boots that big just to have on hand.

"I got an order for them a few years back, but the woman who placed it never returned. Let's try them on, shall we?" He hitched up his floor-length apron and knelt before her once again.

The boots were beautiful—high quality black leather with side button closures. Each jet-black button winked at her from the center of a scallop. The scallops didn't stop there. They continued all the way around the opening. There was even fancy stitching across the instep.

But they had low heels. Very low heels. She'd be surprised if they were half an inch.

He eased her feet into the boots, pulled out his buttonhook and fastened each of the two dozen buttons. "Would you please stand? I need to check the fit."

She obliged, lifting her skirts so he could complete his inspection.

"Seems like you have plenty of room. Why don't you walk around and see how they feel?"

Across the shop she went, taking tentative steps for fear of catching her dragging skirts with a heel. Another lap around the room boosted her confidence. By the third her feet were so happy she practically skipped back to the shoemaker.

"Are they comfortable?"

"Quite." Comfortable didn't begin to describe the cocoon of soft, supple leather caressing her feet. She wanted the boots in the worst way. *Oh, Lord, what am I to do?*

She'd received her pay packet the day before, but when she visited Mr. Hawke's shop to pay for the items he'd set aside for her, she would have to give him half her month's wages. She might have enough left to pay for the repairs her boot needed, but she certainly couldn't afford a new pair like these.

The talented shoemaker crossed his arms. "You're frowning. Don't you want them?"

"Very much, but…" Sometimes being a housekeeper whose handbag held far too few coins had its disadvantages. "The truth, is I'm not even sure I have enough to pay for the repairs."

"I assumed your husband would see to that."

"My husband? No. Spencer—I mean Mr. Abbott—isn't my husband. I'm his housekeeper. I've only been working for him two months and have yet to amass any savings. As difficult as it is for me to say this, I'm afraid I must leave these exquisite boots here and ask you to do what you can for my damaged one."

He stood slowly, grimacing as though in pain, and rubbed his back. "Age isn't for the fainthearted." He chuckled and then sobered. "Those boots you're wearing were ordered by a woman almost as tall as you. A saloon girl who insisted on having lower heels, even though her kind usually ask me to make them as high as I can. She said she'd spent too many years looking down on everyone. I got the feeling she wasn't talking about her height."

The shoemaker paused.

Tess had to know more. "What happened?"

"Even though she'd given me a hefty deposit, she moved on before I'd finished the boots. Since you're the first woman in three years to show an interest in them, I'm willing to entertain just about any offer. I could use the shelf space."

Hope welled up inside Tess. If she asked Mr. Hawkes to hold the items she wanted from his general store for another month… She loosened the drawstrings of her reticule, reached inside to locate every last coin in the silky recesses and laid them on the counter. "This is all I have."

"You've got yourself a deal, young lady." He smiled. "I can take your old boots off your hands if you'd like. I could make use of the leather for patches and such."

She had the distinct impression the kindly shoemaker would have accepted less than she'd given him, but she didn't care. The boots she now wore, abandoned years before, had found a home.

Her transaction compete, she left the shoemaker's shop. A glance at the watch pinned to her bodice showed she had an hour before she was to meet Spencer and the children. She'd entertained the idea of having a glass of lemonade in one of the cafés, but that possibly had evaporated due to her purchase. She might as well acquaint herself with Folsom's shops, so she'd know what was available should she get another opportunity to visit the bustling town.

She meandered through a hardware store, dry goods shop and millinery. Passing by a bakery, she inhaled the inviting aromas of cinnamon, nutmeg and freshly baked bread. The mercantile, with its windows boasting a host of interesting items, beckoned. The bell on the door sent out a melodious chime as she slipped inside.

Stooping to study a display of antimacassars like the one on the back of Spencer's wingback armchair, she was reminded of Polly's suggestion to spend a few minutes with him in the evening. Perhaps she was right. Perhaps Spencer would welcome some company. Even though Tess was eager to work on her sewing projects, taking time to ask him about his day before she headed upstairs might be a way to get him to open up to her again, as he had the day little Petey was born.

"Tess."

She'd recognize that rich voice anywhere. She stood and found herself eye to eye with Spencer. Well not quite eye to eye. He was about an inch taller than she. Due to the lower heels, she'd lost her advantage.

The realization was as startling as an earthquake, shaking her to the core. Had she, like the saloon girl who'd commissioned the boots, enjoyed looking down on people, too?

Chapter Eighteen

Spencer stared at Tess, who stared back at him. Something about her was different. She seemed softer, more vulnerable than ever before. He blinked to break the intense eye contact and shifted his daughter to a more comfortable position. "How did things go at the shoemaker's? Was he able to repair your boot?"

Tess shook her head, causing the peacock feathers on her huge hat to flutter. "I left them with him."

That was it. She was shorter. He glanced at the hem of her skirt, puddled at her feet. "You're not *barefoot*, are you?"

A couple of matrons at a neighboring display case gasped.

"Of course not," she shot back loudly enough for the women to hear.

He'd definitely ruffled Tess's feathers. "I'm sorry, but since your dress is dragging the floor and you said he has your boots, I thought you might not be wearing any."

She lifted that determined chin of hers. "I am wearing boots. Brand-new boots. He had a pair just my size. See?" She hefted her skirts so high he could see a pair of pretty black button-up boots—along with a fair amount of ankle.

"Well, I never…" One of the busybodies cast a withering look at Tess and turned to her companion. "What has come over young people today? Have they no respect for society's conventions?"

Tess let go of her skirts, sending them swishing around her feet. She jammed a fist against her side and glared at the backs of the retreating women. "Some people…"

"Don't worry about them."

She scanned the mercantile. "Where's Luke?"

"At the toy case. He has his eye on a wooden boat. I tried to interest him in the train, but he wouldn't be swayed."

Tess joined Luke, who sat cross-legged with his nose pressed against the display case. Spencer followed her.

She dropped to her knees beside Luke. "Your papa said you like the boat."

"It's not a boat. It's an ark." He jabbed a finger at a set with lots of pieces. "It comes with all kinds of animals—lions and tigers and elephants—and lotsa birds. I like the elephants best because they're the biggest."

"Do you know something, Luke? They're my favorite, too."

His son eyed Tess warily and returned his attention to the toy. How long would Luke continue to push her away? He even refused to use her name. Not that his lack of acceptance stopped her. She kept right on loving him.

Beneath her sometimes-saucy exterior, she had a kind heart. Spencer had no doubt that in time she would overcome Luke's resistance.

She stood. "Which one's your favorite, Spencer?"

"The giraffe…because it's so tall."

The smile she sent his way radiated warmth and light. With Tess around life didn't seem nearly as dark and depressing as before. She could chase away the clouds faster than a delta breeze. He had a sudden urge to spend more time with her. "Do you have any more purchases to make?"

"No. Why?"

"Neither do I, so what do you say we start our picnic early?"

Luke folded his arms and scowled. "I don't wanna go. I want you to buy me the ark."

Tess answered before Spencer could. "He doesn't have to. We can make one ourselves."

Surprise overcame Luke's irritation. "We can?"

"Yes. We'll draw an ark on pasteboard and cut it out. We can make animals, too. Our set won't be as fancy as this wooden one or have as many pieces, but we can still have fun with it. I'll need your help, though. I can't remember all the animals this one has, but I'm sure you can."

Luke nodded. "Yep. I been looking at them a whole long time."

"That's great. I have another idea. Let's see if we can beat your papa and Lila to the river." She grabbed Luke by the hand, hitched up her skirts and took off, with the picnic basket on her arm bouncing and his son scrambling to keep up with her.

Spencer reached the bank of the American River and found Luke sitting on a blanket beneath a massive oak tree crunching a dill pickle. Spencer adjusted Lila's bonnet so her face was shielded from the sun's harsh rays and joined Tess at the water's edge.

She tossed a rock into the murky depths. It landed with a plop. "No matter how many times I try, I can't get it to skim the surface. A boy I supervised tried to teach me, but he declared me a hopeless case in a matter of minutes." She cast a glance at Spencer. "Would you show me how?"

"I would if I could, but unlike my brother, I never mastered the art of skipping stones. I preferred to spend my time throwing a rope."

"What?" She pressed a hand to her throat and dropped her jaw in an exaggerated look of surprise. "You mean there's something you *can't* do? I heard you could do just about anything."

He chuckled. "Who have you been listening to?"

"Your son. According to Luke you're the smartest, most talented man who ever lived. I tried to set him straight, but he'd have no part of it." She laughed. No. That couldn't be called a laugh. That was a giggle. A girlish sound he'd never expected to come out of her.

He couldn't resist the urge to play along and adopted a wounded tone. "And here I thought you were a loyal housekeeper who would uphold my image, not convince my trusting son that I'm actually human."

"But you are a rather nice human." She smirked.

"You're quite nice yourself."

"Why, Spencer, it almost sounds like you mean that."

"I do."

All signs of her playfulness faded. "You do? I— I'm sorry. I didn't mean to question you. It's just that I'm not used to being paid compliments. At least not often. And only by my friends. Polly mostly."

Interesting. Tess didn't consider him a friend. For some reason that didn't sit well. "Then we'll have to remedy that. I'm sure I could come up with at least three more compliments before the day's out."

"Please don't misunderstand. I wasn't asking you to—"

He pressed a finger to her mouth, and her eyes widened. "I'm aware of that. I'm taking it on as a challenge, so you'll just have to accept them when offered. Can you do that?"

She nodded.

"Good." His gesture had rendered her speechless. It had been a long time since he'd had such a marked effect on a woman. But then, Tess wasn't like other women. She appreciated the simplest of gifts. A single compliment could make her lovely face light up. He was eager to see what three in a row would do.

He removed his finger and resisted the almost overwhelming urge to trace her lips with the tip. She surprised him by trailing a finger over the place where his had rested, as though she wanted to imprint the memory of his touch.

She realized he was watching her, blushed bright red and resumed her earlier lighthearted manner. "I thought it would be fun to play some games after our picnic when this little lady takes her nap." She reached out and caressed Lila's cheek. "I know Luke would enjoy that. If you'll agree, I might consider letting you have the biggest piece of Lila's birthday cake. It's chocolate."

His baby girl had turned one three days ago, but they'd agreed to put off celebrating until her teething pain eased, "You drive a hard bargain, Tess, but how can I refuse?"

"You can't. That's the beauty of my plan."

He chuckled. "Your plan, eh? And what comes next? I know it's early, but please tell me it's time to eat. The scents coming from that basket have had my mouth watering all morning."

"A picnic luncheon it is. And then our fun." She headed for the blanket and shot him a playful smile over her shoulder. "Just wait until you see the games I have in mind."

They were sure to be child's play, but he didn't care. He would skip rope or jump through a game of hopscotch if it meant seeing her perky smile or hearing her musical laugh.

* * *

Pleasantly full after their picnic lunch, Tess sat on the blanket she'd spread beneath an aged oak and leaned back on her palms. Luke roamed nearby looking for insects while Lila napped in the shade. Spencer lay on his back with his feet crossed, the sleeves of his white shirt rolled up and his slouch hat covering his face. He looked entirely too appealing in the relaxed pose.

Tess closed her eyes, tilted her head and let the sun kiss her cheeks. She'd expected the day to be unbearably hot, but the temperature had dropped from the high nineties they'd seen the past two weeks to the low eighties, proving a blistering Sierra Foothills' summer didn't last forever.

The heat she was experiencing now was nothing compared to the liquid fire that had coursed through her veins when Spencer had touched her mouth earlier, as intense as it was intriguing. If a brush of his finger across her lips felt that good, a kiss must be beautiful beyond description. His would be, she was sure of it.

"You have a lovely smile."

Her eyes flew open. Spencer was propped on one elbow watching her. "I didn't realize you were awake. Thank you for the compliment." Apparently he was serious about paying her three of them.

"You're welcome. You have two more coming." He flashed her a grin that made maintaining a professional demeanor difficult. If only he weren't so handsome, charming and—

"What were you thinking? It must have been something pleasant."

Very pleasant. And entirely inappropriate. Flights of fancy might be enjoyable, but she had no business engaging in them. "I think it's time we play those games."

"We could, but I think you'll want to remove this first,

won't you?" He tapped the brim of her hat. "I don't see how you could play games with it on. It's rather good-size. Have you ever thought about getting a smaller one?"

"Why would I do that? I like my hat."

"I thought since you got boots with low heels you might want a hat that isn't so—" he swept a hand toward the peacock feathers gracing hers "—lofty."

"Huh! I'll have you know that I didn't set out to get lower heels, but now that I have them I can see the benefits. I could never have raced all the way here in my old boots."

"It's nice to see that you no longer have your head in the clouds." He grinned.

While his words were said in jest, they reminded her of the shoemaker's comment. Why had she worn such high heels? After all, she was already taller than most women.

An image of her sixteen-year-old self facing Mr. Grimsby for the last time came to mind. For years she'd had to look up to him, but that day, wearing the new boots he'd given her as an entirely unexpected parting gift, she'd been on his level.

She could still hear his final words to her. *Keep your head high, Tess, and don't let anyone get the best of you. Remember everything I taught you, and you'll be fine.* And then he'd enveloped her in a brief but awkward hug.

He'd never hugged anyone before, not even the little ones who ached for a loving touch. She'd been with him longer than anyone except Charlie, but the orphanage director's gesture was so unexpected that the scathing farewell speech she'd planned had lodged in her throat. Before she regained the use of her vocal chords, he'd spun on his heel and walked away without looking back.

After all the years under his rule, she'd vowed never to let anyone hold such power over her again. She'd kept that promise—and her hopes and dreams—to herself. Polly was the only one out west who knew about her days in the orphanage and her strong desire to have a family of her own.

Spencer's voice pulled her back to the present. "I'm afraid I might have offended you. I'm sorry."

"It's all right. I was just remembering something. That's all."

"Something unpleasant this time, I'd say. Wouldn't have to do with being tall, would it?"

Her mouth gaped, and she snapped it shut. "How did you know?"

"It makes sense. I was talking about your height. The last time that subject came up, you told me about a painful memory from your childhood. I gather it wasn't easy."

A bitter laugh escaped before she could stop it. "Far from it. I lost both my parents when I was young. The person who became responsible for me was…unkind, but he did equip me to make a living. I had plenty of opportunities to hone my skills."

"A euphemism for hard work, is it not? He must have been happy with yours. I've rarely seen anyone work as hard as you or do as good a job."

"Thank you. That's two compliments in one. You've already fulfilled your quota." She managed a halfhearted smile.

"That wasn't why I said— Never mind. What's important is that you know how much I appreciate you. You do very well with Luke and Lila. Now I know why. You understand what it's like to lose a parent."

She should never have told him about her past, but his perceptiveness had taken her aback. "Please don't feel sorry for me. I love what I do. If there were a way for me to bring joy into more children's lives, I'd welcome it."

Luke dashed over to them, his hands cupped. He couldn't have chosen a better time to interrupt. Her conversation with Spencer had taken her places she didn't like to go.

"Lookee! I found a butterfly." The excited boy pulled his thumbs apart to reveal his find.

Tess didn't have the heart to tell him he held a moth. "That's nice. Don't you agree, Spencer?"

He did, readily, and ruffled his son's hair. "If you'll let it go, we can play some games."

Luke opened his hands to release the insect, and it flitted off. Tess's gaze followed the moth's zigzagging path until it disappeared from sight, once again able to fly freely. What would it be like not to have all the constraints she'd lived with her whole life? To be herself with no thought of ridicule or reprimand? To experience the wild abandon of a child?

She jumped up. "Come on, Luke. We'll start with a game of tag. Your papa can be *it*. Run! Don't let him catch you."

Luke darted away.

Spencer was off the ground in an instant and caught up to Luke. "I've got you, son." He grabbed Luke under the arms and swung him in a circle. The dear boy's joyful shouts were so loud Tess was afraid he'd wake his sister. Thankfully the little girl was a sound sleeper.

Tag led to blindman's bluff followed by Simon Says. Then Tess thought of a way to have some fun herself. What would Spencer think of it? "Have you ever played Barley-Bridge, Luke?"

He shook his head. "What is it?"

"Two people form a double arch. That will be your papa and me, since we're the tallest. You'll run around me, go under the arch, run around your papa and go through the arch again. Keep on going. When I finish the song your papa and I will—" She froze. She'd have to sing, and if Spencer didn't know the words, she'd have to sing alone. How she wished she had a fine voice like his. Even though she didn't, she had no choice but to attempt the tune for Luke's sake and hope Spencer's ears survived the assault.

"Will what?" Luke asked.

"We'll lower our arms to try and catch you between them." She held her raised arms out in front of Spencer. "Take my hands, please."

He laced his fingers through hers without hesitation. Clearly she had no effect on him, whereas the mere thought of touching him had sent tingles racing from her fingertips all the way to her elbows.

Hopefully he wouldn't find her hands revolting. The constant exposure to lye soap, soil and other such things left them rough and chapped.

He gave her hands a squeeze and dazzled her with one of his brilliant smiles so filled with warmth that her concerns dissolved as quickly as butter on a biscuit. Since he didn't seem at all ill at ease—quite the contrary, in fact—she would enjoy herself, too. If anyone saw the two of them holding hands, they would assume she was his wife—the mother of his children. If only that were true...

Where had that thought come from? She loved the children, but she didn't love their father. She did care about him, as she'd told Polly. But love? That was absurd.

They stood face-to-face. Hers was sure to be awash with color, so she avoided looking at Spencer and focused on Luke instead. "Ready to start?"

"Ready."

She launched into the verse slowing the last line so she completed it just as Luke passed beneath the arch. She and

Spencer lowered their arms and captured Luke between them. "We got you!"

Luke's laughter rang out. He begged to play the game another time. Tess started the tune another time, feeling more confident now that Spencer was singing along with her.

Again and again Luke raced figure eights around Spencer and Tess while she did her best to keep her mind on the game and not on the handsome man whose hands she was holding and holding and holding…

She ventured a glance at Spencer, and her breath caught. He was gazing at her with what looked a lot like attraction. Most likely her overactive imagination was at work, but it wouldn't hurt to pretend he was interested—just this once.

"There are advantages to being tall, Tess. We make a good team." He inclined his head toward their linked arms.

Although he was only talking about the arch they'd formed, she wondered what it would be like if they really were a team. A couple. Husband and wife.

Control yourself, Tess. She had no business spinning such tales, even if Spencer was a loving father and would be a wonderful husband.

Lila's chatter drew their attention and brought the game to an abrupt halt.

"Where do you think you're going, princess?" Spencer intercepted his daughter just in time to keep her from crawling off the blanket into the dirt. He tossed her into the air and caught her, eliciting a squeal Tess wasn't sure was caused by fear or delight.

"Mo, Papa. Mo," the little girl cried. Definitely delight.

A short time later they sat on the blanket enjoying generous slices of Lila's birthday cake.

Luke stuffed the last bite into his mouth and licked his fingers. "Is the surprise a cake?"

"What surprise?" Spencer asked.

"The one she said I get in this many days." Luke held up seven fingers.

Tess jogged Spencer's memory. "I told you about it at the depot right before Goliath arrived."

"Ah, yes. I remember now. It's not a cake, son, even though any cake Tess makes would be a right tasty surprise. She's an excellent cook."

Spencer glanced at her, and she acknowledged the compliment with a smile.

"Gumdrops?"

"No. It's even better than that." Tess gathered their picnic items and returned them to the basket.

"You're not the only one getting a surprise, Luke. I have one for Tess, but she doesn't have to wait for hers." Spencer unrolled his shirtsleeves, shoved his arms into his frock coat and pulled something out of the inside breast pocket. He handed her the brown paper package.

"What is it?"

"Open it, and you'll see."

Chapter Nineteen

A frisson of excitement surged through Tess. She'd never received a present from a gentleman. She wouldn't have expected one from Spencer. He tended to be practical and didn't spend money on frivolities, as he called them.

No. He didn't, so why would he now? Her bubble of joy burst. What a ninny she was to think he'd bought her a gift. This must be something for the house. The package was the right size and shape for a saltshaker to replace the one Luke had accidentally broken the week before.

Doing her best to hide her disappointment behind a smile, she untied the string and pulled back the paper. It wasn't a saltshaker, after all. "Oh, Spencer, it's beautiful."

Luke tugged on her sleeve. "Let me see."

"Here." She held out the cylindrical item to him. Clearly unimpressed, he shrugged, plopped down on the picnic blanket and snatched the last slice of cake.

She studied the piece of porcelain from every angle. Sprays of delicate forget-me-nots had been hand painted on the snowy white background. Several holes had been drilled in the top, all of them good-size, with an even larger one in the middle. "I expected a saltshaker, but that's not what it is."

Lila crawled over to Spencer, and he scooped her into his lap. "It's a hatpin holder. When I saw the blue flowers on it, I thought of you. I figured that since you were up much of the night taking care of this little gal while she battled her teething pain this past week and didn't even take your time off, giving you a small token of my appreciation was the least I could do."

Tess's excitement returned with such force she felt lightheaded. It was a gift, after all. "Thank you. It's lovely."

"I'm glad you like it."

"Like it? I love it. I've never been given anything that pleased me more." Perhaps it was a sign that he was developing feelings for her, as Polly had said.

He rubbed the back of his neck. "I was afraid you might not since I've teased about your hat and all."

Eager to dispel any lingering doubts he might have, Tess grabbed her hat, pulled the pins from it and placed them in the holder. "You've done me a favor. Were it not for you, I might have lost my hatpins since I had no special place to store them."

She couldn't resist the urge to tease him. "Without the pins, I would be forced to wear a smaller hat. Although that might please a certain gentleman I know, it would be a *big* disappointment to me." She grinned. "As it is, thanks to that same gentleman I'll be able to wear my *large* hat, knowing it's not going anywhere." She patted her beloved bonnet, knocking it askew.

He reached out to right her hat, lowered his hand and let it hover next to her cheek as though he was contemplating caressing it. If only he would. She held her breath.

"Papa, why are you staring at her like that?"

"Was I? I'm sorry, Tess. That was rude of me." Spencer pulled his hand away so quickly she was certain she felt a breeze. "We should be going. If you'll hold Lila, I'll fold the blanket." He practically shoved his daughter into Tess's arms and jumped to his feet.

Clearly she'd misread his intentions. The gift was a token of his gratitude and nothing more. She'd be wise to curb her vivid imagination and do the job he paid her to do.

A glance out Lila's bedroom window reassured Tess that Luke was engrossed in his play. Woof lay not far away, his muzzle resting on his paws. The watchful dog gave her a sense of peace. Anytime Luke went outside, Woof was with him. If the fearless boy got into trouble, Woof's bark would alert her.

Tess leaned over the side of the crib and kissed Lila's cheek as she slept. Learning how difficult her birthing had been and how close Spencer had come to losing his daughter intensified the love Tess felt for the precious little girl.

She would never understand how a father could walk away from a child the way hers had. The memory of being aban— left at the orphanage refused to dim, even though she shoved it to the most remote recesses of her mind. Recalling it never failed to send searing pain through her, which is why she rarely ever mentioned that agonizing day.

Thankfully, when Spencer had asked her about her past at their picnic, she'd had the presence of mind not to give him anything but the barest of details. She'd been careful to keep their conversations focused on lighter topics ever since. It wouldn't do for him to know her background. He might pity her, and she wanted no part of that. She must focus on doing her best to care for his family.

Luke had been waiting a week for his surprise. The time had come to unveil it. She carried the garments downstairs and had him come inside.

His response exceeded Tess's expectations. He took

one look at the outfit and did so much whooping and hollering it was a wonder he didn't wake Lila.

Tess helped him change into the tunic and short pants, gently instructing him in how the fasteners worked. "Was this worth waiting for?"

He nodded enthusiastically. "I'm a big boy with big-boy clothes."

"You are. Now I'm going to give you a big-boy haircut out on the porch, but you'll have to sit still. Can you do that?"

"Yep."

Luke was true to his word, holding a statue-like pose throughout the cut. She ran the comb through his hair one last time and held a hand mirror so he could see himself. "What do you think?"

"It's short." He turned his head from side to side. "I don't look like a little boy anymore."

"You look very handsome." He was adorable. Her work the past week had been worth the sore back and late nights spent sewing by lantern light.

Because she'd chosen to spend half an hour each evening sitting in the parlor with Spencer before going to her room—just the two of them—her free time had dwindled. Not that she minded. Even though he'd said little, often sitting in silence as he oiled a rope or completed some other chore while she raised the hems of her dresses to accommodate her lower boot heels, the homey atmosphere had filled her with a pleasant sense of belonging.

She wouldn't press him to talk, trusting that in time he'd grow more comfortable. One couldn't expect to bring about a significant change in the space of a week.

Satisfied with the haircut, Tess pulled the sheet off Luke and grabbed the broom. "I'm all done, so you may get down."

"I can't wait until Papa sees me."

Neither could she.

Dust swirled at Spencer's ankles as he neared the house. Woof bounded up to him, his tail wagging so fast it was a blur.

Anytime the Lord saw fit to send rain, Spencer would be grateful. California summers could get mighty tiresome after a while. What he'd give to feel the hairs on his nape rise at the first flash of lightening or hear the rumble of thunder. Surely with October right around the corner, a storm couldn't be far off.

He gazed at the house. A figure stood on the porch. A tall figure. It appeared Tess was watching for him. The thought put a spring in his step.

Something had changed at the picnic a week ago. He couldn't say what for sure, but she seemed more approachable. She'd taken to spending a few minutes with him each evening before retreating to her room. While she said little, he appreciated the companionship. He wished she'd tell him more about her past. She alluded to it briefly that day but had been close-mouthed ever since.

Memories of the outing flashed through his mind. Luke's laughter. Lila's delight at being tossed into the air. Tess's hands in his. She had the hands of someone accustomed to work, and yet those work-roughened hands could caress a child's cheek with tenderness—and had many times.

He hadn't intended to enjoy holding her hands as much as he did. What would she think if she knew how much pleasure it had brought him? Most likely she'd feel sorry for him, a pathetic widower so starved for the touch of another person that he'd allowed the game to go on and on in order to hold his housekeeper's hands longer. He missed the contact with another person. With a woman.

While he hadn't expected to feel any attraction to Tess, he couldn't help but notice her. Although she wasn't a dainty woman by any means, when she gave him one of her playful smiles, she was attractive in her own way.

If only she were more like that woman, Faith, who'd written those introspective letters to her intended. She had no trouble sharing her thoughts and feelings. Should the Lord choose to bless him with another wife someday, he'd want someone like that. Such a woman would be easy to talk with and would make a wonderful partner.

"Papa!" Luke charged down the steps and sped down the drive.

Spencer stopped in his tracks and gaped. His son looked so different. So mature. Tess had taken him from babyhood to boyhood.

Luke reached Spencer and beamed. "The surprise was new clothes. Big-boy clothes. See?" Luke turned in a complete circle. "She cut my hair, too. It doesn't swing around anymore." He shook his head to demonstrate.

A vise-like pain gripped Spencer, squeezing his heart until it ached. He shoved aside the onslaught of memories, both bitter and sweet, and forced himself to share in Luke's excitement. "You look all grown up, son, with your haircut and the new outfit. I like the color, and I like this." He indicated the gold braid decorating the tunic's cuffs and hem.

"And look here." Luke lifted the long top to reveal the short pants beneath. "They got buttons on the front. She made me practice using them lotsa times so I won't have to ask for help when I go to the privy. She said big boys can do it all by themselves. And I can. But she told me not to wait too long 'cause I gotta open the buttons before I can—"

"Take care of business. That's true." He needed to thank Tess, but he wanted her to himself. "Can you run all right in your new clothes, son?"

"Yep. Watch me." Luke took off with Woof right behind him.

Tess balanced Lila on her hip and met Spencer at the bottom of the steps. She watched Luke race around the yard and smiled. "I'm pleased with the way the outfit turned out. He was an absolute darling while I cut his hair. Doesn't he look handsome? Almost as handsome as—" she inhaled sharply and continued in a business-like manner "—as I expected him to."

Spencer tamped down a smile. If he didn't know better, he'd say she'd been about to compare Luke to him. "He looks great. I just wish…" His chest tightened, and his throat grew thick. He cleared it.

Compassion flooded Tess's dark eyes. "I understand. As happy as it made me to sew his big-boy clothes, I couldn't help but think how much joy this would have brought his mother. I'm sure she was looking forward to this day."

"We both were." He couldn't think about that. Life went on despite death and disappointments.

"I'm sorry it's so hard." She patted his arm before removing her hand. It was the first time she'd touched him since the picnic, but this was different—a housekeeper comforting her employer rather than one friend reaching out to another.

Something had caused her to draw back, but for the life of him he couldn't figure out what—or why it mattered so much. "You did a fine job on the clothes. I appreciate your hard work."

"Thank you. I need to go inside and see to supper. Would you take Lila please?" She handed him his daughter, turned and let out with a loud, shrill scream.

"Luke!"

Tess took off running toward the bull's pen.

Luke stood *inside* the fence at the far end, twirling his rope over his head and walking slowly toward Goliath at the opposite end.

Spencer watched in horror as his snorting bull pawed the ground, spied Luke and headed toward him.

Lord, help us! He's going to charge.

Chapter Twenty

Just as Tess reached the pen, Goliath lowered his head, horns forward, and charged.

"Get out, Luke!"

He spun around and pumped his little legs as fast as they could go.

Clutching huge handfuls of her skirt, she raced along the side of the pen.

Goliath picked up speed and gained on Luke.

In the space of a heartbeat, Tess was over the fence. She flew across the hard-packed earth, putting herself between Luke and the bull.

Her petticoats bunched as she ran, and she stumbled. Righting herself, she looked for Luke, jerking her head from side to side.

In a flash of blue, he scrambled between the fence slats.

He was safe, but she was in the middle of the enormous pen.

The pounding of Goliath's hooves, growing ever closer, echoed the frenzied beating of her heart.

There was no way she could outrun the bull.

She yanked off her hat and tossed it over her shoulder

in hopes it might distract the angry animal and buy her precious seconds.

The bull's hooves pounded the ground right behind her, putting wings to her feet.

"Help me, Lord!"

Never in her life had she run so fast.

A thundering crash took place.

She didn't look back as she covered the final feet, scaled the fence and kept on running.

Not until she was several yards away did she stop and turn around. Goliath lay on his side. Spencer leaned over the fence at the far end of the pen by the barn clutching the end of his taut lariat that stretched between him and the bull's right foreleg.

She couldn't believe Spencer had stopped the beast so quickly, saving her from a possible goring—or worse. The man was amazing.

Ignoring the stitch in her side, she dashed over to Luke and held him close as she caught her breath.

"Lemme go." He broke free and stuck a leg through the fence.

"No, Luke! You stay out of there."

"I gotta get my rope."

"Your papa will get it for you. Right now you have some explaining to do, young man." She grabbed his hand and marched toward the corner of the pen nearest the house, where Spencer stood. "Here's your son. I have to get Lila. Where did you leave her?"

"Right where we were standing. Woof's watching her. I'll see to Goliath. You stay put, Luke. I'll deal with you later."

Tess's heart had finally ceased its frenzied beating. She found Lila and the faithful watchdog engaged in what the little girl perceived as a game. Every time she attempted to crawl in one direction, Woof would block the way, so she'd strike out in another, laughing all the while.

"Good job, Woofie. You'll get an extra bone tonight." She patted the dog, gathered the dust-covered girl in her arms and returned to the pen. Luke stood outside the fence watching his father release the rope binding Goliath's leg.

How Spencer could go in the pen after that bull had charged his own son was beyond her. What a courageous man he was coming to their rescue like that. He waited as the enormous longhorn got to its feet and lumbered off.

"Look out, Papa! There's a snake." Luke pointed to a three-foot-long reptile in the center of the pen not far from Luke's rope. A lumpy-looking reptile that wasn't moving.

No! It couldn't be. She patted her head.

Spencer picked up the supposed snake, as well as Luke's rope and her hat. He jogged to the fence and hopped over it.

"Let me see, Papa."

He held Tess's hair switch behind his back, set her dusty but unharmed hat on a nearby hay bale and handed Luke his lariat. "Here."

"I wanna see the other thing. The snake."

Spencer shrugged. "There was no snake."

Luke's face scrunched with puzzlement. "But I saw one. Maybe that's what made Goliath run. Did it get away?"

Tess took pity on the confused boy and held out a hand to Spencer. "May I have it please?"

He hesitated.

"Luke deserves to know the truth."

"If you're sure."

She nodded, and he handed her the hank of braided hair, which she held out to Luke. "It's not a snake. It's a hairpiece."

He looked up at her, his eyes wide. "Your hair broke off?"

"No. It's called a hair switch. It was attached to my head with hairpins. A lady wears one to look..." She searched in vain for a word, but Luke supplied one.

"Pretty?"

Although he was a bright boy, his perceptiveness surprised her. "I suppose that's part of it. But I wore mine to look—" she didn't like admitting it, even to herself "—taller."

Luke glanced from her head to her feet and back again. "But you're already tall. Real tall. Why do you wanna be taller?"

"I don't. Not anymore."

"So you're not gonna wear it now?"

"I'm not." She'd be content with the hair the Lord had given her. "It'll be lighter and cooler without it."

"Can I have it?"

Spencer shot her an apologetic smile. "Son, I don't think—"

"It's all right." While she appreciated his compassion, the loss of her switch was a relief on several counts. She wouldn't have to fuss with her hair as long each morning or worry about the hairpiece coming loose when she practiced roping. "Luke's welcome to it. I would, however, like my hairpins. I appear to have lost several of them in my race to reach him."

Spencer's gaze rested on her disheveled hair. "How many did you lose?"

She patted her head and found two. "Six hairpins—" she glanced at her hat "—and I'm missing two hatpins, as well."

He leaped over the fence in one fluid motion and scoured

the ground. He didn't return until he had every last one of her sterling silver pins. "Here you are."

"Thank you. It was kind of you to get my things for me." And brave. She wouldn't get inside that pen again for anything.

"It's the least I could do after you risked your li—"

"I'm fine." She didn't like cutting Spencer off, but there was no need to frighten Luke more than he already had been. If the terror-stricken look on his face when he'd realized the danger was any indication, he'd learned a valuable lesson. Sometimes experience was the best teacher.

Spencer's narrow-eyed gaze coupled with a subtle shake of his head told her he knew what she was up to but wouldn't be letting Luke off easy. He folded his arms, dipped his chin and faced his son. "What were you doing in Goliath's pen?"

Luke looked up at his father, the picture of innocence. "I was gonna rope him like you did."

Spencer pressed his lips into a straight line. Tess could almost see the steam rising off him. "I told you not to go in there, and yet you deliberately disobeyed me."

Luke tilted his head, a quizzical look on his face. "But you said I could try when I was older, and you told me I looked all grown up."

"When did I say that?"

"When I showed you my new clothes."

Spencer dragged in a deep breath, clearly fighting for control. His frustration was understandable. She couldn't begin to count the number of times the clever boy had tried her patience with his literal interpretations.

"You know now that Goliath didn't see a snake, son. What he saw was you spinning your rope over your head. He was charging at you, and he could have hurt you and

Tess if I hadn't been here to help. You have to mind us, young man."

"I'm sorry, Papa." Luke hung his head.

If Tess had read things correctly, the dear boy was genuinely remorseful. He'd only been acting on the impetuousness of youth and hadn't meant to endanger anyone. "We love you, Luke, and don't want anything bad happen to you. That's why—"

"No!" He stomped his foot. "You're not my mama. You can't love me."

She hadn't meant to say that aloud. While she couldn't help but love her charges, letting a child know how she felt was foolhardy. Her best option was to change the subject as quickly as possible and hope Luke would forget what she'd said—and that Spencer had been too preoccupied to notice.

He spoke before she could get a word out. "You're not to yell at Tess. She's right. We don't want you to get hurt. You're a big boy, but you're not big enough to rope a longhorn bull on your own yet. You have to be at least, um... twelve."

"Twelve?" Luke huffed. "That's *old*. Do I really gotta wait that long?"

"Yes, son. Now go to your room and sit on your bed until Tess calls you for supper. I'll let you know then what your punishment will be."

Luke scowled. Tess expected him to protest, but he turned and trudged toward the house.

As soon as he was out of earshot, Spencer let loose. "What was that boy thinking? He could have gotten the both of you killed. I can't lose anyone else." He grasped the fence with a white-knuckle grip.

She was eager to ease his suffering. If only she could.

"Go Papa." Lila squirmed and reached for her father, almost as though she sensed his need for comfort.

"Come here, my girl." He took her and gave her a peck on the cheek. "At least I have one child who won't make me gray before my time. I don't know what I'm going to do with Luke. He's more trouble than a burr under a saddle blanket."

"If it's any help, I don't think he sets out to get in trouble. What we're dealing with is a bright boy who reasons things out differently than we're used to. I have to be very clear in my explanations. I think he could make a fine lawyer one day." She smiled.

"You're quick to defend him."

"He's special to me."

Spencer grabbed Tess's hat from the hay bale and used it in a game of peek-a-boo with Lila, bringing forth round after round of giggles. "You didn't intend to love him, did you?"

Tess shook her head, causing the braid now hanging down her back to swing from side to side. "It's not wise. I do my best not to give way to my feelings, but despite my best efforts, I can't help myself. And then when I have to leave—"

"You're not thinking of leaving, are you?" He pinned her with a gaze so intense it could bore a hole in a cast iron skillet. "I thought you liked it here."

"I do, but I'm realistic. One day you'll meet someone and won't need a housekeeper. I like to think that when that day comes you'll provide me with a solid recommendation."

"You're doing a fine job. Look at Lila. She was withdrawn when you came, and now she's starting to talk. You've worked wonders with Luke. He's a handful, but you have a knack for knowing what he needs. And your cooking... Well, I've rarely eaten meals as tasty as those you fix. I'm happy with things as they are and have no plans to write such a letter for a long time."

His earnestness touched her, but she knew the truth. She'd seen him with his children and witnessed his grief over the loss of his wife. Spencer Abbott had a great capacity for love. He would find someone, remarry and—Tess could hardly bear to form the thought—send her on her way. When that day came and she was forced to take her leave, she would leave a large part of her heart behind.

Rain drummed on the roof of the main warehouse. A decent storm at long last. Spencer brushed off his frock coat and waited as Peter and his crew transferred freight to a wagon. Their job complete, the baggage handlers dashed off to see to a shipment in another of the warehouses. Peter helped the driver cover his load with tarpaulins, and the fellow set out. Even in his India rubber raincoat, his journey over the Sierras would be a miserable one.

"Sorry to keep you waiting, Spence." Peter led the way to his office and held his hands in front of the stove. "I love my job, but on days like today..." He gave an exaggerated shudder. "I've got hot coffee if you'd like some."

"No thanks. I won't be here long."

"Didn't reckon you would since you don't have your notebook. You're frowning. Something troublin' ya?"

Spencer rested a hand on the window frame and watched rivulets trail down the glass. "I finally got a reply from the gentleman in Sacramento City who'd responded to my inquiry about the letters. Turns out he's misplaced a Bible his great aunt Faith inscribed to him and thought he might have left it on a train."

"What're you going to do?"

"I don't know." Spencer leaned back against the windowsill. "I suppose I could wait a little longer."

Peter plopped into his ancient desk chair, the rickety thing creaking under his weight. "You've waited nearly two months. I say it's time to read the rest of the letters. That's the only way you stand a chance of figuring out whose they are."

"You're right." The trouble was, he had a hard time thinking of reading something so personal. The writer of the letters had poured her heart and soul on the page. How would she feel if she knew a stranger was reading her words? "I'd best get back to work."

Spencer sprinted across the platform. He ducked into the depot and hung his soggy coat on a hook in his office.

A full minute passed as he sat and stared at his bottom desk drawer while a battle waged within. Memories of Faith's words had wound their way into his thoughts for weeks. It was wrong of him to think of another man's fiancée, but he hadn't been able to curb his curiosity.

Her betrothed had been given ample time to send word, provided he'd seen the notice. Apparently he hadn't, or perhaps he didn't realize he'd lost the letters on board a train. Either way, Spencer had no choice but to read the next letter if he wanted to find clues to the man's identity.

He opened the drawer and located the bundle in the back corner. Doing his best to ignore a renewed attack of doubt, he slipped the second letter out of the blue ribbon binding the three of them together. He unfolded the pages and began to read.

Saturday, August 20, 1864

To the man I look forward to marrying,

On that special someday when we first meet, I feel certain I'll know you're the one I've been waiting for all my life. Although the Lord has yet to bring you into my life, I continue to lift you in prayer, asking Him to bless you.

Shock, sudden and overwhelming, gripped Spencer. His hands shook so badly he dropped the letter on the desk.

Faith *wasn't* engaged.

At least she hadn't been as of two years ago. Her supposed fiancé was a figment of her fertile imagination. *She* must have lost the letters.

Surely a woman like her with a romantic bent would want them back. Even Trudy, who'd been more practical than sentimental, had saved the letters he'd sent her during their courtship.

Spencer was filled with a sense of purpose as he picked up the pages that had fallen from his fingers. He would learn all he could about Faith, so he could find her and see that she got her letters back. It was the least he could do. He resumed reading, hoping she'd chosen to include information that would make locating her easier.

Several paragraphs into the letter, he'd learned little about her, since she focused on the husband and family she hoped to have and how eager she was to serve them. While her generous nature appealed to him, he needed facts.

The next section caught his eye and gave him hope.

I realized I've told you little about myself and thought I'd remedy that. My mother died when I was three, and my father left me at the local orphanage, never to return. From that day on, I dreamed of being part of a family again, but the Lord never saw fit to place me in one. He upheld me, though, and showed me a way I could make a difference in the lives of others who'd experienced loss. I spent much of my childhood helping care for the precious little ones who came and went with heartbreaking regularity.

What was heartbreaking was thinking of Faith as a young girl, abandoned by her father and longing to be taken into someone's home. How could a man walk away from his own child? Spencer had heard of others who'd done so, citing financial hardship or other valid reasons, but the mere thought sickened him. Not once, even in the darkest days after Trudy's death when the simple act of drawing his next breath seemed an impossible feat, had he considered giving up Luke and Lila.

He corralled his thoughts and continued reading.

An employment opportunity arose when I was sixteen. Since it allowed me to work with children such as those I'd known and loved, I embraced it. I've been blessed to care for youngsters ever since, and I'm grateful. The work can be challenging at times, especially when I must say goodbye, which happens more often than I like, but the rewards are many.

I hope this glimpse into my past has helped you understand why my dream is to marry and have a family. I've known women with lofty ambitions. While I admire them, my greatest pleasure would be creating a home that's warm and inviting, a place

you'd be eager to return to after a hard day's work.
If that home happened to be filled to the brim with
children, laughter and cherished memories in the
making, I'd be the happiest of women.

A profound sense of satisfaction filled Spencer. The
more he learned about Faith, the deeper his admiration
grew. She was proving to be the kind of woman he'd first
thought. She'd experienced hardships that could have
soured a person, and yet she exuded sweetness.

He could almost picture her standing on his porch with
a child on her hip, greeting him at the end of a long day
with a smile as warm and inviting as the meal awaiting
him. Afterward, when the children were in bed, they'd sit
in the parlor where they'd discuss the day and make plans
for a bright future together.

An image of Tess seated on the settee next to his wingback armchair came to him, and the contrast made him
smile. While she was wonderful with the children and
knew how to have fun, she lacked Faith's gentle spirit
and openness.

He'd witnessed Tess's compassion numerous times, but
she tended to be a private person. Their evenings were
companionable, but he craved a deeper connection.

Even though he'd only read two of Faith's letters, he felt
certain there would be no walls to scale with her. She'd
be the kind of woman who understood him, accepted him
and held nothing back. He was sure of it.

However, the question of how to find her remained. He
could read the third and last letter, but he doubted it would
reveal anything specific, since she hadn't done so in either of the others. Not only that, but once he read it, he'd
have no more of Faith's uplifting words to look forward to.

He'd learned enough to help in his search. He would

start by having Drake send a telegram with an updated notice to the other stationmasters right away. And he would pray that Faith would see it, contact him and turn out to be everything he'd imagined her to be.

Chapter Twenty-One

❧

"I can't believe Thanksgiving will be here in ten days, can you?" Polly patted Petey's back.

Tess divided her attention between Polly and Lila. Ever since the darling girl had learned to walk two weeks before, she fussed if she was held. She toddled over to one of Mr. Hawke's display cases and peered inside, her hands splayed on the glass front. While Luke had gravitated to the toys as always, with Abby his shadow, Lila was content to peer at soap flakes and scrub brushes.

"You certainly have a great deal to give thanks for this year, don't you?" Tess patted the wide-eyed boy in Polly's arms.

"Indeed I do. Petey's such a good baby. Abby fought sleep and caused me to lose plenty of mine, but this little fellow goes down with no trouble and only wakes for a feeding once a night."

The door to the general store opened, letting in a gust of cool air—along with Mrs. Carter. She adjusted her shawl. "Brr. I reckon we're in for another storm. Them clouds off to the west are coming on quick." She cast a glance at the crates Mr. Hawkes was busy filling. "Looks like someone's goin' to have a nice Thanksgiving. Too bad my girl can't come, but at least I'll see her at Christmas."

Tess's heart went out the lonely widow. "I can't abide the thought of you spending Thanksgiving by yourself. How would you like to join us?"

Polly's round face registered shock. "Um, Tessie, have you asked Spencer about this?"

"I'm sure he won't mind, not after all Mrs. Carter has done for him."

The older woman smiled. "Aw, Miss Grimsby, you're too kind. I didn't do all that much, 'cept keep Luke out of trouble. And I didn't do a very good job of that. You saw the state of the place when you first come here, and I know you won't never forget the stink."

Tess laughed. "It's not likely. But the smell didn't last all that long."

"Not after you scoured the place and rustled up them tasty vittles. If you're sure Mr. Abbott won't have no problem with it, I'd be mighty grateful to join you."

"She could find out now." Polly inclined her head toward the front window. "The gentleman himself approacheth."

A quick assessment gave Tess a moment's pause. Spencer wore the frown she'd seen far too many times during her first months in Shingle Springs. He'd been much happier in recent weeks, smiling most days and even laughing on occasion. Something must have happened to dampen his mood.

He entered and strode to the counter, determination dogging his every step. "Ladies." He doffed his hat to them. "Where's Mr. Hawkes?"

"In the back," Tess said. "He's looking for the oranges he ordered. I wanted some for—"

"He won't find them. I've kept Drake busy the past hour

sending telegrams in order to figure out what happened to a shipment that was due Saturday. Turns out a freight handler in Folsom put several orders on the wrong train and sent them back to Sacramento City."

Mr. Hawkes emerged from his backroom. "So that's what happened. Thought I'd misplaced some crates. I've been known to do that." He chuckled. "When can I expect them?"

Mr. Hawke's obvious lack of concern eased the tightness in Spencer's fine features. "Tomorrow morning."

"Very good. Here's the allspice you wanted, Miss Grimsby. That completes your order—less the oranges, of course. Looks like you're going to be busy. Anyone around your table on Thanksgiving is in for a treat."

Tess detected a note of wistfulness in Mr. Hawkes's comment. If she wasn't mistaken, the longtime bachelor would spend the holiday by himself. Unless…

She needed to talk to Spencer. Alone. "Polly, would you please keep an eye on the children for a minute while Spencer and I talk?"

Having received Polly's assurances, Tess headed for the door. To her relief, Spencer followed her. A quick glance over her shoulder revealed curiosity swirling in his bright blue eyes.

His neighbor, that obnoxious Mr. Dodge, entered the shop and barked an order for chewing tobacco at Mr. Hawkes as Spencer and Tess exited. A gust caught her hat, threatening to send it sailing. She held on to the brim.

Spencer chuckled. "You know, if you wore a smaller hat, you'd be less likely to have the wind carry it away."

Not that again. She'd seen the hat in a milliner's shop two years before and been taken in by the frothy sea of teal tulle on an indigo base topped with three gorgeous peacock feathers. Few women, the hat maker had told her, could do justice to such a tremendous creation. "I like my hat. Why do you care about it anyhow?"

He assumed an affronted tone so overdone she couldn't help but smile. "Dear lady, do you doubt my motives? I simply want to make your life easier. I figure if you had a smaller one, you wouldn't have to perform a balancing act to get it to rest on the shelf back home."

She replied with a hefty pinch of spice. "The way I see it, *I* don't need a smaller hat. *You* just need a wider shelf."

His broad grin was disarming. "You got me there, Tess. I'll see to that. So, tell me. What was it you wanted?"

How delightful to have found a way to elevate his mood. Now to secure his permission so she could get back inside where warmth awaited her. "I've been making plans for Thanksgiving dinner. It's going to be quite a feast. I thought it would be nice to share the meal with some who don't have relatives in the area, such as Mr. Hawkes and Mrs. Carter. I'd like to invite Peter, Polly and their children, too, along with the Muellers. I thought you might enjoy seeing so many people around the table for a change."

"No." The single word hung in the chilly air, firm and final, a stark contrast to his jovial mood moments ago.

She wouldn't give up that easily. "Might I ask why?"

"I don't want anyone else there, and I don't want a fancy meal."

Understanding dawned. "You don't want to face Thanksgiving without her."

"What do I have to be thankful for?"

Tess ticked off the items on her fingers. "You have two wonderful children, a lovely home, a job that brings you a great deal of satisfaction, a promising future as a cattle rancher…and a bullheaded housekeeper who refuses to let you hide away and wallow in your grief."

"Are you done?"

"Not quite." She softened her tone. "The day will be difficult no matter what you do. To my way of thinking, the best way to get through it would be to do something for others so you aren't focused on yourself and your pain."

"You're done now."

Tess knew better than to push any harder. Spencer had to wage this battle on his own. She reached out to offer a comforting touch. "I'm sorry it's so hard."

The longing in his eyes as he stared at her hand resting on his was unmistakable. She would have to find creative ways to reach out to him because everything in her told her she was just the woman to meet his needs and fill his life with light and laughter. "We should be getting back inside, but let me adjust your cravat first. It appears to be askew." It wasn't, but he didn't need to know that.

He stood still as she fluffed the silk, rewarding her with the barest hint of a smile. "I've changed my mind. You may invite whomever you'd like."

Mr. Dodge burst out the door. He paused, tossed a bag of pungent-smelling tobacco in the air and caught it in his bony hand. "Apparently you don't listen, Abbott, since I see that rangy excuse of a bull is still in your pen—for now. If you care about your future, I suggest you think twice about your plans to raise cattle, or you'll be sorry."

Spencer glared at the gold-toothed bully. "I told you what I think of your threats."

"It's no threat. It's a promise." The lanky man left without another word, passing the wagon that would soon be filled with crates containing everything Tess needed to make this year's Thanksgiving dinner one Spencer would never forget.

* * *

All her life Tess had dreamed of sitting down to Thanksgiving dinner surrounded by family and friends. Although this wasn't her family, the people with whom she'd be sharing the meal in a few short minutes were her friends.

She peeked in the oven and peered in pots and pans. The air was thick with the delicious scents of a feast in the making.

Polly reached for a wooden spoon. "Quick. Go change. Mrs. Carter and I will see to things until you get back. And don't tarry. These potatoes will be ready for mashing soon."

Tess made short work of slipping into her sapphire silk, a dress she hadn't worn since her days accompanying her charges to events in Sacramento City. With nimble fingers, she transformed the high bun she'd worn earlier—which she'd kept hidden under her hat during the Thanksgiving service—into a chignon at her nape. Spencer had never seen her without her customary braid that, for the sake of ease, she'd taken to wearing down her back when she was at home.

At home? What was she thinking? The festive atmosphere must be getting to her. This wasn't her home. It was his. And he was downstairs with his guests, awaiting the meal that required her finishing touches.

She peered in the looking glass one last time. Thanks to her hours in the kitchen, she had nice color in her cheeks. It intensified at the thought.

A bubble of laughter burst from her. What a silly goose she was. No one cared what she looked like. They just wanted to savor the food she'd prepared.

The final minutes were a flurry of activity as she mashed the potatoes while Polly and Mrs. Carter filled the serving dishes. At last everything was ready, with the rest of the party having taken their places at the table.

Tess picked up the bowl of sage stuffing.

"Oh, no you don't." Polly took it from her. "Mrs. Carter and I will carry in everything except the turkey. Once we're seated, you can bring it in."

"Fine." Tess surrendered the stuffing. Arguing with Polly did no good. Once she put her mind to something, she clung to her plan tenaciously.

The two women worked swiftly. Before long Polly returned for the last item. She grabbed the basket of rolls. "Give Mrs. Carter and me a minute to get settled, and then come on in."

When the rustle of fabric and scraping of chairs ceased, Tess hefted the turkey platter and entered the dining room. A chorus of oohs and aahs greeted her. She paused a moment to savor the scene before her.

She'd never experienced a Thanksgiving like this. Her early ones had been spent around long tables in the orphanage's dilapidated dining hall where the children were grateful to get a sliver of turkey. In recent years she'd sat at tables in the servants' quarters of fine homes, unable to eat until the waitstaff had removed the final dishes following the families' feasts.

The look of gratitude Spencer gave her as she set the browned-to-perfection bird in front of him made her days preparing for this moment worthwhile. Although he would likely say little, he appreciated her efforts on his behalf. She took her seat, her heart overflowing with gratitude.

Tess had outdone herself. Spencer could almost hear his dining table groaning under the weight of the many dishes filled with the tantalizing fare. He'd have to show her how much he appreciated her efforts.

She set the turkey in front of him, took her seat and sent a smile his way before turning to her other side to check on Lila, who sat in her high chair watching all the activity with interest. His daughter had never seen so many people around the table.

Due to her weakened state after Lila's delivery, Trudy hadn't felt up to entertaining. He hadn't realized how much he'd missed having guests. The buzz of conversations chased away the memories of quiet dinners that hovered in the corners of this very room.

Tess had been right—again. Although she lacked the gentleness Faith exhibited, Tess's bold request and refusal to accept his initial reluctance had forced him to overcome his objections.

Faith. How often she entered his thoughts these days. Ever since he'd read her second letter and learned she wasn't engaged, after all, he'd found himself imagining where she was or what she was doing. Was she still pining for a family, or had she found someone deserving of her?

Spencer had the impression there was something holding her back. Some reason she had yet to receive a proposal. There must be, because a woman as kind, caring and warm-spirited as she would surely have received numerous offers.

Perhaps she was plain, walked with a limp or had some other shortcoming that kept men from seeing her inner beauty. Such things might matter to others, but he wouldn't care. He'd gotten a glimpse of her heart, and it was filled with love just waiting to be showered on a husband and children. Some wise man would see beneath the surface and be the richer for it. Or perhaps he would find her and—

"Spencer." Tess rested a hand on his arm, leaned close and whispered. "Are you all right?"

"Hmm?" He gazed into her beautiful brown eyes. A man could drown in their depths. Even in her everyday dresses, Tess could turn heads, but she was a vision in the deep blue gown. Gone was the dutiful housekeeper. In her place sat a beautiful lady with all the charm and poise of Sacramento City's elite.

She smiled, merriment dancing in those captivating eyes, and Tess reemerged. But not the Tess he knew. This striking woman stirred feelings in him he'd not experienced in months. There was more to her than he'd realized. Much more.

"We're waiting for you to say grace."

"So I see." He would pray over the meal now, and later he'd ask the Lord to help make sense of the jumble of emotions tumbling around inside him.

Tess carried the last dirty dish to the kitchen and sighed with contentment. The meal couldn't have gone any better. The sounds of laughter in the parlor tempted her, but she had dishes to wash. She reached for her largest apron, a full-length one big enough to protect her fancy silk dress, and set to work.

"Leave them, Tessie. They can soak." Polly grabbed the stack of plates, set the entire thing in the soapy water and dried her hands. "It's a holiday, and you deserve to enjoy yourself."

"But Spencer expects me to do my job."

"Nonsense. He's the one who sent me to get you."

The spoon Tess had been holding clattered against the side of the metal washtub. "He did? I didn't think he would notice my absence, what with all the people here."

Polly laughed. "He noticed all right. Your appearance in that gorgeous dress captured his attention. He spent the entire meal stealing glances at you."

"Surely you jest. I never once saw him—" That wasn't true. She had caught his eye when he'd put a slice of turkey on her plate. The warmth in the smile he'd given her had sent such a surge of heat into her cheeks she'd wished for a fan to hide behind. "All right. I did see him look my way once. But only once. That doesn't mean anything."

"It could. He's a lonely man. You're a beautiful woman. He's attracted to you, and you obviously care for him. I'd like nothing better than to see the two of you to end up together."

Tess shook her head a bit too forcefully. She pushed a loose hairpin back into her chignon. "It does no good to harbor such dreams. He's a grieving widower who thinks he's responsible for his wife's death."

She gasped and clapped a hand to her mouth. How could she have said that aloud? "Forgive me. It was wrong of me to betray a confidence."

Polly's face registered the same disbelief Tess had felt when Spencer made the surprising confession one rainy October evening. "How could he think that? It's preposterous! Trudy tripped over a rake and fell, was impaled by the tines and died from the resulting infection. It's not like Spencer left the rake in her path on purpose or shoved her so she'd fall on it."

"All I can figure is that in his grieved state of mind he's twisted the facts to support his false belief. Those who've lost loved ones often do. I did my best to get him to tell me more, to no avail."

Polly grabbed the last sweet pickle from the bowl and crunched into it. "Patience, my friend. Patience."

The next two hours were some of the most enjoyable Tess had ever spent. She joined in a lively game of charades, helped Luke search in Hunt the Thimble and watched with rapt attention as Spencer challenged Peter in a fierce arm wrestling competition—and won.

The last guest left, and she went upstairs to change out of her silk dress into one of her more comfortable calicoes. What a glorious day it had been. She couldn't remember the last time she'd felt as carefree.

She returned to the kitchen. Luke sat in the corner with the pasteboard Noah's ark set they'd made, endeavoring to teach Lila the sound for each animal. Her babyish attempts to imitate her brother were adorable.

Water sloshed as Spencer filled a pail from the stove's reservoir and poured it in the rinse tub.

"It's nice of you to help, but I'd be happy to take care of that."

"It's the least I can do after all the work you put into the dinner. Everything was delicious, especially the pies." He rubbed his stomach.

She shot him a smile. "I noticed you sampled all six." She removed the dishes that had been soaking, stacked them on the counter and threw out the cold, greasy water. She refilled the washtub, added soap flakes and set to work scrubbing the plates, carefully sliding them into the steaming rinse water one by one.

To her surprise, Spencer grabbed a dishtowel and began drying them. "I know you appreciated the meal, but I don't expect you to do my work."

"I used to help Trudy. She didn't feel as at home in the kitchen as you do. She said she got lonely, so I took to keeping her company. But if you'd rather I didn't help you…"

"It's all right. I like your company, too."

He deepened his voice. "Do you now?"

The admiration in his eyes stirred feelings she ought not to have. While she enjoyed the surge of warmth coursing through her, she shouldn't encourage him. He was simply a man swept up in memories. Likely he wasn't even seeing her but saw an image of his late wife instead.

"A woman spends hours in the kitchen, so I can relate to your wife's desire to have someone around." Botheration. Desire probably wasn't the best word.

"You looked lovely in that dress today. I liked your hair in that knot thing you wore, but I like it this way, too." He grasped the braid hanging to the middle of her back and ran his hand down the entire length.

"Spencer." She struggled to draw a breath. "The children."

He dropped the braid as though he'd been burned and spoke in hushed tones. "I don't know what came over me. I didn't mean— Please forgive me."

"There's nothing to forgive. You miss your wife. I understand."

"I do, but I wasn't thinking about her, Tess."

He wasn't? Her heart slammed against her corset.

"You worked hard to make this day special for me—for all of us. I haven't had that much fun since—" he took a deep breath and let it out slowly "—since Trudy died. And I have you to thank for it. You helped me through a difficult day, so I'm going to dry every last one of these dishes for you." He shook a finger at her as he did when disciplining Luke, but his grin belied his stern appearance. "And not another word of protest from you, young lady. Understand?"

She couldn't resist playing along, dipping into a deep curtsey and giving a wide sweep of her hand. "Yes, your eminence. Your humble servant hears and obeys."

Never had washing dishes been as enjoyable as it was with him at her side. The task became a game. He pointed out a nonexistent speck of food she'd supposedly missed.

She held out the freshly scrubbed gravy boat and pulled it back before he could take it from her. He flicked rinse water at her, and she retaliated, lifting a handful of soapsuds and blowing it at him.

Luke squeezed in between them. "What'cha laughing at?"

Spencer responded before she could. "Tess is being a pest."

She gaped at him. "Me? You started it."

"I wanna have fun, too. Can I help?"

"Certainly." She handed Luke a towel. "You may dry all the spoons."

Lila tugged on Tess's skirt. "Eff."

"You want to join in, as well, don't you, sweetheart? Let me see." Tess scanned the kitchen. "I know. You may stack the soiled napkins."

Luke scoffed. "She'll just play with them."

Tess leaned over and whispered. "You're good at make-believe, aren't you, Luke? Could you pretend your sister's helping?"

He nodded.

Tess cast her gaze from one of the Abbotts to the next. Although pretending was for children, she couldn't help but imagine what it would be like if the four of them were a family. Based on what had just transpired between her and Spencer, she had her first taste of hope.

And it was far sweeter than any pie she'd ever baked.

Chapter Twenty-Two

The small pine gracing the parlor was nothing like the lavish Christmas trees Tess had helped her previous charges decorate with expensive glass ornaments from the East. She preferred this simple tree. She and the children had draped it with handmade paper chains and popcorn strings before the Christmas Eve service the night before. What she liked best were the pasteboard animals Luke had wedged between the branches, pretending they were hiding in the forest. It was a good thing he wouldn't need them any longer, because they'd become quite tattered.

Tess basked in the warmth of the blazing fire and breathed in the invigorating scent of the freshly cut evergreen. She'd awakened an hour earlier than usual on this frosty Christmas morning. Normally, she hoped the children wouldn't wake until she'd seen Spencer off to work, but she couldn't wait to hear Luke padding down the stairs or Lila calling for her.

Since Spencer had assured Tess he wanted her to be part of their celebration, she'd placed her gifts under the tree. Hopefully he and the children would like what she'd selected.

The front door opened, letting in a blast of cold air.

Tess rushed into the foyer to help him out of his overcoat. "Merry Christmas."

He blew into his cupped hands. "The same to you. Are the children up yet?"

"Not yet, but I'm hoping the smell of hot cocoa in the air will wake Luke. That boy certainly has a fondness for it. I have some ready for you."

No sooner had she set the steaming mug at Spencer's place than Luke popped into the dining room, still clad in his flannel nightshirt. "Is it morning yet?"

"Yes, son. And a very special morning it is. Merry Christmas!"

Lila woke soon after, and they sat down to a quick but hearty breakfast of porridge and canned peaches. Luke wolfed his portion and waited impatiently for the others to finish. Tess understood. She was every bit as eager to gather around the tree, listen to Spencer read the Christmas story in that rich voice of his and watch as the others opened their gifts afterward.

Twenty minutes later, Spencer closed his Bible and laid it on the side table next to his armchair.

"Can we open our packages now, Papa?"

"Yes, son, but we'll start with the ladies first."

The disappointment in Luke's eyes was more than Tess could bear. "I'd be happy to wait until the children have opened theirs."

"So be it. Here's one for you, Luke, and one for Lila. They must be from Tess."

She nodded.

Spencer pulled his daughter onto his lap and helped her remove the paper and string. Lila grabbed the rubber-headed doll the moment she saw it and gave it a kiss. "Baby."

Tess's heart melted.

Luke opened his package and let out a whoop that reminded her of the first time she'd met him. "It's the Noah's ark I wanted! This one isn't paper like the one we made. It's wood."

He examined each and every animal. When he hugged the wooden boat to his chest, it took every ounce of restraint she possessed to keep from hugging him. He turned to her without any prompting from his father. "Thank you."

"You're welcome." She lifted her gaze to the ceiling. *Thank You, Lord, for that most precious of gifts.*

The children opened their presents from Spencer, resulting in more cries of delight.

"Your turn, Tess." Spencer passed her a small package.

She opened it, revealing a bottle of citrus-scented hand cream. He must've noticed how rough her hands were when he'd held them after their picnic in Folsom.

"I hope you don't take offense at such a practical item, but those hands of yours serve me and my children in so many ways. They deserve special treatment."

"Thank you. It's such a thoughtful gift." It was, but his kind words were what she would treasure.

"I have one more for you."

He handed her an envelope addressed to him from someone in Boston. She shot him a quizzical look.

"Go ahead. It's all right."

She pulled out the papers inside. This wasn't a letter at all. It was sheet music. "Oh! It's that new hymn we've been learning at church, 'He Leadeth Me.' How did you know I liked it?"

"I've heard you sing it while you're working. I thought we could try singing it together sometime, the way we did the song at our picnic down in Folsom."

"Are you sure *you*, who have one of the best voices I've

ever heard, want to sing with *me*? I make a crow sound good by comparison."

"What do you mean? You sound fine."

"Really?" She found that hard to believe.

He nodded. "I enjoy listening to you, but you've always stopped when you saw me. I was hoping that might change."

Why, he sounded sincere. She'd love to sing with him. Perhaps he'd be willing to give her a few pointers. "I'd like that."

He unwrapped the leather journal she'd given him and gave her a warm smile. "This is a fine gift. I look forward to using it."

"I thought you might find it helpful to write down your thoughts. I do. As the words flow onto the page, things that were unclear come into better focus. It also helps me see how the Lord has been directing my paths and working out things for my good."

The Lord had led her to this family. To Spencer. She was certain of that. But what would the New Year bring? In April, his mourning period would come to an end. How she prayed he'd be open to new possibilities—and a new woman in his life.

Rain she could handle, but Tess could do without the wind. Its plaintive cry as it swept past the house and rattled the windowpanes filled her with foreboding. She stood at the kitchen window that blustery March afternoon and rubbed her arms. Days like this reminded her of the one on which her father had left her at the orphanage. A gust of wind had sent his hat sailing. He'd run after it—and away from her.

Once this storm arrived and the dark clouds unleashed their burden, she'd be fine. Well, as fine as a person could be during the worst winter on record. They'd had well over thirty storms this season, with more predicted. The latest one had added six feet of snow to the Sierras, bringing the accumulation to over twenty feet in places.

Spencer's concern was that the Central Pacific had kept their crews working to bore tunnels through the mountain passes to the north in spite of the snow pack. He'd hoped for a respite, but the CP's race to lay track faster and further than the Union Pacific continued around the clock. Since his line's monopoly would soon end, he was forging ahead with his plans to establish a herd and had begun to schedule appointments with the ranchers ready to make use of Goliath's services.

Her primary concern was how to occupy an active boy tired of being cooped up. If it wasn't for the wraparound porch, she didn't know what she'd do. It gave Luke a place to work off some of his abundant energy. He'd declared the area a race track and went round and round, straddling the stick horse Spencer had fashioned out of an old shovel handle, a short section of rope and a pasteboard box he'd painted to look like a horse's head.

A door banged in the distance, and Tess jumped. She was sure she'd slid the latch into place when she'd let Woof out of the barn earlier.

She rushed to the foyer and peered out the window. Someone slinked from the barn, hunched over to avoid the buffeting winds. It couldn't be Spencer. He wasn't due for another hour.

Woof raced across the yard and barked at the figure beneath the hooded rain cloak. A trouser-clad leg kicked at the loyal watchdog. The man appeared to be clutching something to his chest. Had he taken something from the barn?

Uneasiness dug in its claws.

The intruder stood just outside Goliath's pen.

Oh, no! She wasn't about to let him near the bull. Spencer's hopes for the future hinged on that longhorn. She reached for the rifle over the front door.

Luke looked up from the settee in the parlor where he and Lila were playing with their Christmas toys. "Why did you get that down?"

She forced herself to remain calm. "I'm going to see what Woof's barking at. You stay here with your sister. Don't go anywhere near the fireplace, and don't go outside. Do you understand?"

Luke nodded and returned his attention to his ark.

"I'll be right back." *Please, Lord, let that be true.*

Hefting the rifle into place, she stalked toward the pen, her skirts whipping about her ankles. The man slipped a foot through the fence slats and crouched.

When she was close enough for him to hear her over the howling wind, she shouted. "What do you think you're doing, mister?"

He turned, saw the gun pointed at him and took off limping across the field with surprising speed for one with such an affliction.

She called Woof over to her and fired a single shot in the air to send the prowler a warning.

The man stumbled. He straightened and resumed his flight with his limp more pronounced than before.

Raindrops pelted Tess. The storm had arrived at last. She lowered the rifle and moved away from the pen.

Goliath was snorting and butting the fence. She'd learned that loud noises caused the otherwise docile animal to become agitated, as was the case the day she'd seen Luke in the pen and shrieked. She wasn't overly concerned. The bull would soon settle down now that things were back to normal.

A quick perusal of the barn helped slow her racing heart. The animals were fine, and nothing appeared to be missing, although a trail of oats led toward the doors. That must have been what the trespasser had taken. It made sense, considering he'd headed straight from the barn to the bull's pen.

She returned to the house, rested the rifle on its pegs and had Luke and Lila join her in the kitchen. Luke insisted on taking his ark with him, so Tess gathered all the animals on the settee into her apron and hustled the children to their play corner by the pantry where she could keep watch over them. She did her best to remain outwardly calm as she continued her supper preparations, but inside she quaked.

Spencer couldn't get home soon enough to suit her. She stirred the potato soup and sang the hymn she now thought of as their special song, hoping the words would ease her fears.

She'd just started the final chorus when he arrived and added his glorious voice to her shaky one. She ceased singing and spun around. "You're here! I'm so glad."

Before she could tell him about the trespasser, Luke blurted the news. "She shot the gun."

Spencer crossed the room in three strides and faced her. "What happened? Are you all right?"

"We're fine." Speaking in hushed tones so she didn't alarm Luke, she filled Spencer in.

Concern creased his brow. "Do you have any idea who he was?"

"I can't be sure, but the intruder walked with a limp. When Mr. Dodge dropped by the house last fall, I noticed that one of his driver's boot heels was twice the size of the other. I didn't see him walk, but I would imagine he limps. You don't suppose…?"

"That's the logical conclusion, given Dodge's threats."

A chill swept over her, and she shivered. The thought of Mr. Dodge's henchman prowling about the ranch made her mad enough to...to spit. On his boots. At least she'd run the scoundrel off before he did whatever it was he'd come to do. "What if the children had been outside? What if he comes back?"

Spencer placed his hands on her shoulders. "I won't let any harm come to them—or to you. Keep supper warm. I have a message to deliver to Dodge."

Half an hour later hoofbeats signaled Spencer's return. She met him in the foyer. "How did it go?"

"Dodge denied having anything to do with the incident, but I gave him fair warning. If he or any of his men are caught skulking around the ranch, he knows the guns aimed their way won't be pointed at the sky. I'll ask Frank to check on the place regularly and to come right away if he hears any shots fired over here. I'm also going to teach you how to hit your target when you fire my rifle. I'll give you a lesson this weekend."

"Good." She gave a firm nod. "No one's going to hurt the children when I'm in charge—not if I can help it."

"You have no idea how much peace of mind it gives me knowing Luke and Lila have such a fierce defender."

His compliment warmed her clear through. She hastened to put the postponed meal on the table, and everyone took their seats.

They bowed their heads, and Spencer said grace. "And, Lord, I'd ask you to place a hedge of protection around my family and keep us from harm. In your Son's precious name. Amen."

Tess marveled at his use of the word family. Did he consider her part of it now? The possibility fanned the flames of her lifelong dream. She couldn't let herself get

too excited, though. As much as she'd like to believe his
word choice had been intentional, habit was a more likely
explanation. Even so, she couldn't help but hope that someday, the good Lord willing, she'd have a family as wonderful as this one.

Where had that boy gotten off to now? Tess stood in
the foyer and shook her head in exasperation. She'd asked
Luke to stay indoors until it warmed up outside. Although
the rain had let up the day before, the air that sunny mid-
March morning had a bite to it. Not only that, but an
abundance of muddy brown puddles dappled the satu-
rated ground. No doubt the adventurous boy had found
them irresistible. She dreaded seeing the state of his boots.

"He's not out front, so let's look in the backyard." She
shifted Lila higher on her hip, stepped onto the porch and
paused. "Do you hear that?"

Woof was far afield, barking continuously.

Luke!

Tess rushed into the kitchen, dragged the large bath-
ing tub from the pantry and lined the bottom of the high-
sided metal container with the blanket from the children's
play area nearby. "In you go." She placed Lila inside and
flew out the door.

Grabbing her skirts, Tess hefted them all the way to
her knees. She raced across the soggy field toward Woof.
He ran back and forth near the spot where Dodge's man
had stumbled. The memory of that terrifying ordeal sickened her.

The vigilant watchdog saw her, ceased his frenzied
pacing and stood in one spot, his tail wagging wildly. The
tone of his bark changed, no longer a cry for help but one
of encouragement, urging her forward.

As she drew near, she heard someone call her name. She

spun in a circle, scanning the clumps of weather-beaten bunchgrass, but saw no one. Only when she reached Woof and he ceased his barking could she make out Luke's muffled voice coming from beneath a wooden covering. Two of the weathered slats had given way, leaving a hole large enough for—

Her stomach lurched. Was that a well shaft?

"Luke! Is that you?"

"Yep. I fell in a great big hole."

"I'm going to help you." She peered through the opening into an inky black pit. "Are you hurt?"

"I hit my bottom real hard, and I'm all wet. Get me outta here!"

It was definitely a well. "How high's the water?"

"It comes to my belly button, and it smells real bad. My b-b-boots are gonna be ruined." He let loose a heart-wrenching sob.

"Don't you worry about that, sweetheart. If they are, I'll buy you a brand-new pair." She had to see him and assure herself he was all right. "I'm going to move these boards, so you'll hear some noise."

With a series of kicks, she broke off the stakes holding the cover in place. She stooped, grabbed one side of the pallet-like structure, stood and flipped it over, nearly losing her footing on the rain-soaked earth. The mass of dry-rotted boards landed with a thud. Sunlight flooded the shaft, but her angle of vision made it difficult to see inside.

Her first thought was to get Spencer's lariat and pull Luke out herself, but as slippery as the ground was, she risked sliding into the hole, too. "I have to get someone to help, but I'll be back as fast as I can. You'll hear the gun go off, but it will just be me sending a signal to Frank."

"No! Don't leave me here all by myself."

"You're not alone. Woof's here." At the sound of his

name, the helpful dog gave a reassuring yelp. "See if you can sing the alphabet song five times before I get back. Will you do that?"

Luke hesitated briefly but launched into the song, his voice wavering.

Tess sped to the house, peeked in the kitchen to make sure Lila was all right and grabbed Spencer's repeating rifle. She stepped outside and fired three shots into the sky in rapid succession. The noise left her ears ringing, and the smoke made her cough, but she didn't care. All that mattered was getting Luke out of that horrid hole as soon as possible.

She hung the rifle back on its pegs, grabbed Spencer's lariat from the barn and raced back to Luke. Desperate to reassure the frightened child, she flattened herself on the muddy ground and shimmied forward until she could see into the well shaft. Although fear had her in a chokehold, she did her best to sound unconcerned. "How many times did you sing the song all the way through?"

"Three."

"I told you I'd be fast, didn't I?" She kept him talking as she kept up a silent prayer, asking the Lord to send someone. Soon.

One minute turned into two, three and four. At last she heard a sound that changed her pleas to praise. Hoofbeats were coming her way. A quick glance revealed Frank's pinto bearing down on her location. She scrambled to her feet and waved her arms.

Luke whimpered. "Don't leave me again."

"I'm not going anywhere. Frank's coming to help."

Their young neighbor reached her in no time. "Am I ever glad to see you." She pointed at the hole. "Luke's down there. Get him out. *Please*."

"Don't you worry. We'll haul him up in no time. I just need to go for a rope."

"I've got one. Here." She shoved Spencer's lariat at him.

"You're prepared." Frank jumped to the ground. He formed a slip noose in one end of the rope and tied the other around his saddle horn.

"Are you having your horse pull him out? Is that safe?"

"I'll do it. This is just a precaution in case I slip. Would you hold him so he doesn't go anywhere?"

"Certainly." Tess gripped the bridle.

Frank stood at the side of the shaft, dug in his boot heels and lowered the loop. "All right, Luke. Let's pretend you're a miner and I'm pulling you out of a mineshaft. I'm sending your papa's rope down. When you have it, tell me."

"I got it."

"Good. Put the loop over your head, and then stick one arm through it at a time. Tell me when you're ready, and I'll pull you out."

A few tense moments later Luke hollered. "Ready."

"All right. Up you go." Grasping the rope, Frank used steady hand-over-hand movements to raise the brave boy.

The minute Luke cleared the gaping hole, Tess rushed to him, dropped to her knees and crushed him to her in a fierce hug. "My dear boy. You're safe now."

"I was calling you and calling you, Tess. I knew you'd come." He burst into tears and buried his face in her shoulder, trembling violently.

"Of course I did. I'd do anything to help you, Luke. I love you." As much as she wanted to relish the feel of his arms around her, she had to get him out of the cold and into dry clothes right away.

"Poor little tyke." Frank shook his head.

Tess stood and snuggled the dear boy to her. "Thank

you so much for coming. You've already done so much, but would you be willing to ride to the station and—"

"Get Mr. Abbott? By all means." He handed her the lariat, mounted his horse and took off.

Chapter Twenty-Three

Luke had fallen asleep clutching his mother's quilt in one hand and an elephant from his Noah's ark set in the other. Tess planted a kiss on his cheek and sank into the rocking chair by his bedside. She'd left him just long enough to change out of her soggy, mud-encrusted dress.

Lila padded over and placed a wooden bear by her brother. "Wuke?"

Tess pulled the precious girl onto her lap and rocked her, the rhythmic creaking of the chair lending much-needed comfort. "He'll be all right, sweetheart."

If only that were true. He'd been in that putrid water for who knew how long and gotten a chill.

The front door opened and closed. Spencer was home at last. Tess breathed a prayer of thanks.

He thundered up the stairs and burst into Luke's room. "How is he?"

"Sh." She pointed at Luke. "He's fine, for the most part, thanks to Frank's quick response."

"My poor boy." Spencer sat on the edge of Luke's bed and caressed his son's face with such tenderness Tess had to blink back tears. For Spencer's sake, she must remain strong.

He plunked himself in the extra rocking chair she'd dragged in from Lila's room and gripped the armrests so hard his knuckles turned white. "I don't understand how this could have happened. The cover was intact the last time I checked it."

"That question's been plaguing me, too. I think Mr. Dodge's man—or whoever was snooping around that day—ran across it after I fired my warning shot. Apparently the boards broke under his weight, creating the opening Luke fell through."

Spencer said nothing for the longest time. He just held Luke's hand and gazed at his son.

At length he spoke. "Being a parent is the most challenging job I've ever had. It's as though part of your heart is walking around outside your body. If any harm comes to your child, you feel it as intensely as if it were you."

When she'd first arrived, Tess would have been surprised to hear Spencer say such a thing, but it hadn't taken long to see what a loving father he was. "I'm not a parent, but I have a great deal of empathy for those who are."

"Do you think he has any broken bones or sprains?"

"I doubt it. He was moving normally and didn't complain about anything—other than his…backside. I gather he landed on it. He might have a bruise or two that hadn't developed yet, but the only things I saw when I bathed him were the few scrapes he got when he fell through the covering. My concern is that he might have swallowed some of that stagnant water."

"He cut himself?" Spencer's curt question startled her. He threw back Luke's blankets. "Where? How badly?"

"On his legs mostly, although there are a couple of scratches on his arm. I wouldn't worry too much. I don't think they'll get— I don't think they're serious."

She'd caught herself just in time. She didn't want to

mention the possibility of infection and trigger painful memories.

He ran his hands over Luke's limbs, exploring the abrasions with his fingertips, and faced his fear without hesitation. "Infection isn't something to be taken lightly."

Infection of Luke's wounds didn't worry her nearly as much as infection of his intestines. She'd heard about people succumbing to cholera after ingesting contaminated water. But based upon Spencer's experience, his concerns were understandable.

"I'll stay by his side and see that his wounds are cleaned regularly and the air in his room kept fresh. One of my former employers—a doctor—believed cleanliness could help prevent infection." She would ensure Luke got plenty to drink, as well. From what little she remembered about cholera, the resulting dehydration could lead to death.

Spencer returned to the rocker. "I'm in awe of your ability to keep a level head, Tess. I know Luke's in the best of hands with you, but I'm staying here until I'm certain he's out of danger."

"I would have expected no less. That's why I asked Frank to get you."

All day and into the night they sat by Luke's bedside as he slept, exchanging whispered words on occasion. They only left one at a time to eat the simple meals Tess prepared or to tend to Lila.

Around two in the morning, Spencer shifted his position. "I need to rest my eyes a minute. Please wake me if there's any change."

He quickly dozed off. Tess spread a blanket over him, brushed a lock of golden hair off his forehead and fought the urge to plant a kiss on it.

She kept vigil. Although silence was her only companion, she found Spencer's presence comforting. He was there if she needed him. Should the situation worsen, she'd welcome his quiet strength.

He woke as the mantel clock in the parlor chimed six times and rubbed the stubble on his jaw. "How is he?"

"Doing well so far. He roused an hour ago, asked for a drink and guzzled a full glass of water." She endeavored to sound encouraging, but Luke's thirst troubled her.

"That's good."

"I fried some ham and diced potatoes. Would you like me to get you some?"

"I'm going to see to the animals, so I'll grab myself a plate."

She leaned her head on the rocking chair and prayed.

In no time, Spencer returned, clean-shaven once again, and checked on Luke. The flush-faced boy coughed, and she gasped.

Spencer pinned her with a penetrating gaze. "What is it? You're as white as my shirt."

She felt fuzzy headed after her sleepless night. Her thoughts tumbled over one another like leaves in the wind, but one stood out. "I didn't want to tell you, but I think he might have a case of cholera coming on."

"He doesn't."

His certainty surprised her. "How can you be sure?"

"I've seen the disease. He hasn't complained of any stomach pain or vomited, and he doesn't have, um…intestinal issues."

"I'm relieved it's not cholera, but what could it be? Influenza? Pneumonia?"

"Time will tell."

They sat in silence for several minutes. Her head lolled to the side. She jerked herself awake and cast a glance at Spencer, who was watching her intently.

"You need some sleep. I'll sit with him while you rest."

She should protest, but he was right. Keeping her eyes open required tremendous effort. She staggered to her room, removed her boots and climbed beneath her blankets fully clothed. Sleep claimed her the moment her head hit the pillow.

A knock on her door hours later roused her. "Just a minute." The afternoon sun slanted into the room. She threw back the covers and opened the door.

Spencer flashed her a blinding smile. "Someone wants to see you."

Luke slipped past his father. "Papa fixed stew, Tess. Can you smell it?"

"My dear boy." She gave him a hug but released him before he could protest. "You're up and dressed. You must be feeling better."

"Yep. Papa said I could go out and play, but I gotta be careful 'cause I got scabs on my scratches. See?" He pulled up the legs of his short pants, revealing dark red patches covering his abrasions.

She gave him ample attention for his injuries. They left, and she took a few minutes to freshen up. She checked on Lila, who was napping, and joined Spencer in the kitchen.

Tess looked out the window and watched Luke throw a stick for Woof. "It's wonderful to see him doing so well, isn't it?"

"Thanks in large part to you." Spencer's rich voice came from right behind her.

Guilt ate at her. She took a deep breath, faced him and launched into her confession. "It's my fault Luke fell in that well. I'd told him to stay inside and didn't hear him go out. If it weren't for me, he—"

Spencer held up a hand. "You did nothing wrong."

As much as she wanted to believe that, she couldn't. "I didn't watch him like I should have, and then I couldn't even get him out on my own." Her voice broke. "What kind of housekeeper am I?"

"You do an excellent job caring for the children. If anyone's to blame, it's my son. Luke should have obeyed you. Perhaps he's learned his lesson and won't be so quick to go running off in the future."

"He *was* terribly frightened. I'll never forget the look on his little face when Frank pulled him out. He wept in my arms. And he—" she drew in a steadying breath "—he called me Tess."

"It's about time. You've showered him with loving care. I couldn't ask for more. Thank you."

A ragged sigh rushed from her. She blinked to keep tears from spilling over. "I'm sorry. It's just that when I saw him in the bottom of that horrible pit…"

"Come here." He eased her into his embrace. "Everything's going to be fine."

She rested her head on his shoulder, grateful for his strength, and savored his scent—part smoky, part earthy and all male.

Far too soon, he released her. They remained toe-to-toe, his hands resting on her upper arms. He was so close she could feel his breath on her cheek. His gaze roved over her face and lingered on her mouth. Her heart beat erratically.

With no warning, his entire demeanor changed. He blew out a long breath, dragged a hand through his hair and turned away. "The stew's on the stove." He flew through the house, letting the front door slam shut behind him.

Disappointment engulfed her. One minute she was sure he'd wanted to kiss her, and the next he looked as though he found the idea revolting.

No matter what he was thinking, she knew exactly what she'd wanted—to feel Spencer's lips on hers.

* * *

Try as he might, Spencer couldn't deny it. He'd been about to kiss Tess.

He saddled his horse and rode toward the high point at the edge of his property where he'd taken Trudy the day she arrived at the ranch. He crested the hill, slipped from his saddle and plopped down on a large slab of granite. They'd sat in that very spot, and he droned on and on about his plans. She'd given him that indulgent smile of hers, the one that let him know she didn't mind listening to his dreams. The one that made him forget all else but her. How he missed her.

He was lonely. That's why he'd hugged his housekeeper and come dangerously close to kissing her. Or perhaps he was simply relieved. After all, he and Tess had spent hours at Luke's bedside, afraid he was in grave danger. People had been known to act impulsively at times like that.

It was no use. He had to face the facts. He'd wanted to kiss Tess because she was Tess, the strong, hardworking woman who loved his children as if they were her own. The self-assured woman who wore that ridiculous hat and didn't care what anyone thought about it. The outspoken woman who had an uncanny ability to shift his focus from the past and help him experience the joy to be found in the present.

Tess was right. He had to move on. It's what Trudy would have wanted. She'd said so herself when it became clear the infection was going to take her from him. *Don't spend the rest of your life alone, Spencer. The children will need someone to care for them, and you'll need a partner.*

When Trudy had said those words eleven months ago, it didn't seem possible he could ever care for anyone else, and yet he'd developed feelings for his housekeeper. If that wasn't bad enough, a woman he'd never met had been occupying his thoughts with unsettling frequency. He'd insisted the other stationmasters keep his latest notice on their boards—to no avail. Five months had passed without a single inquiry. Faith was out there somewhere, but despite his efforts and his prayers, he'd been unable to locate her.

He slapped his riding gloves against his leg, his decision made. If he wanted to find Faith—and he most definitely did—he had no choice but to read the last of her letters. He would, first thing tomorrow.

Chapter Twenty-Four

"What can I get for you, Mr. Abbott? A piece of pie, perhaps?"

Spencer set the packet of letters on the table. Miss Minnie's baked goods couldn't compare to those Tess served, but he needed a few minutes to himself before heading home. "I'd like a slice of peach."

"I'll have it for you in two shakes."

His duties at the station had kept him busy all morning, and he hadn't had a moment to himself. He'd have to be quick, though, because Tess was probably eager to enjoy her afternoon off after the ordeal with Luke.

He could finally read Faith's last letter, but he dreaded doing so. While he hoped for information that would lead him to her, there was a strong possibility she'd provided no more clues to her identity or whereabouts than she had in her first two letters.

If that was true, he'd have no choice but to abandon his search and give up the idea of meeting the warm-hearted woman who'd captivated him. That's exactly what he would do if this letter revealed nothing that would help him find her.

He reached for the packet of letters and slipped the

bottom one from it. With one quick motion, he unfolded the letter and braced himself for whatever it contained.

Sunday, August 20, 1865

To the man I look forward to marrying,

I'm relishing the freedom of my day off. While the temperature has soared as it always does this time of year, I'm sitting on my favorite bench by the river, grateful for the shade provided by one of the many trees stretching its limbs toward the water's edge. The riverboat Confidence, visible in the distance, is enjoying her day of rest, as well.

Hope flowed through Spencer. Faith was in Sacramento City. She had to be. The paddle-wheeler she'd mentioned traveled from the San Francisco Bay, up the Sacramento River and back again. His rail line often received passengers who'd arrived in the capitol city via one of the river steamers.

Since he knew where she was, he could renew his search in earnest. He would place advertisements in all the Sacramento City newspapers seeking a woman named Faith who worked with children and had lost important documents aboard an eastbound train. Even if she wasn't a subscriber, someone she knew might see one of the notices and contact her.

"You're looking mighty happy. Wouldn't be the anticipation of sampling my delectable dessert, now would it?" Miss Minnie grinned and set the piece of pie before him.

"I'm sure it's every bit as tasty as usual."

"That's right nice of you, but I know flattery when

I hear it. Enjoy your letter, er, pie." The jovial woman winked and hustled to another table.

He read while he ate, tasting nothing as he savored Faith's words. Unlike her previous letters, this one had a lighter feel, almost as though she sensed the Lord at work in her life and trusted Him to bring her dreams to fruition.

I've spent far too many years bemoaning my lot in life, but no more. The Lord has showered blessings on me, and I can choose to embrace them with a grateful heart. If you're out there—and I firmly believe you are—I trust He will cause our paths to cross. When He does, I shall rejoice.

Until that glorious day when my wait is over and you ask for my hand, I'm hoping all is well with you and praying you feel the Lord's presence in a mighty way.

With love from Faith

He was here all right, and he would find her. He had to. Faith embodied all the traits he wanted in a wife. Kindness. Goodness. Faithfulness. And a heart so full of love it overflowed. A woman like her would make the world a brighter place.

Reaching for the packet of letters, he spied the ribbon. Blue. Tess's favorite color. An image of her in the dark blue silk she'd worn on Thanksgiving flashed through his mind. She'd never looked as beautiful as she did that day.

He held the ribbon in one hand and Faith's letter in the other. Guilt gnawed at him. He didn't want to think about what God would have to say to a grieving widower who had feelings for not one, but two women.

The sooner he found Faith, the better. Perhaps she was

nothing like he envisioned. If that was the case, he could silence his persistent thoughts, focus on what was right in front of him and begin a new chapter of his life free of doubts and unrest.

"No! Goliath can't be gone." Tess stood beside the empty pen shivering in the cold night air. The past two hours had crawled as Spencer searched for his missing bull. She buttoned the cloak she'd thrown on when she heard him ride into the yard moments before.

"I didn't want to believe it, either, but I've been over my place twice, and he's nowhere to be found."

"What do you think could have happened to him?"

His reply was clipped. "I can answer that in one word. Dodge." He removed his hat and raked a hand though his hair. "I didn't tell you before, but when I noticed Goliath was gone, the gate to his pen was closed. My longhorn didn't let himself out. He had help."

Icy fingers of dread gripped her. "I'm afraid you might be right. Mr. Dodge has made it clear he doesn't want you to raise cattle. What can you do about it?"

He slammed his hat back on. "Nothing at this point. He would deny having anything to do with Goliath's disappearance. I have no proof—just suspicions. I'll have to wait and see if the big fellow shows up, but I'll be watching Dodge like a cougar ready to pounce."

The sadness in Spencer's voice tore at her heart. He'd hung all his hopes for starting a cattle ranch on his prized longhorn. "I'll pray that if Goliath's out there somewhere, he'll find his way back."

Spencer urged her to get in out of the cold, and he led his horse to the barn.

Minutes later Tess bent over the quilting hoop in her room. She had less than a month to finish the quilt. She kept her needle sharp so it would pierce the pages of the letters she'd added to each square.

She was still at it when the parlor clock chimed twelve times. Her restless thoughts had kept her awake. If she couldn't get to sleep soon, she'd be bleary-eyed in the morning. She had to make sense of the turmoil within and knew of only two things that helped.

Since she'd already prayed, she reached for her journal. She opened the leather bound book, dipped her pen in the inkwell and began writing.

> My heart aches for Spencer. Losing his wife was hard enough, but having his dream threatened by that conniving neighbor of his has to be a tremendous blow. If only I could do something to ease his pain. I know the Lord will uphold him, but I long to find a way to comfort the man I love.

She stared at the words she'd written. The truth was there in India ink. She'd fallen in love with Spencer Abbott.

Spencer passed the hand mirror to Tess, rose and stood at the porch railing, his back to her. "Thank you for the cut."

"You're welcome." She flung the sheet over the porch railing, snapped it to remove the hairs and did her best to silence the doubts gnawing at her.

Ever since the near-kiss after their night spent at Luke's bedside, Spencer had been withdrawn. He'd spoken to her only when necessary. The long, searching glances he'd been sending her way puzzled her.

She joined him at the railing. "I'm sorry you haven't

found Goliath yet, but I trust you will. Things have a way of showing up when we least expect them."

He moved two steps to the side, adding literal distance between them. "That's true. Some things can be hard to find. But I won't stop looking."

She had the feeling he was no longer talking about his bull, but it was clear he wasn't going to confide in her. "I'd like your help with something this afternoon."

"You're not going to hole up in the kitchen creating new recipes?"

That was how she generally spent her Saturday afternoons off, but Lila wouldn't be asleep long. "Not just yet. Luke's still having those nightmares. I thought they would have stopped by now, but he's had one every night this week. I want to see if we can help him."

"I assume you have a plan."

She faced him, but he wouldn't look her way. "I'd like you to let him help you build the new well cover. Perhaps seeing the process for himself would ease his fear of falling down the shaft again."

He nodded his approval. "That's a good idea. Frank will be here with the supplies soon, and we'll get started." He strode toward the barn without another word.

Minutes later Tess accompanied Luke to the worksite. Spencer had removed the hastily patched cover from the abandoned well. The traumatized boy stayed well away from the dark, dank hole.

Spencer's wagon lumbered across the field. Frank reached them and brought it to a stop.

Tess pointed at the load. "Do you know what those big pieces of wood are, Luke?"

"Yep. Railroad ties."

Spencer pulled on his leather work gloves and grabbed the end of one of the massive ties. Frank took the other.

"That's right, son. They'll make a strong cover. Nothing—not even an elephant—could fall through the one we're making."

The two men soon had the ties in place. They wired them together into a square and drilled a hole in each of the cover's corners.

"It's time for you to help." Spencer gave Luke the task of inserting a metal spike in every hole.

Tess sighed. Spencer was as patient with his son as ever and was laughing at Frank's jokes. It seemed she was the only one getting a chilly reception.

His job complete, Luke quickly lost interest in the project and wandered through the knee-length clumps of greening bunchgrass nearby in search of dragonflies. How nice it was to see him acting like his carefree self again.

She watched with admiration as Spencer wielded the sledgehammer and drove the first spike deep into the ground until it was flush with the cover. What a strong, handsome man he was. How sad that he'd reverted to wearing a frown much of the time.

Luke stooped to pick up something and darted over to her. "Look what I found." He handed her a strangely shaped piece of wood and dashed off again.

She clapped a hand to her chest. "Well, grease my griddle!"

Spencer completed his swing and stopped. "What is it?"

"A boot heel. A very high man's boot heel. This is where the trespasser stumbled when I fired the warning shot that day. It had to be Mr. Dodge's driver, and this—" she held out the heel to Spencer "—would explain why his limp was so much worse than it had been before."

He grabbed the incriminating evidence. "I've got my proof now." He shoved the boot heel in his coat pocket.

"I'm going to pay my scheming neighbor a visit. And it won't be a friendly one." He took off running toward the barn.

Luke rushed over to her. "Where's Papa going?"

"To look for Goliath."

Spencer appeared minutes later astride his big black horse and came to a stop beside Frank. "I forgot to ask. Would you finish up here?"

The young man smiled. "Sure thing."

Tess wished him well.

He worked his fingers over the reins and avoided looking at her. "Don't wait supper for me." He tore off toward the east without a backward glance.

She'd keep his meal warm and keep him company while he ate it, no matter how late he returned. And then they would have a talk.

Chapter Twenty-Five

Elmore Dodge stepped onto his porch with his driver and spat a stream of foul-smelling tobacco juice, which narrowly missed Spencer's feet. "What do you want?"

Spencer forced himself not to plant a fist in Dodge's gut. "I have reason to believe you're harboring my bull. The deputy and I are here to take a look around." He'd known better than to go alone, so he'd dropped by the sheriff's office with his evidence and found a ready ear. Turned out others had lodged complaints against Dodge, too.

The seasoned lawman standing beside Spencer spoke with authority—and an impressive show of cordiality. "You don't have a problem with that, do you, sir?" He tossed the boot heel in the air and caught it.

Dodge's driver followed the journey of the mud-encrusted chunk of wood with a telling lift of his chin. His face drained of color. So, the heel lost near the abandoned well must be his, as Tess had suspected.

Dodge sent them a too-wide smile. His gold teeth flashed in the sunlight. "I don't know why you think this is necessary, gentlemen, but feel free to search my barn."

The barn was the last place Dodge would hide the bull

because it was the first place anyone would look. Even so, the deputy had advised Spencer to accept the anticipated offer and give Dodge time to make a telling mistake, which guilty parties often unwittingly did.

Spencer and the sheriff waited while Dodge's driver opened the barn's double doors. The weasel of a man limped inside and stood half hidden behind a bale of hay, but Spencer had seen the uneven boot heels. He had no doubt he'd found the person Dodge had ordered to carry out the crime. Now to find his bull.

Their investigation complete, Spencer and the deputy followed Dodge and his driver out of the barn. Dodge linked his thumbs behind his suspenders and jutted his jaw forward. "I told you I didn't have your bull. Are you satisfied?"

Spencer bit back an unsavory retort. "For the time being, but you don't mind if we take a short ride around your property, do you?"

The scoundrel gave a dry laugh. "You're a persistent one, aren't you, Abbott? I have nothing to hide, but unless you've come bearing a note signed by a judge, I reckon you've seen enough for one day."

Dodge's driver cast a furtive glance at a ramshackle outbuilding in the distance, caught himself and flinched. That was the sign Spencer had been waiting for. He looked at the deputy and received an answering nod.

As planned, the lawman didn't argue with Dodge. "I don't think a visit to the judge will be necessary. We've seen enough." He mounted his horse, and Spencer followed suit.

Counting on the fact that Goliath would react to a loud noise as he had before and that the rundown shack would be no match his bull, Spencer enacted the final step in the plan. He tipped his head back, opened his mouth wide and let out with the longest, loudest, shrillest scream of his life.

The answering bellow and unmistakable sound of splintering wood did his heart good. Goliath burst out of the shed, horns down, heading straight at Dodge and his driver.

The terror on their faces was priceless. They took off running in opposite directions like the spineless chickens they were.

"I'll take his henchman," the deputy hollered to Spencer. "You get Dodge."

"Gladly." Spencer coiled his rope, urged his horse into action and raced after his wily neighbor.

One toss of Spencer's lariat was all it took. He caught Dodge around the ankle, brought him down and dragged him a few feet over the soggy ground before his horse came to a standstill.

Spencer dismounted, bound Dodge's hands behind him and flipped him over. "I have half a mind to let my bull have some fun with you."

Dodge spat once again, but this time he spewed muddy water. Served the slimy snake right. "You haven't seen the last of me, Abbott. I've got money. I'll get the best lawyer money can buy."

Spencer removed his lariat from Dodge's ankle. "No lawyer can help you when you're caught red-handed."

The lanky man lying in the puddle glared at Spencer but said nothing more.

The deputy shoved Dodge's driver forward. "I'll haul these two in, Spencer. You go get your longhorn." He inclined his head toward the north, where Goliath was a speck on the horizon. "I'll stop by your place tomorrow to take care of the paperwork."

"Sounds good."

Spencer coiled his lariat and hung it over his saddle horn. He couldn't wait to see Tess's smiling face when he returned with his bull.

"Welcome home, big fellow." Spencer slipped from the saddle and led his bull into the pen.

The five days his bull had been missing were some of the longest Spencer had ever lived. Had he lost Goliath, his plan to build a herd by receiving calves in exchange for providing his bull's services would have been stopped in its tracks. But he'd found his longhorn well cared for and unharmed.

An idea struck Spencer and lifted his spirits. If he'd found Goliath when he thought all hope was lost, surely he could find Faith. Perhaps it was time to do more than rely on notices and advertisements. He patted Goliath one more time and led his horse toward the barn.

Tess hurried across the yard. "You got here in time for supper, after all. How did everything go?"

He tilted his head toward the pen. "Goliath's back."

"Oh, Spencer! You found him. That's wonderful." She threw her arms around him.

He tensed. As much as he'd like to crush her to him and inhale her citrusy scent, he couldn't. Until he put the matter of finding Faith to rest, he wasn't free to act on his feelings for Tess. She deserved more than a man torn between two women.

She released him and stepped back. "I'm sorry. I don't know what came over me." She clasped her hands, and her shoulders curled forward. "Wh-what happened? Over at Mr. Dodge's place?"

"I got the deputy, and we went there together and presented my evidence. Dodge denied everything and refused to let us search anywhere but his barn, but we didn't need to." He recounted the encounter, ending with Dodge eating dirt. "I knocked that smug smile off his face."

"I wish I could have seen that." She glanced at the bull and back at Spencer. "I'm glad Goliath's all right. What will happen to Mr. Dodge and his driver?"

"They're in jail awaiting trial and are sure to be convicted. The sheriff will be out tomorrow to take your statement. Dodge no longer poses a threat to you, my children or my bull."

"That's a relief." Her smile held little warmth. "I should get inside and put supper on the table."

"Not yet. I owe you an apology." He held the reins in both hands. Keeping them busy would keep him out of trouble. He wanted to caress Tess's cheek in the worst way and show her how sorry he was for shutting her out, but he wasn't about to mislead her.

"I know I've been a bear the past few days. Can you forgive me?"

She nodded. "I know you've had a lot on your mind, what with Luke's accident, Goliath going missing and..." She picked up a piece of straw and rolled it between her fingers.

"And what?"

"It's getting close to April. I thought perhaps— Never mind. You don't need me to remind you about what's coming up."

"I appreciate the thought, but I'll be fine."

"I know. It's not my place. I'll see to supper." She broke the straw in half, threw the pieces down and set out for the house.

Her slumped shoulders spoke volumes. His preoccupation and need to keep his distance had hurt her, and that knowledge stole his appetite.

The time had come for him to take a more active role in

the search for Faith. As soon as possible, he would travel to Sacramento City and start knocking on doors.

The Flynns filed into their customary pew and took their seats. Tess joined them.

Polly handed Petey to Tess, who was delighted to hold the good-natured baby. She leaned close to Polly and whispered. "He's gotten so big. I can't believe he's six months old already. Then again, I can't believe Luke will turn five the day after tomorrow."

"Are you planning anything special?"

"I'll bake him a chocolate cake, and Spencer's giving him a wooden train."

"That's nice." Polly reached for the hymnal and flipped to the opening hymn. "And speaking of Spencer, how are things progressing?"

"Not well. He seems to be avoiding me. Ever since he got Goliath back, he's gone straight to the bunkhouse after we tuck the children in."

"He's had a lot to deal with lately. Perhaps he's just tired."

There was more to it than that. There had to be. "He didn't come home this past Thursday. He said he had business down the hill, but he didn't tell me what it was. I can't help him if he pushes me away."

Polly smiled. "You've fallen pretty hard for him, haven't you?"

"No. Yes. I didn't mean for it to happen. I don't know what to do."

"Pray, Tessie. Pray. Long and hard and often."

Reverend Josephs entered. The room quieted, and he delivered the opening prayer. The quartet led the congregation in singing "Guide Me, O Thou Great Jehovah." As she did each Sunday, Tess listened for Spencer's voice behind her, reveling it in as she sang.

The final note faded, and Reverend Josephs rose. "Brothers and sisters, do you worry and fret, wondering what the future will hold? That's understandable. The world is changing before our eyes. Before we know it, our country will be connected by a ribbon of rails. One can't help but be amazed, but at the same time uncertainty can gain a foothold."

How true. She'd certainly been feeling lost and confused.

Everything had changed after the vigil at Luke's bedside when Spencer had held her in his arms. She'd seen the attraction in his eyes. He must regret his momentary lack of control.

She understood. She'd berated herself numerous times for throwing herself at him the night he'd returned to the ranch with Goliath. He'd been downright rigid. She might as well have hugged a broom handle. While she could understand his surprise, he didn't have to take such drastic measures as leaving town to avoid being around her.

She leaned forward eager to hear more of the minister's message.

"Take heart, dear ones. God has a plan for our nation— and for each of us. Listen to His words in Proverbs 16:9, 'A man's heart deviseth his way: but the Lord directeth his steps.'"

Truth pierced her willful heart. She wasn't in charge. God was. She wanted a family in the worst way, but that might not be His plan for her. Who was she to tell Him what was best for her?

She drank in the rest of the sermon, filling her parched soul. God knew. He cared. And He wanted good things for her. They might not be the things she thought would bring her happiness, but she could trust Him. All she had to do was let Him lead the way.

Spencer was an extraordinary man with more depth than most people knew, and he was an excellent father. While she'd imagined herself at his side more often than she cared to admit, that wasn't her place. She was his housekeeper and the woman privileged to care for his children for as long as the Lord saw fit. And she would do so with a grateful heart.

Tess had left the general store and was on her way to Miss Minnie's café when the postmaster dashed out of his office and called her name. "Yes?"

"You received a letter."

"I did?" She couldn't think of anyone who would write to her.

"Looks to be from your father or brother."

"I beg your pardon." The last time she'd seen her father was that dark day when he left her at the orphanage.

"It's from Charles Grimsby."

Charlie wasn't her brother, but the orphanage director had given his surname to the pesky boy when he was left on the orphanage doorstep as a baby, just as he'd given it to her when she'd been left there four years later.

"Thank you." She took the letter, and the postmaster returned to his office.

She plunked herself on one of the benches in front of Mr. Hawke's store. Memories assailed her, none of them pleasant. Not only had Charlie coined that detestable nickname. He'd made it his mission to torment her on a regular basis. No doubt he'd gotten into some kind of trouble and wanted her help, her money or both.

Using a hatpin, she slit the envelope, which bore a Sacramento City postmark. Apparently Charlie had come west. She scanned the few lines written in an elegant hand quite unlike the scrawl he'd used when they were young.

April 4, 1867

Dear Tess,

I'm sure you're surprised to hear from me. I've spent months tracking you down and am glad I finally located you. It's urgent that you come to Sacramento City to meet with me at your earliest convenience. I have an important financial matter to discuss with you.

He concluded by asking her to contact him at the office of a prominent lawyer with an office in the heart of the city. It would appear Charlie had tangled with the law, as many of the orphanage staff had predicted.

She shook her head in disbelief. As if she would hop on a train at his request. If he wanted to see her, he would have to make the trip up the hill. She shoved the note in her reticule and snapped it shut. Once she reached the ranch, Charlie's plea would serve as fuel for the fire. Right now she'd enjoy a rare afternoon off spent in town—and a piece of pie someone else had made.

Tess reached Miss Minnie's café minutes later. The outgoing owner hustled to her table.

"Good afternoon, Miss Grimsby. I haven't seen you in a month of Sundays, but Mr. Abbott was here a couple weeks back. I caught him reading letters from his sweetheart and wearing a big ol' grin. His head's clearly been turned. I'm guessing it won't be long before you'll be serving a new mistress. That's exciting, isn't it?"

She fought a wave of nausea. Somehow she had to

squeeze a response out of her throat even though it had gone dry. "I'd like nothing more than for him to be happy and his children to have a new mother." Apparently it wouldn't be her.

Her shocking news delivered, Miss Minnie took Tess's order and bustled off, leaving her shaken. Despite the roiling in her stomach, she must press on. Just last Sunday she'd decided to let the Lord direct her path. She could trust Him, and she could hope. Miss Minnie might not have her facts straight. Perhaps the letters weren't from a sweetheart at all. Spencer had mentioned an aunt. Maybe he'd been rejoicing to receive news about his relatives back in Texas.

Tess left the café a short time later, set out for the ranch and ambled along the rutted road singing "He Leadeth Me" while tears streamed down her cheeks.

Chapter Twenty-Six

"I'm sorry, son, but we've never had anyone with that name work for us." The white-haired merchant's wife gave Spencer a sympathetic smile.

He resisted the urge to pound a fist into the doorjamb and excused himself with the cordiality of a gentleman. Despite having visited every hospital, orphanage and school in Sacramento City on his two previous trips looking for women who worked with children, he was no closer to locating Faith. He'd taken to calling on individual homeowners, thinking she might work as a governess, as Tess had.

If anyone had told him a year ago when he'd laid Trudy to rest that he would come to care for two women before his official mourning period was over, he would have scoffed at the idea. And yet here he was, the very day he'd removed his black armband, searching for Faith while Tess was back home awaiting his return. How could he be so fickle?

Weary from knocking on doors all afternoon, he plunked himself on a bench by the river, leaned back and listened to the medley of birdsong. The lilting notes of a lark sparrow reminded him of Tess. How she loved to sing. He'd lost count of how many times they'd sung her favorite hymn, her alto and his baritone blending well.

And then there was the day she'd finally let him give her tips on roping, allowing him to stand behind her and guide her arm as she swung her loop. The braid hanging down her back had tickled his chin as it bounced from side to side, and that citrusy cologne she wore had teased his senses. She'd finally lassoed her first fence post and done the cutest little jig afterward.

Tess was quite a character. Not only was her hat as big as Texas. So was her heart. She loved Luke and Lila deeply and without reservation. But did she love him? He'd thought she might, but then he'd tried to kiss her and made a mess of things. He couldn't forget the shocked look on her face. Ever since then, he'd kept his distance, biding his time until he met Faith.

A church bell chimed nearby, sending out an invitation to anyone seeking the Lord. Spencer answered the call. He could use some guidance, and there was no better place to find it.

He entered the redbrick building, sat on a back pew and bowed his head. Instead of praying, he listened. The Lord had led him here, so surely He had a message to deliver.

For several minutes all Spencer heard was the rumble of wagons as they passed by. Then came muted footfalls and a rustle of skirts. Someone else had come to spend time with the Lord. A woman.

She sneezed, and Spencer looked up. She was tall and wore a huge hat that rivaled Tess's in size. It was unlikely to be her, but...

The woman sank onto a pew and rummaged in her sleeve as though searching for a handkerchief but found none. He reached her in a few strides and held out his crisp, clean one. "You may have mine if you'd like."

"Thank you, young man." The woman with many years etched in her friendly face took it and wiped her nose daintily. She tucked the soiled square in her drawstring bag and smiled. "Was there something you wanted?"

"What? No. I'm sorry. I didn't mean to stare. I thought you were someone else. Forgive me."

"I know that look. It's the one my dearly departed Abner wore when we first met. The look of a man in love."

He hadn't realized his feelings were so obvious.

"Who is she?"

"Tess. My housekeeper. She came after my wife died and helped us learn to live again."

"A recent loss?"

He heaved an audible sigh. "One year ago today."

"So your mourning period is over, and you're torn."

She didn't know the half of it.

"You didn't ask, but I'll give you a bit of advice. If you've found the woman of your dreams, tell her how you feel. You'll regret it if you don't. I speak from experience. I held on to my grief far too long and missed out on the love of a fine man who came into my life several years after I lost Abner."

"I have found her." Although he'd been infatuated with Faith, Tess was the one he loved.

A glance at his pocket watch showed he had just enough time to visit a jewelry store before the shops closed. He'd return to his hotel, get up early tomorrow morning and take the first train up the hill.

If all went according to plan, he'd arrive in Shingle Springs before noon, make sure everything had gone all right at the station in his absence and head home. After dinner he would invite Tess into the parlor, ask her to marry him and hold his breath.

* * *

Polly went to the window to check on Luke and Abby. They were out on the porch that sunny April morning playing with his new train, adding the sounds of hissing steam, wailing whistles and clacking wheels. She repositioned the crocheted antimacassar straddling the back of Spencer's armchair. "I have something to tell you, Tessie, and it's not something you'll want to hear."

Tess focused on Petey. He sat on the rug in the middle of Spencer's parlor watching Lila build a block tower. The little fellow shot out a hand and knocked it over. Tess had a sinking feeling her dreams were about to come crashing down around her, as well. "Don't keep me in suspense. Just say it."

Polly plopped on the settee next to Tess. "Peter received a telegram from Spencer right before quitting time last night." She pulled a slip of paper from her reticule.

Tess's vision blurred as she read the ten words. Found woman of my dreams. Back tomorrow. Wish me well.

"Oh, Polly, I thought I was prepared for this, but..." Two tears escaped, and Tess flicked them away.

Lila toddled over, climbed into Tess's lap and patted her damp cheeks. "Ess no cry."

Tess blinked to prevent the torrent that threatened from spilling over. "It's all right, sweetheart." She pressed her lips to Lila's golden hair.

Polly rested a hand on Tess's arm. "What will you do when he gets here? Tell him, or act as though nothing's changed?"

"I can't face him. I love him." She drew in a shaky breath and continued. "I tried so hard not to, but I do. He'll see it my eyes, so I can't be here when he gets back. I must go. Now. I'm sorry to have to ask, but could you watch the children until he can find someone else?"

"Of course. But do you really have to leave? I like having you here."

"I like being here and will miss everyone terribly, but I can't stay. Not when he loves another."

"I understand. I'm so sorry it turned out this way. I was certain he cared for you."

As quickly as possible, Tess packed. She took a lingering look around the room that had been hers the past seven months but would soon belong to Spencer and his new bride.

The quilt had turned out well and looked lovely on his bed. Tess took comfort in the fact that she was leaving a part of herself behind, but she would love to have seen Spencer's reaction when he saw the results of her handiwork. If only he hadn't chosen to leave when he did. She'd been eager to give him her gift the day before as a memorial to his late wife, but perhaps he'd preferred to mark the anniversary of Trudy's passing at a place that wasn't filled with reminders.

Most likely he'd been spending time with his intended. That was a good thing. It meant he was embracing life.

A shuddering sigh escaped Tess. That's what she'd wanted, so she ought to be happy for him. Maybe in time she could be, but her pain was too fresh. "Goodbye, Spencer. I'll miss you more than you know."

She went downstairs, lifted her hat from the shelf for the last time and closed the door on the happiest days of her life.

The ride to the station passed in silence. Tess held Lila. Luke sat beside them, his face pinched and his arms crossed, looking like the sullen boy she'd met that memorable July day. Leaving Luke, Lila and their wonderful father was the hardest thing she'd ever had to do.

The Lord had led her here for a reason, but her work in

Shingle Springs was done. Another woman would come and take her place. *Lord, please let her be a good mother to the children and the doting wife Spencer deserves.*

Polly parked her wagon alongside the platform.

Peter met them. "I'm sorry, Tess. I didn't expect him to find her."

She took a steadying breath. "I'm glad he did. He deserves to be happy."

Polly patted Peter's arm. "Would you please help Tess with her luggage and buy her ticket? She has a train to catch."

"Sure, but I think you should stay until he gets back, Tess. I don't think Spence would want you to leave. He speaks so highly of you."

She produced a weak smile. "Thank you for that, but I don't want to be in the way."

Peter took her money and headed for the ticket window. She led Luke aside and knelt before him.

His lower lip trembled. The dear boy was trying not to cry but failing miserably. "Why do you have to go, Tess? I love you. I know I been a bad boy sometimes, but I'll be better. I promise."

She placed her hands on Luke's arms and gazed into his watery eyes, her own just as full of unshed tears. "I love you, too, Luke. I wish I didn't have to go, but your papa's found a new mama for you. She'll be taking care of you now."

"I don't want a new mama. I want you." He threw himself into her arms and sobbed.

The shrill whistle of the train pierced the air, and the conductor hollered "All aboard."

"Come, Luke." Polly placed a hand on his back. "It's time for Tess to go. Let's stand here so we can wave goodbye."

"No!" He took off running.

Peter handed Tess her ticket, wished her well and set out after the heartbroken boy.

Polly stood by her wagon fighting tears as she balanced Petey on one hip and held Abby to her side. "The children will miss you greatly, but so will Spencer. I hope he knows what he's doing, because he's losing someone very special."

Tess reached into the wagon to pick up Lila and plastered the little girl's cherubic face with kisses. "Goodbye, my sweet." She set Lila down, gave Polly a fierce hug and boarded the train.

With a clatter of steel wheels on iron rails Tess was on her way, leaving Shingle Springs and the family she'd longed to call her own behind. She watched the depot grow smaller and smaller through a sheen of salty tears.

Chapter Twenty-Seven

Something was wrong. Spencer knew it. Polly rarely came out to the ranch without Peter, but the Flynn's wagon was in the yard. Since the horses had been unhitched, she must have been there for some time.

He ran up the steps, burst inside and raced to the kitchen. "Tess!"

Polly stood at the stove stirring something. She spun around, a wooden spoon in her hand. Her face was red and puffy, as though she'd been crying.

Nothing had happened to Peter. Spencer had seen him at the station deep in conversation with a baggage handler. He made a quick count of the children. Two babies in the corner, and the two older ones out back. They were fine.

"Where's Tess?"

Polly's chin trembled. "She left."

He struggled to make sense of the shocking news. "When? Why?"

"First thing this morning. I showed her the telegram you sent Peter, and she said she had to go."

"I don't understand. I was coming home to her."

The wooden spoon clattered on the floor. "You mean…?"

Polly stared at him. "*Tess* is the woman of your dreams, isn't she? But she's gone. This is terrible."

Spencer staggered backward and clutched the edge of the kitchen table. "No. Tess wouldn't walk out like that. She loves the children, and they love her. She wouldn't do anything to hurt them."

"She thought…we all thought that you'd found the woman in the letters."

"Peter told you about them?"

Polly shook her head. "Miss Minnie mentioned to Tess that she'd seen you reading letters from your sweetheart in her café. I asked Peter about it, and he said it was true— that you were smitten with the woman who'd written them and were searching for her. And then we got the telegram. It said you found her."

"But I didn't. I realized Tess is the woman for me."

She jabbed a fist against her side and scowled. "Well, you certainly didn't make that clear."

He gripped her by the shoulders. "I've got to find her. Where is she?"

"I don't know. She rode the train to Sacramento City, but she didn't have any idea where she'd be staying. I made her promise to write as soon as she gets settled."

He released his hold and dragged in a breath. "I'll go look for her."

"I know you want to find her, but she'll be roaming the city in search of a job. You won't even know where to look. She said she might be forced to explore options elsewhere, as well. It would be best if you wait for her letter to arrive."

"I can't." He paced. "I have to do something."

"Oh, Spencer, you do have it bad, don't you?" Polly gave him a weak smile. "I must say, I'm relieved. When

I thought you'd chosen someone else over Tess…" She growled playfully.

He ceased his restless wandering. "I was blind. I read those letters and imagined the woman who'd written them. After a while she became almost real to me, and I had to find her."

"What made you stop looking?"

"A very large hat and the advice of the wise woman wearing it. She told me not to lose the woman of my dreams. But I've gone and done just that, haven't I?"

Polly rested a hand on his arm. "Don't you dare give up that easily, Spencer Abbott. Tess *will* write, and you *will* go get her and bring her home."

The back door flew open, and Luke rushed in. "Papa, something real bad happened. Tess got on the train and went away. She said you found a new mama for us, but I don't want one. I want Tess."

Spencer ruffled Luke's hair. "I want her back, too, but it might take me a while to find her. You'll have to be patient, son." So would he, although everything in him revolted at the idea.

It took some talking to get Luke to understand the situation. Once he did, he trudged back outside.

Polly stood at the stove again and glanced over her shoulder. "Tess left you something. It's upstairs in your room. Dinner won't be ready for a few minutes yet so why don't you go take a look."

He stood in the doorway to his bedroom moments later. Tess had made him a beautiful quilt with red-and-blue Ts. The red ones must be for Trudy and the blue for Tess. He traced the brightly colored letters with a fingertip and smiled. Now he knew why Tess's light had burned so late at night. She'd spent countless hours making this just for him. What a thoughtful, generous, talented woman she was.

Grabbing a corner of the quilt, he squeezed it. Something inside crinkled. What was it? He bunched the quilt again and heard a rustle that could only be paper. Tess must have hidden the letters he and Trudy had exchanged inside after he'd told her never wanted to see them again. How clever.

If only he were clever enough to find her, but he had no choice. He had to wait for Polly to hear from Tess.

She'd better write soon, or he'd go mad.

Lifting her face to the April sky laced with a few wispy clouds, Tess sent a prayer heavenward. "Lord, please help me find work."

Without a recommendation from Spencer, her chances of finding a position in Sacramento City were slim. She had nothing to show for her work the past nine months, and her previous employer's recommendation was not very flattering.

She strolled down the street, turned the corner and found herself on the block housing the office of the lawyer Charlie had asked her to contact. Thankfully she'd heard no more from her childhood tormentor. Since he was likely long gone by now—or behind bars—she might as well pay the lawyer a visit and ask if he knew of anyone seeking a governess. If he happened to recognize her name and give her some indication of the trouble that had led Charlie to contact her, so be it. Not that she was curious. Well, not overly much.

The rich scent of wood polish greeted her when she stepped into the paneled interior. A young clerk seated at a gleaming walnut desk rose. "May I help you?"

Tess assumed her most businesslike manner, grateful that her silk gown disguised her perilous financial position. After paying her train fare, she had precious little money left. "I wondered if I might have a word with Mr. Livingston."

"I'm sorry, but he's in court. I'll get his partner for you. Please, take a seat." He indicated a waiting area heavily populated with plush chairs and disappeared through a door with a frosted glass center.

The end table beside the chairs bore a display of newspapers from around the state. If the lawyer had no leads for her, perhaps he'd let her peruse the advertisements placed by those in need of hired help. Although she had no desire to relocate, she couldn't be choosey. She had to find a job right away.

The door opened, and an impeccably dressed gentleman with glittering green eyes entered the reception area. She shook her head in disbelief. He looked a lot like— "Charlie? Is that you?"

"Tess." He beamed. "You haven't changed a bit."

"You're a lawyer? I thought…" She waved a hand dismissively. "Never mind."

He laughed. "You probably thought I was on the other side of the law, but I'm no longer the rapscallion I once was."

"So I see."

The clerk joined them, and Charlie clapped a hand on his shoulder. "This is the woman I crossed the country to find, Jones. Meet Miss Tess Grimsby."

"Oh." The color drained from the young man's face. "I'm sorry I didn't think ask her name, sir."

"It's fine. Please see to it we're not interrupted." Charlie turned to Tess and held out a hand. "If you'll come with me, I have good news for you."

Tess preceded Charlie into his office, took a seat in front of his massive desk and folded her hands in her lap. He offered her a cup of tea, which she declined. All she wanted was to find out what he'd meant by "good news." She could use some.

He sat in his oversize leather desk chair, rummaged through a stack of files on his credenza and pulled out a thick folder. "I've been helping Mr. Livingston prepare for his court case. Otherwise I would have headed up the hill to pay you a visit. I've decided to stay here and had looked forward to seeing more of my new state."

She was in no mood for small talk. "Why were you looking for me?"

Charlie smiled. "Direct as always. I like that. I won't mince words, then. Mr. Grimsby named you as a beneficiary in his will. He entrusted me to see that you receive your inheritance."

"Inheritance? Are you saying he's no longer with us?" The news saddened her more than she would have expected.

"His heart gave out a year ago. I was with him at the end. He went peacefully."

"I'm sorry to hear he's passed on."

"I know you remember him as a gruff man, but he changed soon after you left. He missed you greatly. He began attending that church you did and gave his life to the Lord, as did I. His transformation was as remarkable as that of Ebenezer Scrooge."

"He missed *me*?" The idea was inconceivable.

"He loved you, Tess. You were like a daughter to him, and I was the son he never had. Six years back his wife's parents died and left their fortune to him. He adopted me and put me through law school. Said I'd make fine lawyer, since I knew how to argue." Charlie chuckled.

"He was married? I had no idea."

"It's a tragic tale. He was a poor boy deeply in love with the daughter of a wealthy man. Her dream was to open an orphanage and better the lives of children like you and me, but she took ill on their honeymoon trip abroad and died soon after. Although Mr. Grimsby was heartbroken, he forged ahead with their plan. The man you knew was an embittered widower." Wistfulness filled Charlie's eyes. "I wish you could have seen him as the loving father figure he became."

"I can't believe it. I mean, I'm glad he changed, but he made my life so difficult."

"Yes. And he regretted that. He wished he could've adopted you, too, but he did the next best thing. He left you a third of his estate, as he did me." Charlie reached for the folder, pulled out a sheet of paper and handed it to her. "You're a wealthy woman."

She stared at a page titled Tess Grimsby: Portfolio. A list of investments was tallied, the sum staggering. Despite the warm spring day, a chill washed over her. "This can't be. You're teasing me, aren't you?"

"Not this time. When your father walked away that day, Mr. Grimsby's heart ached for you. He didn't know how to show his love back then, but he was determined to see that you'd be able to make your way in the world. That's why he pushed you so hard. You were special to him. Bright, caring and determined, like his beloved bride…Tess."

Her mouth fell open. "He gave *me* her name? Then it's true? He really did care about me?"

"Very much. You reminded him of her. She was tall, like you. Your height is what first endeared you to him. You weren't too tall, Tess. Not in his eyes—or mine. It was wrong of me to pester you the way I did." Charlie leaned forward, sincerity clearly evident in the face of this man who was almost a brother. "Can you forgive me?"

"Yes. I do. We're not who were, Charlie, are we?"

"We're not. The Lord's been at work." He resumed his businesslike manner. "Now, let's discuss your inheritance, shall we?"

"What about the orphanage?" She held up the list of investments. "I can't accept this if it means those poor children—"

"They're fine. Mr. Grimsby had me set up a trust with the remaining funds. There's enough to cover the orphanage's expenses for a good twenty years. Maybe more. He wanted you to have the money and enjoy it."

"I'm curious. If you received a share like mine, why are you working?"

Charlie took a sudden interest in his inkstand. "I felt the Lord leading me to help those less fortunate, so I do a good deal of pro bono work." He returned his attention to her. "But enough about me. Let me go over things with you so you understand your financial picture."

They spent the next hour discussing her holdings. As they talked, a sense of purpose enveloped her. Like Charlie, she could use her wealth to better the world. The thought lifted her spirits.

She bid Charlie farewell. "Thank you for everything. I'll contact you once I've decided what I want to do." She gave him a sisterly hug and left the office.

When the train had pulled out of Shingle Springs the day before, she'd had no idea where the Lord would lead her or how He would provide. Never in her wildest dreams could she have imagined the blessings He'd showered on her. Her future was secure. Not only that, but she would be able to enrich the lives of many others.

In time the gaping hole in her heart would heal, but she would never forget Spencer Abbott and his children.

Spencer stared at the ledger lying open on his desk. Normally he enjoyed completing the tallies, but he couldn't concentrate that morning. All he could think about was Tess. The three days she'd been gone seemed like an eternity.

Perhaps a slice of Miss Minnie's pie would ease his edginess. It would definitely give him a respite from Mrs. Carter's cooking. The widow was doing her best, but her culinary skills were no better than before. He donned his hat and coat and strode to the café.

"Afternoon, Mr. Abbott." The affable owner smiled. "What can I get for you today? Pie? Or would you care to try my special. It's chocolate cake."

"Cake please."

She set a piece before him in no time and flitted off to wait on another customer.

He took a bite. While the cake was good, Miss Minnie wasn't half the baker Tess was. She'd made chocolate cakes for his children's birthdays. Hers were so moist and tasty he always ate two large slices. Luke had begged her to make another one just last week, but she said chocolate cake was a special treat and that she wouldn't make one again until the next birthday. That would be Spencer's, which was the thirteenth of May. He hoped Tess would be back well before then.

Wait. She'd baked a chocolate cake a few weeks after she'd arrived. Could it be…? He tossed some coins on the table, apologized to Miss Minnie for his hasty departure and sprinted across the street to the Flynn's place.

Polly looked up from where she was hanging clothes on the line. "What's the matter, Spencer? I've never seen you run before. Peter's all right, isn't he?"

"He's fine. Everything's fine. When was Tess born?"

"In '41. That makes her twenty-five, if you have to know."

He waved a hand. "Not the year. The month and day."

"August twentieth. Why?"

Excitement surged through him. He pulled Faith's letters from his frock coat pocket, unfolded all three and fanned them so the dates showed. "Look."

Polly trailed a fingertip across the pages. "Are these the letters?"

Spencer nodded. "They're from Faith. She was raised in an orphanage. Was Tess?"

"Yes."

"I think she and Faith are the same person."

Compassion filled Polly's eyes. "I know how much you want to find Tess, but I'm sure there are many orphaned women born on that day."

"But how many of them rode the train to Shingle Springs? It could be her. If it is, I know where to find her." Both women liked to spend time at the same place. "I have to go back to Sacramento City right away."

"She might not even be there, though. She was afraid her poor recommendation from the banker she'd worked for prior to coming to Shingle Springs would prevent her from finding a position. I got the impression she was only going to spend a few days looking for work there before she moved on."

He refused to lose hope. "It hasn't been that long. Will you help Mrs. Carter if she needs anything?"

"Yes. And I'll pray the Lord leads you right to Tess."

"Thanks. I'll tell Peter what's happening, and then I'll be off."

If all went well, he'd hold the woman he loved in his arms before nightfall.

Chapter Twenty-Eight

A stiff breeze off the Sacramento River riffled the sheaf of papers in Tess's hands and sent several of them sailing. She jumped to her feet and made a grab for the pages, catching all but two. They flitted toward the riverbank.

Footfalls raced toward her from behind. A tall man in a short black frock coat and top hat dashed to the water's edge, catching the sheets before they met a soggy end. She'd recognize him anywhere.

Spencer.

He scaled the bank and held out her sketches. "Here you are, Tess."

"Thank you, sir." She snatched the drawings from him.

"It's about time you showed up. I've spent the past four days looking for you. I started by visiting every hotel and boardinghouse in the city, but apparently you aren't staying in one."

"No." She hadn't had the money for that when she'd returned to the city, so she'd been sharing a room with a girlfriend who'd taken pity on her.

"I took to strolling along the river. I figured a woman who likes to sit at the water's edge would have to make an appearance sooner or later."

Memories of their picnic in Folsom rushed in, bringing with them a flood of feelings she'd tried so hard to keep at bay. "I'm sorry you were inconvenienced, but I didn't expect you to follow me."

"I had no choice. The woman of my dreams is here."

Her lashes grew damp, and she blinked to keep the tears from escaping. "So I've heard."

He cupped her chin, forcing her to meet his gaze. Never had she seen such joy in his brilliant blue eyes. All those months she'd longed for Spencer to look at her that way, and yet another woman had captured his heart, shattering hers. She'd tried her best not to think about him and to immerse herself in her plans, but her thoughts strayed to him by day and her dreams revolved around him by night.

Not trusting her wobbly knees to support her, she sank onto the bench and stuffed the drawings in her satchel. He sat beside her and gave her one of his most dazzling smiles. While she was happy for him, saying goodbye would be easier if he wasn't so charming—and totally disarming. She drew in a shaky breath, willing herself to remain strong.

"Polly told me I'd made a mess of things, so let me make things clear. You're the woman of my dreams, Tess." He dropped to one knee, pulled a small box from his pocket and opened it to reveal a ring with a deep blue sapphire. "I'd like you to be my wife."

"Me? What about the telegram and the letters Miss Minnie saw you reading? I thought the woman who wrote them was the one you—"

"I can explain." He shoved the jewelry box in his pocket, returned to the bench and took her hand in his, rubbing the pad of his thumb over the back of it and sending tingles racing up her arm. "Last fall Peter brought me a packet of letters that had been left on a train. There were no envelopes or identifying information, so I had to read them to see if I could find the owner. But they weren't just any letters. They were written by a kind, loving, sensitive woman to the man she looked forward to marrying. Her name is Faith."

Tess gasped and began trembling. "You... They... It can't be. Do you have them?"

He slipped his free hand inside his coat and produced the packet of letters she'd thought were long gone. She took one look at them and squealed. "I can't believe it."

"Polly was afraid I might be mistaken, but I see I was right. You and Faith are one and the same, aren't you?"

She nodded. "Faith was the name my parents gave me. Mr. Grimsby changed it."

"I see. Well, here's the best part. You wrote these letters to me. I'm the man you've been waiting for, Tess. At least I want to be. Will you marry me? Please, say you will."

All the love she'd held inside for months broke free. "Yes, Spencer. Yes. A thousand times yes. You're everything I dreamed of and so much more."

She threw her arms around him. This time he hugged her back, holding her tightly and whispering "Tess" over and over with such feeling that she couldn't stop the tears from flowing.

All too soon he ended the embrace. He reached in his pocket once again and produced one of the snowy-white handkerchiefs she'd washed, ironed and folded while praying for the wonderful man who would use them. He wiped her cheeks with such tenderness that another wave of tears threatened.

"If I hadn't read your letters, your reaction would have surprised me. I've seen the bold, confident Tess who speaks her mind, but there's more to you than that. You're every bit as tenderhearted as I thought. You've kept it hidden, but you don't have to any longer. I love you, Tess—both sides of you." He took her hand and slid the ring on her finger.

His declaration left her so lightheaded she feared she might swoon. She took a series of calming breaths as she stared at the ring. Once she'd regained control, she gazed into the eyes of her beloved.

"I love you, too, Spencer. So very much. I have for the longest time. I didn't mean to. A housekeeper isn't supposed to fall in love with her employer, but I couldn't stop myself. You don't say much, which can be a bit challenging at times, but the few times I did get you talking, it was wonderful. You're good and kind and loyal and…" She paused. "Why are you smiling?"

"Because you love me, and because you understand me like no one ever has." He studied her, his forehead furrowed. "There's something I need to know. Do you really like it here—in California?"

"I've come to love the wide-open spaces and the ruggedness of it. Why?"

"Trudy tried, but she wasn't happy here. She came expecting life to be easy and money plentiful. What she didn't know was that when I left Texas, my father disinherited me. I wasn't the wealthy man she expected, but she agreed to marry me anyhow. I gave her all I could, but it wasn't enough. I denied her the one thing that could have saved her. It's my fault she died."

The anguish in Spencer's eyes tore at Tess's heart. She took his hands, gave them a reassuring squeeze and received a grateful smile in return. "You said that once, but you never told me what you meant. Please. I'd like to know."

"She wanted me to hire a housekeeper, but I wanted to use the money to build a herd. I put my dream ahead of her. She never regained her strength after Lila's birth, which made seeing to her chores taxing. If I'd gotten her help…"

Tess tugged a hand free and, emboldened by his earlier response to her touch, caressed his cheek. "You can't blame yourself. She fell. She could have done that anytime, anyplace. It was an unfortunate accident and nothing more."

"I've tried to tell myself that, but hearing you say it makes it easier to believe."

"It's true. Trudy was blessed to have a man who loved her the way you did. And now that blessing is to be mine. I'll do my best to be the wife you deserve."

"You'll be a wonderful wife and mother, my darling." He captured her hand and pressed a kiss to the back of it, the warmth penetrating the thin cotton glove and setting her senses spinning.

His gaze rested on her mouth, and he leaned toward her. She waited with baited breath. And then he gave her a fleeting kiss, feather-light and far too short.

He pulled back and studied her. "What is it? You look… disappointed."

"I liked it. I just thought it would be different somehow."

He smiled. "You've never been kissed before, have you?"

"Not until now."

"Well, then, let me give you a proper kiss. I'll start by getting rid of the obstacles." He took off his hat and removed hers, too. "Close you eyes, tilt your head and trust me."

She did as he asked. He cradled her head in his hands. His lips met hers—warm, soft and oh, so wonderful. Just when she thought the kiss couldn't get any better, it did. As many times as she'd dreamed of this moment, her imaginings had failed to do it justice.

Long before she was ready, he brought the kiss to an end.

"Was that more to your liking?"

"It was incredible. You're very good at it."

He grinned and glanced at the path behind them, where others were coming their way. "Now that I've gotten a taste of you, I don't want to stop, but this isn't exactly the time or place. Here's what I propose—we get a license and go straight to a church right here in the city. Today. Then tomorrow I'll take you home where you belong. If you're certain you want to marry me, that is. I'm not a rich man, but I'm a hard worker who intends to make a good living as a cattle rancher."

She smiled. "I can help with that. An old friend contacted me a few weeks ago, and I paid him a visit when I reached the city. His name is Charlie. He grew up in the same orphanage I did. He's a lawyer now. He told me that Mr. Grimsby, the director, left us both a sizeable inheritance. That's why I was sitting here making plans to open an orphanage of my own."

Spencer's face fell. "That changes things."

"No. It just means we have more options. I could buy you another bull if you'd like so you can build the herd faster." She chuckled. "What am I saying? I could buy you an entire herd. I'm what Charlie referred to as 'a woman of substance.'"

"I don't want your money, Tess. I just want you."

He couldn't have said anything that pleased her more. "I'm afraid you can't have one without the other. I could use your help managing my portfolio. I've never had more than a few dollars to my name, so the thought of handling my investments is a bit overwhelming."

"In that case, I'd be happy to help, but you'd have to tell me what you want."

"What I want? That's easy. What I want more than anything is to have a family—your family. I want to be your wife and fill your life with as much joy as possible. I want to have lots of children who know they're loved. I want pictures of Luke and Lila to put in my locket. And I hope this won't offend you, but I'd like the house to be painted blue."

"That's all you want?" He deepened his voice and caressed her with his gaze, giving her a delicious case of the tingles. "Nothing more?"

"There is one more thing. Since I want a whole lot more of your kisses, I'd like to get married right away."

His face lit up. "I was hoping you'd say that."

The following afternoon Tess rested her hand on the crook of Spencer's arm as they strolled from the railroad station to the ranch. *Their* ranch. Very soon she would hug *their* children.

"I've been thinking."

"Yes?" Spencer drawled.

"I'd still like to open an orphanage."

"I'm glad to hear that, Mrs. Abbott."

How she loved hearing him use her new surname. Not that she minded the name Grimsby as much as she used to. "Good. Then I can contact Charlie and ask him to scout out possible locations."

"You don't need to do that. We can open it here—" he gestured down the road "—at the ranch. I could teach the boys all I know about raising cattle, and you could teach the girls to cook and sew and garden."

She squeezed his arm. "Oh, Spencer, that's a terrific

idea. And when their lessons were over, the children could play, the way children should."

"Exactly."

"Are you sure you wouldn't mind having a dormitory full of children to care for? Orphans can be quite needy. They often arrive with wounded hearts and require a lot of love and attention."

He placed his hands on her shoulders and gazed at her with such love and admiration she felt dizzy with delight. She'd left Shingle Springs expecting never to return, but the Lord had brought her back to serve this special family—her family.

"I've never met a woman with a heart as big as yours, Tess. I watched you reach out to Luke day after day. You never stopped loving him, no matter how cantankerous he was. I don't have your way with children, but I'll do my best to be a father to the fatherless. Above all, I'll teach them that they have a heavenly Father who loves them and will never leave them."

Tess smiled. "A father to the fatherless. That's what God's been for me. No matter how difficult things were, I always knew He was there. And now He's led me home."

They ambled along talking and talking. She marveled at how much Spencer had to say. Ever since he'd found out she was the one who'd written the letters that had captivated him, he'd opened up to her the way she'd always hoped he would.

"I have a surprise for you. Look." He held out a hand to the arch at the ranch's border. A freshly painted sign bore the words *The Double T.*

"I love it. That's the name of the quilt pattern I used."

"About that quilt. It's beautiful. I can't thank you enough for your months of hard work. I appreciate the way you honored Trudy. I'm not surprised, though. You've always been selfless."

She snickered. "Me? Selfless? I'll have you know I'm a very demanding woman, Spencer Abbott. For instance, right now I'm going to demand a kiss." She tugged on the lapels of his jacket.

"So, you want a kiss, do you, my lovely wife? Well, then, I'll give you a kiss you won't soon forget."

He pulled her to him and, true to his word, gave her a kiss she would remember for a very long time. When he finally released her, she heaved a contented sigh.

"Satisfied?"

"Very much so." She gave him a coquettish smile. "For now anyhow."

"That's what I like to hear. I plan to spend the rest of my days making sure you're a happy woman. Now, let's go see our children."

They neared the house, and Luke flew out the door. "You're home!" He raced toward Tess with his arms open wide.

She caught him in an embrace. He hugged her back. Then, to her surprise and delight, he kissed her cheek.

Spencer inclined his head toward the house. "Someone else wants to see you."

Polly stood on the porch with her children. Lila bumped down the stairs on her bottom the way Tess had taught her and took off running the minute she reached the ground. Tess met Lila halfway and scooped the little girl in her arms.

She patted Tess's cheeks. "Tess."

"No, Lila." Luke tapped Tess's arm. "She's Mama."

Spencer smiled. "Yes, son. She is."

Tess wanted to respond, but her throat was too thick. God had given her the desire of her heart. She was a wife and mother with a family of her own. A wonderful family that would expand to include many more children through the years. And she would shower each and every one of them with love.

* * * * *

Dear Reader,

Thank you for taking time to read *Family of Her Dreams*. I hope you enjoyed spending time with Tess, Spencer and the children.

As a native Californian, I love including aspects of the state's rich history in my stories. When I learned that the sleepy Gold Rush-era town of Shingle Springs, not far from where I live, had once been home to one of the busiest rail stations in the West, I decided to set this story there. I endeavored to show how the rapid changes taking place in the state's early days affected those who helped settle this area.

Tess was such fun to write, although doing so was a bit of a stretch in some ways. At six foot, she has ten inches on me. Watching her overcome her painful past and discover what the Lord had planned for her was exciting. Like me, Tess has trouble relinquishing her dreams and letting God lead her at times. I hope witnessing her journey to His destination is a source of encouragement.

I enjoy hearing from readers and cordially invite you to pay me a visit at my Victorian-style cyber home at www.keligwyn.com. Look for my next Love Inspired Historical, coming early 2016. Until then…

Happy Reading!
Keli Gwyn

COMING NEXT MONTH FROM
Love Inspired® Historical

Available July 7, 2015

THE MARRIAGE AGREEMENT
Charity House
by Renee Ryan

Fanny Mitchell has cared for her boss, hotelier Jonathon Hawkins, since they met. When they're caught in an innocent kiss, Jonathon proposes marriage to save her reputation. Can Fanny turn their engagement of convenience into one of love?

COWGIRL FOR KEEPS
Four Stones Ranch
by Louise M. Gouge

The last thing Rosamond Northam wants to do when she returns to her hometown is help a stuffy aristocrat build a hotel. But her father insists she work with Garrick Wakefield, and now it's a clash between Englishman and cowgirl.

THE LAWMAN'S REDEMPTION
by Danica Favorite

Wrongly accused former deputy Will Lawson is determined to clear his name. His search leads to lovely Mary Stone, who seems to know more about the bandit who framed Will than she lets on...

CAPTIVE ON THE HIGH SEAS
by Christina Rich

When ship captain Nicolaus sees a beautiful woman in a dire situation, he offers to rescue her from slavery. As their friendship grows at sea, Nicolaus wants to offer her freedom—and his heart.

REQUEST YOUR FREE BOOKS!

2 FREE INSPIRATIONAL NOVELS
PLUS 2 *FREE* MYSTERY GIFTS

Love Inspired® **HISTORICAL**

YES! Please send me 2 FREE Love Inspired® Historical novels and my 2 FREE mystery gifts (gifts are worth about $10). After receiving them, if I don't wish to receive any more books, I can return the shipping statement marked "cancel." If I don't cancel, I will receive 4 brand-new novels every month and be billed just $4.99 per book in the U.S. or $5.49 per book in Canada. That's a saving of at least 17% off the cover price. It's quite a bargain! Shipping and handling is just 50¢ per book in the U.S. and 75¢ per book in Canada.* I understand that accepting the 2 free books and gifts places me under no obligation to buy anything. I can always return a shipment and cancel at any time. Even if I never buy another book, the two free books and gifts are mine to keep forever.

102/302 IDN GH6Z

Name _____ (PLEASE PRINT) _____

Address _____ Apt. # _____

City _____ State/Prov. _____ Zip/Postal Code _____

Signature (if under 18, a parent or guardian must sign)

Mail to the **Reader Service**:
IN U.S.A.: P.O. Box 1867, Buffalo, NY 14240-1867
IN CANADA: P.O. Box 609, Fort Erie, Ontario L2A 5X3

Want to try two free books from another series?
Call 1-800-873-8635 or visit www.ReaderService.com.

* Terms and prices subject to change without notice. Prices do not include applicable taxes. Sales tax applicable in N.Y. Canadian residents will be charged applicable taxes. Offer not valid in Quebec. This offer is limited to one order per household. Not valid for current subscribers to Love Inspired Historical books. All orders subject to credit approval. Credit or debit balances in a customer's account(s) may be offset by any other outstanding balance owed by or to the customer. Please allow 4 to 6 weeks for delivery. Offer available while quantities last.

Your Privacy—The Reader Service is committed to protecting your privacy. Our Privacy Policy is available online at www.ReaderService.com or upon request from the Reader Service.

We make a portion of our mailing list available to reputable third parties that offer products we believe may interest you. If you prefer that we not exchange your name with third parties, or if you wish to clarify or modify your communication preferences, please visit us at www.ReaderService.com/consumerschoice or write to us at Reader Service Preference Service, P.O. Box 9062, Buffalo, NY 14240-9062. Include your complete name and address.

LIH15

Jonathon's eyes roamed Fanny's face, then her gown.
Appreciation filled his gaze. "You're wearing my favorite
color."

"I…know. I chose this dress specifically with you in
mind."

Too late, she realized how her admission sounded, as
if her sole purpose was to please him. She had not meant
to reveal so much of herself.

He took a step forward. "I'm flattered."

He took another step.

Fanny held steady, unmoving, anxious to see just how
close he would come to her.

He stopped his approach. For the span of three heart-
beats they stared into each other's eyes.

She sighed.

"Relax, Fanny. You've checked and rechecked every
item on your lists at least three times, probably more. Go
and spend a moment with your—"

"How do you know I checked and rechecked my lists
that often?"

"Because—" his expression softened "—I know you."

There was a look of such tenderness about him that

for a moment, a mere heartbeat, she ached for what they might have accomplished together, were they two different people. What they could have been to one another if past circumstances weren't entered into the equation.

"We're ready for tonight's ball, Fanny. *You're* ready."

She drew in a slow, slightly uneven breath. "I suppose you're right."

He took one more step. He stood so close now she could smell his scent, a pleasant mix of bergamot, masculine spice and…him.

Something unspoken hovered in the air between them, communicated in a language she should know, but couldn't quite comprehend.

"Go. Spend a few moments with your mother and father before the guests begin to arrive. I'll come get you, once I've changed my clothes."

"I'd like that." She'd very much enjoy the chance to show him off to her parents.

He leaned in closer. But then the sound of determined footsteps in the hallway caught their attention.

"That will be Mrs. Singletary," she said with a rush of air. The widow's purposeful gait was easy enough to decipher.

"No doubt you are correct." Jonathon's gaze locked on her, and that was *not* business in his eyes.

Something far more personal stared back at her. She had but one thought in response.

Oh, my.

Don't miss
THE MARRIAGE AGREEMENT by Renee Ryan,
available July 2015 wherever
Love Inspired® books and ebooks are sold.

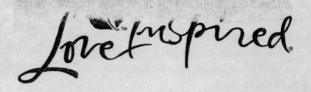

Love the Love Inspired book you just read?

Your opinion matters.

Review this book on your favorite book site, review site, blog or your own social media properties and share your opinion with other readers!

Be sure to connect with us at:
Harlequin.com/Newsletters
Twitter.com/LoveInspiredBks
Facebook.com/LoveInspiredBooks